AGED TO PERFECTION

Also by Joyce Henricks (J. E. Henricks)

Dying to Fit In

AGED TO PERFECTION

JOYCE HENRICKS

iUniverse, Inc.
Bloomington

Aged to Perfection

This is a work of fiction. All of the characters, names, incidents, organizations, and dialogue in this novel are either the products of the author's imagination or are used fictitiously.

iUniverse books may be ordered through booksellers or by contacting:

iUniverse
1663 Liberty Drive
Bloomington, IN 47403
www.iuniverse.com
1-800-Authors (1-800-288-4677)

Because of the dynamic nature of the Internet, any Web addresses or links contained in this book may have changed since publication and may no longer be valid. The views expressed in this work are solely those of the author and do not necessarily reflect the views of the publisher, and the publisher hereby disclaims any responsibility for them.

ISBN: 978-1-4502-7196-7 (sc)
ISBN: 978-1-4502-7197-4 (ebook)

Printed in the United States of America

iUniverse rev. date: 11/12/2010

In loving memory of my parents, Ann and Fred

Acknowledgments

Special thanks to Alice Littlefield and Dennis Thavenet for their willingness to read the whole manuscript and offer suggestions for improvement, to Larry Reynolds for his creative suggestions for a title, one of which was actually usable, and to Guy Meiss for his excellent proof-reading skills. And to my family and friends—whose support is always appreciated, even when unacknowledged—my thanks for always being there when I need you.

Chapter 1

Hannah Lowenstein stepped off the bus and hesitated. She stood in front of a large brick building with fake stone columns in front—a building clearly designed by someone who wasn't limited by good taste. Disapproval clearly visible on her face, she entered the building, muttering to herself, "My God, the inside is even more depressing than the outside."

Hannah was a small woman, smartly dressed in a gray pantsuit with a bright red silk scarf trailing behind her as she walked briskly down the hallway of the nursing home. Anyone observing her would have thought she was a busy administrator on her way to an important meeting, not a seventy-eight-year-old grandmother on her way to visit a friend.

The hallway walls of *Sunset Manor* had originally been painted the pale green used by nursing homes in the belief that it calms patients' fears and anxieties, but, after many years without repainting, the flaking green paint had turned bilious, somewhere between yellow-green and brown. They were, however, well lit, which simply magnified the imperfections in the walls. The patients sitting in wheelchairs outside their rooms, waiting for the lunch cart—a high point in their day—added to the depressive atmosphere. A staff member stood by one of the patients, an agitated old man in a brown robe, pajama legs hanging down over legs as thin as a two-inch pipe, trying to convince him that lunch would soon be arriving, while another staff member, seemingly oblivious to the calls of patients asking to be helped into their rooms, continued the conversation on her cell phone. An old woman dressed in a colorful caftan, shuffled down the hallway leaning on her walker. She looked up and nodded when Hannah smiled at her.

The smell of urine mingled with a cheap floral air-freshening spray accosted her senses as Hannah continued down the hallway. Not seeing anyone at the nursing station, she checked the name tags on the doors in search of her friend. She stopped outside a door with *Ruby Shapiro* written on it and peeked in. The walls were painted the same color as the halls. All she could see was a pale, deeply-lined face, with gray hair coming loose from the hairpins that tried to hold it in a bun, huddled under a faded blue blanket.

Thinking that her friend was asleep, she started to turn away when Ruby raised her head. She was all of eighty but still had the hearing of a teenager, something Hannah greatly envied. Janice, her daughter, had been after her to get a hearing aid for over a year now, but Hannah was convinced she wouldn't need one if only people talked louder.

"Oh, please come in," pleaded Ruby. "I'm not sleeping."

When Hannah entered, she noticed that the room was unusually dark for that time of day. The laughter of children at play in the schoolyard across the street was audible, even through the painted-shut windows. The gray blinds—originally white?—were drawn, shutting out the daylight. Hannah was appalled, thinking that this was the gloomiest room she had ever seen: ugly walls, dirty windows, an old faded blanket, and a tiny lamp which barely gave any light.

She went over to Ruby and gave her a hug. "So how are you?"

"I'm fine," Ruby started to say—and then burst into tears. "I'm so sorry," she hiccoughed between sobs, "it's just that I've been so scared. They moved me here—from the hospital—two days ago and there's no phone so how could I tell anyone where I am?"

"I know, I know. I've been trying to find you for two days. Every time I called the hospital I got the run-a-round. First, they said you weren't in your room, then they didn't know where you were. Finally, some nice nurse checked and told me you were here. I was beginning to think they had used you for parts—you know, like in that book where they take healthy people and use their parts for transplants."

Ruby laughed and dried her tears. "What parts would they want from me?" she asked.

"Don't laugh. We may be old, but there are still things they could use from us—like our eyes, although mine aren't so good any more—I think I'm getting cataracts. Anyway, what are they saying? Are they giving you therapy? You know it's important you should take the therapy seriously if you want to get out of here. How long do they think you'll be here, anyway?"

Ruby started crying again. Hannah looked around and found a box of tissues on the table. "Here, it's all right. Are you in pain? Should I call the nurse?"

"No, no, no. It's just that I'm so confused. I don't understand. Harold, my son, tells me that he's selling my house. He says I can't live alone, and the only way is for me to stay here or some other place—like assisted living—and in order to do that he has to sell my house to pay for it. He's already contacted a real estate agent."

Ruby dabbed at her eyes with the crumpled tissue and took a deep breath. "I don't want to stay here, but maybe assisted living wouldn't be so bad."

"How could he sell your house? Without even asking you?"

"Well, he owns the house. A few years ago he figured out that if I put it in his name he wouldn't have to pay taxes on it when I died. And I could live there just like normal. He figured it out and it made sense, so I signed it over to him. The house was all paid for—no mortgage—so I just pay the utilities and the taxes."

"Did he pay you for it?"

"No! I couldn't take money from my own son! It was all done legally, by a lawyer. He would own it, but I would live there."

"I see." And Hannah was beginning to see, but was reluctant to say anything to upset Ruby. She was just glad that her daughter would never treat her that way. Instead, she asked, "Have you seen your son? Has he visited you?"

The tears started flowing again. "No, he just phoned and told me what he was doing. He says he's too busy to visit, but he'll call again when everything is settled."

At that moment, the lunch cart appeared in the hall, pushed by a young woman wearing jeans and a t-shirt with the words "I'M A VIRGIN—NOT" on the front. Hannah went to the door to help her and, taking the tray, inquired if Ruby was on any special dietary restrictions. "No, she just gets the food everyone else gets," the young woman replied, shrugging as she left the room.

When Hannah removed the cover, she found a limp sandwich composedof a slice of bologna between two pieces of white bread, a cup of chicken noodle soup, apparently without chicken or noodles, and a small container of applesauce.

"Is this what they've been giving you here?" she asked Ruby.

"Yes, it's not very appealing, is it? I don't have an appetite anyway, so it doesn't matter."

"Well, of course you don't have an appetite! This would make *me* lose my appetite—and you know how hard that would be. Listen, tell me what you want to eat and I'll bring it by tomorrow. But aren't you supposed to be on a salt free diet? Bologna's not good for you."

"They don't know from salt free here. Everyone gets the same no matter what you have. You could have heart problems, like the woman down the hall, and they give you hamburgers and cheese."

"You need to get out of this place. That's irresponsible! How about I bring you some chicken stew tomorrow—you know, that dish I made for the senior reception a few months ago?"

"Oh, that was good. Do you think they'll let you bring it in here?"

"They'd better not try to stop me. Okay, that's settled—Janice's been asking me to make that dish so I'll be killing two chickens—literally. Now, let's catch up."

They chatted for over an hour, Hannah bringing Ruby up to date on what was going on at the Senior Center, including how Charlie Bernardi kept asking about her but was too timid to visit her at the hospital.

"He's a good man—a little shy, you know," Hannah chuckled. "That woman at the Center—you know the one, she's always flirting with the men?—well, she invited Charlie out to a show at the college and you'd have thought she asked him to sleep with her! He turned beet red and stammered something about being busy. If I hadn't felt so sorry for him, I'd have laughed."

Ruby did laugh. "He is nice," she agreed, then changed the topic to her garden. "I'm so worried. Who's going to take care of it if I go into assisted living? The tomatoes are ready to can and there's so much zucchini. I was going to do all that before I fell—you know, can the tomatoes, make zucchini bread—now they'll all rot. And the plants—the roses, azaleas—they have to be prepared for the winter." It was clear that Ruby was getting upset, so Hannah volunteered to look after the garden until Ruby left the nursing home—a big commitment for her as she hated gardening and didn't know how to can anything. By the time Hannah left, Ruby was tired, but more cheerful.

As Hannah waited for the bus, she thought over her reaction to her visit with Ruby. She was pleased that she had left a more cheerful Ruby than she had found when she arrived. But why did she have this feeling of unease? Visiting friends in hospitals and nursing homes had become a common occurrence in the last few years, so that wasn't it. Was it the place? It was certainly gloomy, but she had seen worse. These thoughts were interrupted by the arrival of the bus. Hannah's attention was now on finding enough scattered coins at the bottom of her purse, pushing the feeling of unease from her mind.

She sat back in her seat, pleased that there were other passengers, relieving her of the responsibility of holding a conversation with the driver, a lovely woman whom she occasionally chatted with. Today she just wanted to relax and think.

The friendship between Hannah and Ruby was most unusual. All they really had in common was the fact that they were New York Jews of a similar age transplanted to the Midwest. Hannah was small, round, and dynamic;

Ruby was tall, thin, and lethargic. Hannah was a political activist, even in her new surroundings; Ruby didn't show any interest in politics, not even the local issues that might have an impact on her. Hannah was feisty, ready to fight when she perceived an injustice; Ruby was timid, reluctant to get involved in anything controversial. Hannah had no problem confronting people, even if it meant offending them; Ruby could never bring herself to do anything that might upset others.

They came from different backgrounds, too. Ruby had been raised in a wealthy neighborhood in upper Manhattan, the daughter of a textile factory owner and a stay-at-home mother. In her youth she had been a beauty, courted by many of New York's most eligible bachelors. She had attended private schools and had just finished her second year at Bryn Mawr when she met Bernard Shapiro, a young man just out of law school, clearly on a quick path to success. They were married two months later, with the blessings of her parents, who saw in Bernie a man who would be able to provide the good life for their daughter. He joined a prestigious law firm in New York, whose primary clients were large financial institutions, but his premature bid for partnership was turned down. Seeing this as the handwriting on the wall, he resigned and took a position at a smaller, less prestigious firm, one where he felt his talents would be more appreciated. When he again didn't make partner, he decided to leave the competitive scene of New York and moved the family to Michigan, where he set up a private practice which dealt with family issues: divorces, real estate, and accidents. He never made the money he had expected to be earning by the time he was in his fifties, even though he worked long hours.

Ruby never held a paying job, but spent her days, before her son was born, attending social events and playing bridge. It became clear that her main function was to be attractive, pleasant, and keep whatever opinions she might have to herself. When they moved to Michigan, she found herself alone, without any family for support. Bernie was busy at work. Even before Harold went off to college she didn't see much of him when he was at home, so she spent her days reading romance novels and watching soap operas. She hated the Detroit suburbs and moved to Brewster when Bernie died, thinking that a small college town would provide her with the cultural opportunities she craved in a more comfortable environment.

Hannah, on the other hand, had never been a traditional beauty. With a crooked tooth, thin lips, a short compact body, and a mass of unruly dark hair, her beauty only surfaced after one talked with her. Her eyes sparkled as she gestured her way through a conversation; her smile—with crooked tooth—captivated her audience, and her energy was contagious. People couldn't help but notice her, and, when they did, they were drawn to her.

Born and raised in a working-class neighborhood in Brooklyn, the daughter of a postal worker and a mostly stay-at-home mother, who worked at the neighborhood grocery store when Hannah was in school, Hannah went from high school to a full-time job as a waitress in a local diner. She met Leo Lowenstein at the diner, noticing him when he came in for breakfast, lunch, and dinner every day for two weeks. He was shy and didn't speak to her, but his eyes followed her as she carried trays from the kitchen to the tables, joking with the regulars, and fussing over their children. She finally made the first move, telling him that he had better ask her out before he ran out of money. He did, and they married the following summer. Leo worked as a typesetter for the local newspaper—*The Brooklyn Gazette*—and she continued at the diner until Janice was born.

Always interested in politics, she became even more involved after she married Leo, a union rep for the newspaper. After participating in demonstrations, protests, and boycotts, she and Leo joined the Socialist party, delighted to meet other like-minded activists. When he left the *Gazette* to work for the *New York Daily,* they moved to an apartment in lower Manhattan, worlds apart from Ruby's upper Manhattan home. By this time, Janice had finished college and was working on her master's degree at Columbia, visiting home once a week to have dinner with her parents.

Hannah was a voracious reader, trying to make up for the lack of a college education. But when she wasn't reading, her interests ranged from politics to poker to cooking to sticking her nose into other people's business.

Hannah and Ruby were as different as two women could be—yet, they were friends.

· ·

The bus let her off at *Marty's Market*, the local supermarket, where she could buy the chicken for the stew she was going to make. She loved to cook, but found that she now had to use recipes for dishes she'd been making for years. Janice kept telling her it was normal to forget things as one got older, but Hannah didn't buy that excuse. She claimed that it was because she hadn't cooked much for herself since Leo died and she began living alone. With Leo gone, and so many of her friends dead, in nursing homes, or just waiting to die, moving to Brewster, Michigan, from New York was the best thing for her—though, she had to admit, it was quite an adjustment to live in a small town. Brewster would not have been considered a small town by its 50,000 residents, but to Hannah anything less than a million was small.

She bought the chicken and, as usual, also some items that weren't going into the stew but would be nice to nosh on while watching TV.

Janice only watched news programs and PBS, but Hannah could usually get her granddaughter, Madison, to watch her kind of programs: *Desperate Housewives, Grey's Anatomy*, things like that. She could never get Madison to watch *Walker, Texas Ranger*, though, so she "TiVo'd" it—an accomplishment she was quite proud of—and watched it when no one else was home. Her grandson, David, was another matter. At twelve, five years younger than Madison, he couldn't sit still long enough to watch any program on TV. But give him a video game—one that involved lots of killing and torture—and he could sit for hours in front of the screen.

Fortunately, *Marty's* was close to home, the day was beautiful—warm, but with the smell of fall in the air—and the groceries weren't heavy, so she walked the short distance. The house was in an older section of Brewster, where maple trees grew large and full, casting welcome shade in the summer. Situated back from the street, with juniper bushes bordering the driveway, the two story house appeared smaller than it was. Originally containing three bedrooms, it had been expanded to include a separate bedroom and sitting room for Hannah on the ground floor. She loved the privacy that the sitting room provided, with its own small TV and lounge chair. However, she found herself spending most of her time in the kitchen—where most of the family discussions were held—and in the living room, where she watched her favorite programs on the large family TV.

Janice and the children were not home yet so, after putting away the groceries, Hannah turned on the TV and watched last night's episode of *Walker*. "What a handsome man he is—reminds me of Leo," she sighed, as she removed her shoes and settled into the recliner Janice had bought especially for her.

Chapter 2

Janice was a forty-two year old attractive woman with a successful career—principal of the high school which had the lowest drop-out rate in the county—and yet her mother made her feel like a child. Oh, she knew Hannah didn't mean to do it, but she couldn't help herself. It's as if she reverted back to childhood, reacting in ways that she was embarrassed for Madison to see. Hannah just knew how to push her buttons—all in a sweet, passive-aggressive way.

Take last night, for example. Janice was dressed for dinner with Paul and Hannah looked at her and said, "Is that what they're wearing these days?" Now why didn't she just say she didn't like the outfit, or that Janice didn't look good in it? But, no, that's not Hannah's style—she has to say something "neutral" so she can always respond, "I didn't say anything was wrong."

Well, Janice fell for the trap—and went into a long diatribe about how, yes, this was what people were wearing these days, and she liked it, and that fashion had changed since Hannah's time. Janice was angry and showed it. And Hannah said, as predicted, "I just asked a question—why are you so upset?" Madison glanced up from her homework and rolled her eyes—whether at her mother or her grandmother wasn't clear.

Well, Janice thought, I've had a good day, we're going to have a good dinner and, hopefully, there won't be any crisis to deal with. I just want to relax, have a nice warm bath, and read my book.

When she arrived home she found Hannah asleep in the recliner, with the TV blaring away. As she turned off the TV, Hannah awoke. "I wasn't sleeping, just resting my eyes. What do you want I should make for dinner?"

Janice sat down on the couch next to Hannah's recliner. "I thought we'd have a big salad with some of the salmon we had last night. How does that sound?"

"Fine….So how was your day?"

"Actually, pretty good. The faculty meeting went pretty well—the only one who objected to the new curriculum proposal was Mike, and nobody agreed with him. He took twenty minutes to explain all his objections, but it passed anyway! How about you? What did you do today?"

"Oh, it was so depressing! I finally found where Ruby was. They had her hidden away in some nursing home. I visited her there—such a terrible place: gloomy, bad food. And her son, that son-of-a-bitch, is selling her house so she'll have to go into assisted living. Assisted living, my *tuchis*—she's perfectly capable of taking care of herself. She just fell—anybody can fall—but she's getting therapy and should be able to walk in a couple of weeks. And she's not at all senile. Just because you're eighty years old doesn't mean you're senile."

"Ruby—she's the one you met at the Senior Center?"

"That's the one. She's a widow and lives over on Fancher St., in that big white house with the beautiful garden. And that's another thing—she's worried about the garden so I promised I'd take care of it."

"You? What are you going to do—go over every day and look at it? I can't see you weeding."

"No, I don't do weeding. But I could water things—that should be easy enough. And besides, it's only until she gets out of that place."

"But you said her son is selling the house—how can he do that?"

"Because he's a son-of-a-bitch, that's how."

"That doesn't tell me much, Mom."

"Well, it seems that Ruby's son convinced her that it would be a good idea to sell the house to him—for tax purposes, or something like that. Anyway, she would live there but he would own the house. So now he can sell it if he wants. I think he's up to something—I think he's going to use the money from the house for his own advantage and leave her in some terrible place that doesn't cost much."

"Do you know him?"

"No, but I know he's no good. What kind of a son does that to his mother? He didn't even visit her when she was in the hospital and he lives only two hours away."

"Well, he does sound like scum, but don't get yourself involved in anything. Ruby should get a lawyer to help her. This is beyond anything you can do to help."

"I know; but I feel so sorry for her. You know, she was the first one to go out of her way to make me feel welcome when I arrived here. I met her at *Marty's*. She helped me figure out what the different cuts of meat were—you know they do things different here. I couldn't find any Delmonico steak and she explained that it's called rib-eye steak here. Strange! Anyway, she invited me to have lunch at the Senior Center, and then she introduced me to the people there. And, as they say, the rest is history. The fact that she's Jewish, and from New York, doesn't hurt. You know, there aren't many Jews in this town—not that it matters, of course, but it's nice to have someone to talk to about the old days. Anyway, she's become a good friend and I want to do what I can to help her."

Just then the door opened and Madison burst into the room and yelled, "I'm home!"

"Hi, honey, we're in the living room." Janice smiled as her daughter entered the room. Madison's long brown hair was pulled back into a ponytail, tendrils falling forward over her cheeks. She was on the short side, obviously a family characteristic, but was slender with ample curves. She wore no make-up, but her full lips and large dark eyes, with lashes so long and full it was hard to believe they were real, made enhancements unnecessary. At seventeen, she combined the innocence of a girl with the blossoming beauty of a young woman.

"How did the math test go?" Janice asked.

"Terrible. All that studying and then he asked questions that we haven't even gotten to yet. What a jerk."

"A jerk? You call your teacher a jerk?" This was asked by Hannah, who had such respect for educators that she couldn't imagine a teacher being, no less a student calling one, a jerk.

"Oh, Grandma, you just don't understand. He doesn't teach, he just reads the textbook to us and gives us problems to work on in class. I can read the textbook by myself. I need someone to explain it to me!"

"Well, you're lucky then. Your mother was always good at school—she can explain it."

Janice laughed. "Not in math, though. Okay, let's get started on dinner. Maddie, how about putting your stuff away and helping me in the kitchen? We can let Grandma rest a little bit before dinner—she's had a tough day."

Madison's ears perked up. "Why, what happened, Grandma?"

"Oh, it's nothing serious, darling. A friend of mine is having troubles. Her son, that son-of-a-bitch, is selling her house and she'll have no place to live and will have to go into an assisted living place, even though she's perfectly capable of living alone once she finishes her therapy."

"Assisted living? What's that?" inquired Madison.

"It's a place they put old people when they don't want them around any more."

"That's terrible."

"You got that right, kiddo."

"Now Mom, that's not fair," interrupted Janice. "Some assisted living places are quite nice. And sometimes that's the only solution for people who really can't live alone any more."

"So that's what you're going to do to me when I get old?"

"Grandma, you're already old," said Madison in her matter of fact voice. "You don't need to go into one of those places. You have us."

"I know, darling, and I love you both for letting me live here." Hannah smiled and looked at Madison. "But some people don't have such a good daughter—like my friend Ruby and her son-of-a-bitch son!"

"Enough with the son-of-a-bitch son. I'd prefer not to use that language in this house," declared Janice.

"Oh, Mom, I've heard that word before. In fact, that's rather mild—at least Grandma doesn't call him that mother-fucking son-of-a-bitch."

"Madison! That'll be enough….Come help me get dinner ready."

"What are we having? I'm really starved. Lunch was yucky today—no pizza or tacos, just some kind of slop with vegetables I've never seen before. Suzanne had to add hot sauce to give it any taste. I didn't eat any of it though. I just had some yogurt and chips."

"Your brother's eating at Billy's house tonight, so we're having salad with salmon—his least favorite dish!"

As Janice and Madison went into the kitchen, Hannah thought back over dinner times when she was a child. Whatever was put on your plate, you ate! To even make a face about the food served was followed up with such a withering look from both her parents that she learned early on to say nothing, but just eat. Occasionally she slid the lima beans—her least favorite but often served food—into her napkin, hoping her parents wouldn't notice.

However, she was pleased that Madison didn't seem to have fallen into the compulsion to be overly thin. She ate when she was hungry and she ate well. Some of her friends seemed anorexic to Hannah—skinny, not slender. Where were their mothers, she wondered.

. . . .

They had a pleasant dinner at the table in the kitchen. Good food and good conversation. Madison was in fine form, entertaining them with the antics of her friends and describing her plans for the homecoming dance in two weeks.

"I'm going with Kenny—he's not a boyfriend," she insisted, "just a friend. Have you seen my dress, Grandma? It's beautiful. We found it at the local consignment shop. Mom noticed it first and she was right—it's perfect: red with thin straps and it fits just right." She hesitated. "But I have to find shoes to go with it," she said, glancing over at Hannah, who, over Janice's objections, promised to take her shopping.

The dinner conversation lasted longer than usual. By the time they had finished eating, it was time for Janice to listen to the 7:00 PBS news. Madison scooted off to her room, there to listen to the latest *Lady Gaga* CD while she studied her French verbs, and Hannah stayed behind to clean up the kitchen. When she joined Janice in the living room, Jim Lehrer was reporting on the latest Washington scandal involving payments by a lobbyist to a Senator. Hannah restrained herself from commenting that this was nothing new, not wanting to interrupt Janice's concentration.

When the program was over, Janice retreated to her study down the hall to work on plans for the next day's meetings, and Hannah took over the TV to watch her evening dose of *Walker, Texas Ranger*. Fortunately, the show was in syndication and reruns were available every evening on cable. She didn't care that she had seen most of the episodes before. She still enjoyed them and found that she often didn't remember how they ended, which added to her enjoyment.

Chapter 3

Madison was trying to concentrate on the conjugation of irregular verbs in order to prepare for a quiz in her French class the next day, but found herself zoning out and listening to her iPod. She loved the iPod—she could listen without her mother complaining that it was too loud, or commenting on her choice of music. Why couldn't old people understand that music was different these days? Her mother listened to jazz and blues, which was not too bad, but her grandmother thought that no one could compare to Frank Sinatra. Fortunately, they didn't have any Sinatra CDs so she was spared having to listen to Hannah explain why he was so good.

Grandma was funny. In some ways, Madison thought, she was really young—for her age. But in other ways, she was really out of touch. Like when she first came to live with them. She arrived in March, and looked out the window one morning and asked, "Why do you have all those dead trees on the lawn?" She had lived all her life in New York City and obviously had never noticed that trees shed their leaves in the fall and then grew them back in the spring! And then there was the time they had taken a ride into the country to get pumpkins for Halloween and Hannah had said, "Look at all this wasted space—they should build a shopping center here." She seemed skeptical when Janice pointed out that this was farmland and in the spring things would be growing in the fields. Hannah didn't appear convinced, which caused Madison and David to look at each other with amazement.

But then she could be fun to be with. Even David thought she was okay, and that was high praise for him. Madison enjoyed being with Hannah, who was easy to talk to and, most of the time, defended her in the many arguments she had with her mother. But she couldn't understand why her mother found Hannah so frustrating and why she reacted the way she did to Hannah's questions. Grandma never criticized her mother, just asked questions—what was wrong with that?

Madison heard the downstairs door open and slam. Obviously, David was home. Any minute now, he would stomp up the stairs and into her room with tales of his latest adventure. He and his friend Billy were into some new video game and he kept Madison up to date on his wins—and infrequent losses. She couldn't understand his interest in the games; they were too violent for her. But she accepted the fact that boys were different, less mature than girls!

. . . .

Downstairs, Janice was trying to get more than the usual responses from David to her questions: "What did you do today?" "Nothing much." "Well, how was school?" "Okay." "What did you and Billy do after school?" "Nothing much." "Did you play video games?" "Yeah." "What did you have for dinner?" "Some kind of meat."

Janice gave up and told David to get ready for bed. He bounded up the stairs, charged into Madison's room, and proceeded to relate his afternoon victories to her.

Janice looked at her mother and sighed. "I don't know what to do with him. I know he's a good kid, but he never tells me anything."

"But he's doing well in school, isn't he?" asked Hannah. "So don't worry. He's at that age, you know, when boys get involved in their own world, with their own friends. Family just doesn't seem important to them. He'll change."

"But he spends so much time on those video games. That worries me. He and Billy spend almost all their free time playing them, and they're so violent. I try to monitor which games he plays, but who knows what goes on when I'm not around or when he's at Billy's."

"Have you talked to Billy's mother?"

"She has the same worries I do. She and her husband both work so no one is there when the boys come home from school. Who knows what they're doing—especially since he won't tell me!"

Hannah knew she had to tread lightly as she asked the next question: "How do they get the games?"

"What do you mean? They buy them, they don't steal them!" Clearly, Janice had once again misunderstood Hannah's point.

"I know that, darling. But isn't there some way you could, you know, like monitor what he buys? I know it's his own money, but could you maybe put some restrictions on the games that he can buy with his money?"

Janice shrugged. "I tried that. He doesn't buy any of those really violent ones, but they get them from the other kids at school and somehow copy them. I'm sure it's illegal, but that's the least of my concerns. Sometimes I think that if his father took some responsibility for his children things would be different. But Jim barely has contact with either of them. Madison accepts that, but I sometimes think that David is really angry about his father."

"Well, that's hard for children—to be ignored, almost abandoned, by a parent. But don't be so hard on yourself. Obviously Billy's father hasn't been able to make a difference either."

Janice smiled at her mother. Here she had done it again! Hannah was clearly trying to help, and she had jumped on her for asking an innocent question. Madison was right—she was unfair to Hannah.

The two women sat in silence for a while, watching a rerun episode of *Sex and the City*. Hannah's only comment was, "Who would pay that much for shoes!" Janice didn't share how much she paid for the red sandals she had just bought. No need to tell Hannah everything.

At the end of the program, Janice went upstairs to ensure that both kids were ready for bed, and Hannah dozed through the next program, awaking only when she heard Janice turn off the TV. She got up, bid goodnight, and went to the kitchen to make herself some herbal tea before she retreated to her own suite. Sometimes she just liked the privacy that the suite afforded.

. . . .

The next morning, after the usual hectic breakfasts—Madison arguing with Janice that oatmeal wasn't real food, David gulping down cereal, toast, and a banana while dashing out the door to join Billy, and Janice trying to finish her coffee before heading off to work—Hannah sat at the kitchen table with her second cup of coffee. She cherished this time of the day, a time when she was alone in the house and could visit with her thoughts and make plans for the day. She was a planner, a list maker. Every night before turning in, she made a list of things to do the next day. Sometimes, the same items appeared on subsequent lists, but eventually they got done and she could permanently erase them.

The kitchen had always been her favorite place in a home. It symbolized family to her, reminding her of when that had been the hub of her household, with her cooking while Janice did homework at the table. Even in the years when Hannah worked outside the home as a saleswoman at *Macy's*, she had always found time to cook a hot meal for Leo and Janice. It was clear to her that if her job interfered with her family, the job would go. Of course, that was easy for her to do as Leo's income was sufficient for a comfortable life. Not all women were as lucky as she.

And this kitchen was special. Larger than any of the kitchens she had ever had, with its bay window overlooking the back yard, and its yellow walls, it was bright and cheerful. She enjoyed looking out the window at the occasional bird at the bird feeder, which occasionally had some birdseed in it! There was a formal dining room, but most of the family meals were taken in the kitchen at the large round table. The house was a standard 1980s model, but with a large kitchen. The appliances were not new—no stainless steel stove and refrigerator—but the space was more typical of those found in old country kitchens.

This morning, she was going to prepare the chicken stew to take to Ruby when she visited later in the day. But while that was baking, she would do some detective work—find out about Harold. All she knew was his name and that he had a car dealership. She wasn't sure what she would find out, or even how to go about finding out, but she could certainly make a start. She knew how to use a computer and had googled all sorts of things. That would be a starting place.

She put the chicken stew in the oven, cleaned up the kitchen, settled down in front of the computer in Janice's study and typed in: "Harold Shapiro." Unfortunately that was also the name of the former president of Princeton! After browsing through twenty pages of items, she gave up and redid the search for "Harold Shapiro car dealership." That didn't work, either. She had to get more information to narrow down the search.

It was now 11:00 and another of her favorite programs was on—*The View*. Seated in her recliner, with a third cup of coffee, she tried to concentrate on the program but her mind kept going back to Ruby and her son-of-a-bitch son. She would have to get more information about Harold from Ruby without upsetting her. No mother wants to think that her child is crooked—although, Hannah had to admit, she really had nothing but a gut feeling about Harold's motives.

By noon she was ready to leave. She called the local bus company. Brewster didn't have public transportation, but they did have a bus service available on request. Coming from New York, she found this quaint, but rather charming, and so had adjusted easily. Often, however, Hannah would drive Janice to work and then use the car for her errands and lunches at the Senior Center. Today Janice had needed the car and so Hannah boarded the bus, carefully carrying a big red casserole dish.

When she entered Ruby's room, Ruby looked up and exclaimed, "They let you in with that? Nobody noticed?"

"Noticed, schmoticed—those two out there are so busy talking to each other they wouldn't notice if I was carrying a machine gun! It's a wonder anybody ever checks up on you."

"Well, that they don't do either. But I'm getting better. I can get out of bed by myself and if I use the walker, I can get to the bathroom and even down the hall. But, let me smell the chicken."

Hannah lifted the lid off the casserole dish and Ruby breathed in the aroma. "Ah, real food. Could I have some now?"

"Of course—that's why I brought it. Here's a plate and fork. It's so tender you don't need a knife, but I brought one anyway."

As Hannah dished out the chicken, Ruby started to cry again. "I'm sorry for being such a burden. I don't deserve such a good friend."

"Nonsense! Everyone deserves a friend—so why wouldn't you? Besides, you're the one who was a good friend, making me feel comfortable when I first arrived. Remember how you helped me at the meat counter at *Marty's*? And then introduced me to the Center? You remarked that my New York accent made you homesick. And when you heard I was Jewish, well that did it. Two old Jewish ladies reminiscing about the old days in New York. But enough about that. Have you heard from Charlie? He said he was going to call you."

Ruby, smiling, replied, "Yes, he called this morning. He said he'd try to visit me today, but he thought he was coming down with a cold and so might not make it. He's a nice man, but I really don't think I want to get involved with him—or with any man. At this age, they come with so many troubles it's not worth it."

Hannah agreed. Most of the men she knew who were her age were either lifelong bachelors who were used to their own ways, or widowers who were in the market for a new wife to take care of them. Better she should stick to her women friends.

"Okay, so what's the plan? When do you get out of here?"

"You think they tell me anything? I haven't seen a doctor since the first day I was here. The only people I see are that girl who brings the food—you know, the one with the terrible writing on the t-shirts—and the people in physical therapy."

"Have you heard from your son?"

"He's coming down this weekend to discuss his plans for me. I keep telling him I don't want to stay here, that I want to go home. If I could be there, I could afford some home-care—I don't need help all the time, just a little in the morning getting ready. But he keeps saying he's already put the house up for sale."

"Do you have anyone you could bring in—like a lawyer?"

"No, who knows a lawyer who works for nothing!" Ruby paused, then looked up. "Hannah, would you be here when Harold comes? It would make me feel better to have you here. It might make him listen to me."

"Of course. Just let me know when he's coming. If it's the weekend I'll probably be able to use Janice's car, so I could come any time. But, look, your chicken is getting cold. Eat!"

. . . .

When Hannah returned, she was surprised to find David at home, sprawled on the couch, reading a comic book. "Darling, are you sick?" she asked.

"No, it was just a half day. Teachers' conferences or something," he replied.

"Are you hungry? Do you want a nosh?"

"No thanks, I had lunch."

"David, I have a favor to ask of you." David's ears perked up. It was unusual for his grandma to ask for anything. "I need to get some information about a man and his business and I haven't been able to find anything about him on the computer. Do you know how to do that—get information about someone?"

Now she had his attention. David was twelve, going on eight! But he knew computers and he loved intrigue. He was short for his age, with light brown curly hair which he kept short, arguing that that way he didn't have to comb it. He had inherited his father's blue eyes, combined with the full eyelashes of his mother. He showed signs of becoming a handsome young man, but at present all that one could see was a small, thin boy in constant motion, dressed in whatever was at hand when he awoke. No matter how much time Janice spent making sure he left the house with at least clean clothes and matching socks, by the time he arrived at school he looked as if he had just finished a ten mile marathon, smudges on his clothes and face.

"Sure," he replied. "Is he a bad guy?" he asked with glee. Clearly, a bad guy would be fun to track down.

"Well, I don't know that he's a bad guy—but I think he is. That's what I want you should find out. Can you do that?"

David leapt off the couch and ran to his computer. "What's his name?" he asked.

"Harold Shapiro—but I checked and there are too many Harold Shapiros. I know he's in cars—you know, selling cars."

"Okay, but then we need to know where he lives, his relatives, where his business is, things like that. Maybe get his middle name. You know, narrow things down."

"All I know is he lives in Broomfield something—that's in Michigan—and I guess his store is there, too."

"I think you mean Bloomfield Hills. That's near Detroit. I went there once with my dad when he had a friend living there. It was a cool house—had a swimming pool and a tennis court. And horses! It was awesome!"

"Ah, so it's a ritzy neighborhood. That makes sense. Okay, see what you can find out. Tomorrow, when I see my friend, I'll get more information about him. And, darling, let's keep this to ourselves. I wouldn't want we should worry your mother."

David nodded agreement, although he looked puzzled. Why would his mother be worried about getting information about this man? This was going to be excellent! He might even get his buddy, Billy, involved in this. This could be as much fun as playing *Grand Theft Auto*. In fact, it might be better—it was like being a spy!

Hannah smiled as she left David hunched over his computer. She, too, felt the exhilaration of "spying."

Chapter 4

THE LINE OUTSIDE JANICE'S office was finally disappearing—only three students remained. It had been a hectic afternoon. Midterm grades had been distributed and she had been meeting with students who were failing their various courses. It was something that wasn't required of a principal. After all, if students failed, they failed! But Janice believed that taking a personal interest in students' performances motivated at least some of them to do better.

Janice was liked by most of the students, and respected by her teachers. It was the superintendent she had trouble with! He was a "bottom line" person—interested in how many students graduated within the typical four years. State funding, while never adequate, was now allocated on the basis of the number of students who graduated in four years. Drop-outs obviously hurt the budget but, given the new funding system, so did "laggers." Janice was concerned with these students and did what she could to keep all students in school. But she understood why it took some students an extra semester or so to graduate. Given the economy, many of the older students worked too many hours after school, sometimes instead of school. This clearly affected their grades, requiring them to repeat courses. Since she had taken the job of principal, the four-year graduation rate had gone down. Previously, the pressure was on to promote everyone, even if they had not mastered the course material. No one had received a grade lower than a "C" and everyone graduated on time. That had changed when Janice became principal. Now, teachers were free to grade a student's performance more honestly, which resulted in more of the students repeating courses, thereby delaying their graduation.

After the last three students had left, Janice sat back in her chair and took a sip of the now cold coffee on her desk. She was preparing to work on the new curriculum proposal when Madison came in. "Hi, honey. What's up?" she asked.

"Mom, is it okay if I go shopping with Grandma for shoes after school today? I know it's my turn to take Max for a good run, but I could do that after dinner. Okay?"

Max was the big loveable golden retriever that had been in the family since David was born. Twelve years old and still a puppy! Janice had been reluctant to add a puppy to the family, especially since at the time she was pregnant with David. But Jim had brought home this adorable puppy and she couldn't resist, even though she knew she would end up being responsible for its training and care. They had built a large pen in the backyard where Max could frolic during the day when everyone was away, but it wasn't enough to dissipate the dog's energy. So it became the children's responsibility to take him for a run every day.

"Have you talked this over with Grandma? You know she's spending a lot of time with her friend these days. She may not be up to shopping."

"I'll ask her, but I'm sure she'll say okay. You know she really likes to shop—more than you."

'Okay, but don't pressure her. Remember, she may think she's young, but she's not. She sometimes forgets that and overdoes it."

Madison kissed her mother and left. Janice smiled to herself. She was proud of her daughter. At seventeen, she was turning into a lovely young woman. And she was proud of her mother. At seventy-eight, Hannah was handling widowhood well. Leo had died four years ago and Hannah had stayed on in New York for two years, living alone, until Janice had convinced her to come to Brewster. It hadn't been easy. Hannah had to adjust to a small Midwest town and Janice had to adjust to living with her mother again. Hannah had been such a strong presence in Janice's childhood that she was still working out how to have an adult relationship with her mother.

The last four years hadn't been easy for Janice either. Divorced, with two teenagers and no financial support from her ex, she was worried. Even with a principal's salary, which she had to admit was certainly more than most people earned, she was constantly concerned about money. Would she be able to put the kids through college? She had seen what happened to students who had to work thirty, forty hours a week to pay for school—she didn't want that to happen to her kids. And she worried about her mother. What if Hannah needed more care than Janice could provide? At present, Hannah was perfectly capable of taking care of herself, and others. But what about the future? Janice clearly felt herself a part of the "sandwich generation"—the generation caught between responsibility for one's parents and one's children.

At least, she thought, there have been no complaints about her dating again. Everyone seemed to like Paul Burrows. But with both of their schedules so crowded they barely found time to be together. Once every two weeks was typical, and even then privacy was difficult to find. Paul, also divorced, shared custody of his ten-year-old daughter, Sandy, who alternated weekends between him and his ex-wife. Working around all these schedules made romantic evenings rare.

. . . .

By the time Janice arrived home, the kitchen was filled with the aroma of chicken and spices, Madison was on the phone, and David and Hannah were huddled over the table peering at papers. Surprised at seeing David so involved in something other than his video games, Janice resisted disturbing them—but she was curious. She knew that David was fond of Hannah, but she couldn't imagine what interests they had in common.

She uttered a cheery, "Hi, folks. Smells good, Mom," as she hung up her jacket.

Hannah looked up from the jumble of papers on the table and smiled at Janice. "It's the chicken stew I made for Ruby. I kept some for our dinner. So how was your day, darling?"

"Pretty good. A lot of conferences with students, but it went well."

Madison hung up the phone and ran to Janice. "See?" she said, pointing to her feet. "These are the shoes Grandma bought for me. Aren't they beautiful? I'm breaking them in so they'll be ready for the dance."

Janice looked down at the delicate black straps wound around Madison's feet. "They're very pretty, but can you walk in them? That's a rather high heel."

"It's only three inches—and that's why I'm practicing walking in them. I'll be fine by the dance."

Janice looked at Hannah, who shrugged and proclaimed, "Well, they *are* pretty!"

By this time, David's interest had evaporated and he rose from the table. "Can we eat now? I have soccer practice at 7:00."

. . . .

The next morning, determined to find out more about Harold, Hannah dropped Janice off at work and then drove to *Sunset Manor*. Again, she went unnoticed by the staff, who seemed to be looking at magazines, ignoring the bells ringing from patients requesting help. She found Ruby sitting up in the wheelchair. Ruby smiled. "I got into this on my own, no help at all. I could get along at home with just a little help for a while. Then I'll be as good as new."

"Well, I don't know about 'new'—none of us is as good as new. But you look better. I brought you a salad for your lunch—it's got tuna and a hard-boiled egg in it—but it should be all right without refrigeration. I'll leave it here next to the bed. Do you want I should push you outside to get some fresh air? It's a nice day. Just put a sweater on so you don't get a chill."

Ruby, pleased at the promise of fresh air, pointed to the closet where her sweater was, and together they left the room, Hannah pushing Ruby in her wheelchair as if on a mission. Part of Hannah's agenda, aside from getting Ruby out from that depressing room, was to get her talking about Harold.

She parked Ruby's wheelchair in front of the ugly building in the small area that served as a garden—even though there was nothing in it but piles of dried leaves—and sat down on the bench next to her. "So, tell me about Harold. What does he do? Is he married? Children?"

"He's married—her name's Mimi—and they have two children, both boys. I haven't seen them in years. They must be in their teens already, maybe even in college. They used to visit when Bernie—my husband—was alive, but in the last few years I rarely hear from them."

"What does Harold do? Does his wife also work?"

"He has a car dealership. He does very well—he's so smart, you know! They have a nice house in Bloomfield Hills—that's a wealthy area near Detroit—and the boys both go to private schools, so he must be making good money. And his wife, she doesn't work—not even at home! They have maids for everything. She doesn't know from cooking or cleaning, and to go without having her hair and nails done every week—well, that would be a disaster!"

"What's the name of his store?"

"Oh, it's a lovely name. He used his father's name—Bernard—and called it *Bernie's Bloomfield Buys.* Isn't that nice?"

"Adorable! What are the boys' names?" Hannah asked, thinking that the more specific the information she got the easier it would be to track down information on Harold and his business.

"Martin is the oldest and Samuel is the younger one. Martin must be about 19 now and Sam is two years younger. They're good boys. I'm sure if they lived closer I'd see more of them."

It was clear to Hannah that Ruby was protective of her son. No mother wanted to think that her child was a son-of-a-bitch, to use Hannah's favorite expression. It was going to be difficult to convince Ruby of that, though, without strong evidence. She just hoped that David was up to the challenge.

Ruby drew closer to Hannah. At first, Hannah thought that she was getting chilled and suggested they go inside, but Ruby shook her head and said, "I don't know if having nothing to do all day has made me imagine things, but I'm worried about some of the people here."

"Worried, why?"

"You know I have therapy twice a day here. And it's good therapy, I think. Anyway, it's helping. We do the therapy in a group—the same people every day. But some of the people show up for only a few times and then never come back. I don't know what happens to them."

Hannah could see that Ruby was clearly concerned, but she didn't understand what was so problematic about people finishing therapy. She asked, "Maybe they got better and went home?"

"But they were in worse condition than I am. Some could barely get out of their wheelchair, and some had trouble breathing—I think they had heart problems. Why would they be released before they were better? They won't release me until I can get in and out of my wheelchair and walk down the hall by myself."

"Well, it does sound strange. But maybe they went to live with their families, or maybe they didn't have enough money to stay here—although it's hard to believe you have to pay to stay in this place."

"Maybe. But one of them, Mrs. Johnson, told me that she had no family—and besides, her name is still on the list of patients but I never see her any more."

"That is strange. But there must be some reasonable explanation. Have you asked about her? Maybe the nurses could explain what happened."

"You see nurses? That's how I see nurses! The only one I see is the therapist, and she never says anything, except to give us orders. I really think something's not right here."

"Well, all the more reason to get you out of here. We need to discuss that when Harold comes tomorrow. What time is he coming—so I could be here when he comes, like you asked?"

"He said sometime in the afternoon, but he wasn't specific. It would be after lunch, that I know. He wouldn't want to miss his lunch! He was always such a good eater and never put on weight until this past year. I guess that's typical of men when they get to his age—sixty. Could you be here like 1:00? I wish I could be more specific, but he never gives me details."

"No problem. How about I bring you some lunch and then I'll just wait until he arrives. Maybe I'll work on the scarf I'm making Maddie for the holidays. She picked out the pattern—it's not difficult, and I'm almost finished."

They chatted a while longer and then Hannah wheeled Ruby back to her room, helped her into bed and left, leaving Ruby to her tuna fish lunch, most likely followed by a nap.

Chapter 5

Driving home, Hannah tried to keep in mind all the information she had received from Ruby. *Bernie's Bloomfield Buys*—what a silly name, she thought. But it obviously was a successful business, so who was she to criticize. Private schools for the boys, a maid for the wife—he must be doing okay. She only hoped that David was up for the job of finding out what made Harold run. Did he need the money from Ruby's house or was he just a son-of-a-bitch, as she suspected.

She was concerned about Ruby, though. She had seemed genuinely worried about the missing Mrs. Johnson. Hannah was sure Ruby was just confused and that her own anxiety was coloring her perceptions. Once she was out of that place, she'd be better. And that was the problem to concentrate on—getting her out of there. But to go where? If she couldn't convince Harold to let Ruby stay in her own home, where could she go? Even if he paid for her care in some assisted living place, that wasn't what Ruby wanted.

It wouldn't be what Hannah wanted either, which made her again realize how fortunate she was to be able to live so comfortably with Janice and the children. She made a mental note to remember that and not annoy Janice so much, though she couldn't understand why Janice always turned what she said into a criticism. Truly, she marveled at Janice and what she'd accomplished with her life. Who knew that the adorable, chubby little girl, who was so shy she hid behind her mother whenever anyone was around, would turn into a beautiful, accomplished, assertive woman? And even though Janice was now a single parent—doing an amazing job, no thanks to that no-good-nik ex-husband of hers—she had made a place for Hannah where she felt wanted and loved. If only Ruby had a child like that!

It was close to noon by the time Hannah arrived home. Hungry, she made herself a salad with the remainder of the tuna and sat down at the kitchen table with the day's crossword puzzle. But today she couldn't concentrate on the crossword puzzle. She was anxious to get to the computer to see if she could find anything out about Harold. She knew David would be more successful, but her curiosity was at too high a level for her to wait.

She sat down at the computer in Janice's study and typed in *"Bernie's Bloomfield Buys"* and up came a page of information. But it was all about the cars they had in stock, what services they provided, and promotional material. That wouldn't help her find out what she needed—was he in financial troubles? That was beyond her computer abilities, perhaps also beyond David's. Disappointed, she went into the living room and settled in her recliner to watch *Oprah.*

When David came in he found her snoring away in her chair. He tried not to wake her, but she was a light sleeper and he was a heavy walker. Hannah looked up. "Sorry to wake you, Grandma," he said. "Oh, no, darling. I was just resting my eyes," she replied. David looked at her and smiled, but didn't say anything.

"David, I have some more information about that man. But I don't know if we can get what I want. I know his business name, and the names of his family and where he lives, but how can we get information about his financial situation—you know, whether his business is in trouble? Do you have any idea how to find that out?"

Hannah knew that expecting a twelve year old to have access to that sort of information was foolish, but perhaps he knew how to hack? Would that be wrong? Would she be aiding and abetting? Surely, there must be some public record of how well a business was doing. Who could she ask?

"No, but I can at least see what's on his site. Maybe we could take a trip down there and see if his business looks good—you know, see if anybody's buying his cars."

Hannah laughed. "You mean a free trip down to Detroit, right? And maybe while we're there we could take in a Tigers game? Good try, kiddo."

Just then Madison and Janice could be heard at the front door. Madison was pleading with Janice to let her go to a sleepover the night of the homecoming dance. Janice wasn't responding, which indicated to Hannah that she had already issued her decision and wasn't going to be influenced by Madison's well-rehearsed arguments and threatening tears.

"Hi, Mom. How was your day?" Janice was clearly ignoring Madison, which caused her to tromp upstairs, as she shouted, "You're so unfair. Suzanne's mother agreed. I'll be the only one who can't go. I won't be able to face my friends. It's so humiliating."

Hannah looked questioningly at Janice, who simply said, "Don't ask."

Not hearing the usual noise from upstairs of monsters being zapped, Janice inquired, "Where's David? Isn't he home from school yet?"

"He's upstairs—working on something on the computer, I think." Hannah was reluctant to let Janice know of her plans. Janice would be "sensible," pointing out that it wasn't Hannah's problem, that Ruby should be the one to deal with her son, and that there was nothing Hannah could do anyway: Ruby's son legally owned the house and could do what he wanted with it. But Hannah didn't want sensible. She wanted justice—at least that's what she told herself.

Her thoughts were interrupted by shouts from upstairs. Madison had shared her list of grievances with David, who responded that dances were a waste of good time and couldn't understand why Madison was so upset. "Anyway," he said, "I'm busy with something important, so go away."

This interchange could have been accomplished quietly, but both of them were shouting at top volume. With apparent frustration, Janice asked Hannah to start dinner while she went upstairs to see what was going on.

'Maddie, that's enough. We'll talk abut this later—when you can discuss it like an adult. And, David, what are you doing that's so important you can't be civil to your sister?"

"I'm working on this project for Grandma. We're going to get that guy."

"What guy? What project? What are you two up to?"

"You know, the guy who's making Grandma's friend go to that bad place. We're going to find out about his business and then…." David shrugged—he didn't know what happened next! He'd leave that up to Hannah.

"Mother!" Janice yelled as she came downstairs. "What are you up to? What have you got David involved in?"

"Darling, calm down. It's perfectly legitimate. I just need a little help finding out some information on the computer and he's helping me. You know, these young people are so good at that sort of thing."

"He says you're trying to 'get that guy.' What the hell does that mean?"

Their conversation was loud enough to get the attention of Madison, who was now standing in the hallway, having at least momentarily forgotten her own problems.

"What's going on?" she asked.

"Nothing, darling," Hannah answered. "Your mother and I were just having a conversation. Come, help me set the table. Dinner will be ready in about twenty minutes. We're having pot roast—it's almost done."

Janice realized that this was not the time to pursue the issue. "It's all right, Maddie," she smiled. "We didn't realize we were talking so loudly.

Come, help us in the kitchen—and then, later…well, we'll see…" leaving the thought unfinished.

. . . .

Dinner went smoothly, everyone on good behavior. As usual, David was the first one to ask to leave the table. As he headed up the stairs, Janice called out to him, "Homework before anything else."

Madison, however, captivated by the bits and pieces she had heard earlier, was anxious to pursue the topic. "Grandma, what's happening with your friend, the woman in the nursing home? Is she going to have to move out of her home because of her son?"

"Not if I can help it, darling."

Janice looked at her mother, but said nothing. There would be time for that after Madison went to bed.

"But what if she has to? Where will she go? Is she going to be homeless like the people you see on TV?"

"No, she just needs help because she can't take care of herself. She'll probably go to an assisted living place…"

Here Janice cast a warning glance at Hannah— "where there will be people to take care of her," Hannah continued. "She won't be homeless."

"What's assisted living?" asked Madison, not having previously received an adequate answer to the question.

"It's where you have your own place," answered Janice, "usually a nice room, or even a small apartment, where you can have some of your own things with you, and there are people who help you with things like bathing, getting dressed, getting you in and out of bed or wheelchairs. And there's a dining room where you can go to eat and a lounge where you can be with other people to talk, play cards, watch TV—things like that. It's usually a very nice place. Do you remember Mrs. Lorenzo, who lived next door? Well, when she got old and couldn't take care of herself she went to an assisted living place. Her daughter told me that she was very comfortable there and had made new friends whom she played cards with. They even had parties and dances; it was a very nice place."

Hannah sat quietly through Janice's idyllic description of assisted living, not mentioning that the kind of place she had described cost quite a bit of money, money that Ruby will not have. But Janice was right; it wouldn't do to have Madison worry about Ruby—at least not yet. Eventually, however, she thought, children need to know the realities of life or they never develop the compassion for others that makes a *mensch.*

After Madison had cleared the table and gone upstairs to finish her homework, Janice turned to her mother and asked, "More coffee, Mom? We need to talk."

"No, no more coffee for me. So, talk!"

"Mom, what are you up to? I know you. You notice something wrong and you have to fix it. I love that about you, but sometimes you get involved in things you can't fix. Ruby's situation seems like one of those. What can you do? And what is David doing? I don't want him getting into trouble with hacking or anything like that."

"Darling, I'd never get him involved in something illegal or dangerous. It's just that he's so much better at getting information than I am. You know I don't know much about computers. I can do email and order things on-line, but that's about it. He knows how to get information that's on there that I can't get to. But, yes, I am trying to find out why Harold—that's Ruby's son—is so anxious to sell her house. I know, I know. It's not her house any more, but even that makes me suspicious. Why did he convince her to sign it over to him? Why wasn't there some guarantee in the agreement that she could live there until she died? A lot of agreements put that in to make sure there isn't any hanky-panky going on. If I find out that he doesn't need the money, that his business is doing just fine—well, then he's just a son-of-a-bitch. But if I find out that he has money troubles, well, then, that's a different story."

"So, what will you do in either case? Tell Ruby her son is no good or that he's kicking her out because he has financial problems? Will that change anything for her, except open her eyes about her son? She still has to find someplace to go."

Hannah sighed. "I don't know. It just makes me angry that a person could treat someone—especially a parent—that way."

Janice got up from the table and went over to Hannah. Hugging her, she said, "Mom, you know you never have to worry about anything like that happening to you. Even when you get old—older—and can't walk, and keep forgetting things, and frustrate me even more than you do now, you'll always have a place here—even if we have to bring in help."

Hannah replied, "I know, darling, I know." Fighting tears, she said, "I think I'll have some more coffee—and some of those cookies you got the other day."

Janice smiled and went to the counter, returning with cookies and coffee. The conversation turned to Madison and what to do about the sleepover the next weekend. Pros and cons were discussed as the two women sat, drinking coffee and eating cookies.

Chapter 6

THE NEXT MORNING, HANNAH took special care with dressing. She didn't want Harold to think of her as a frumpy old woman. She was wise enough to know that she couldn't appear young, but she could present herself as a confident, knowledgeable older woman, one who wouldn't be impressed by his bullying. Of course, never having met him, she didn't really know that he was a bully, but it helped build her confidence to prepare for the worst. She just hoped he didn't turn out to be an utterly charming, loveable man really concerned about his mother's well-being!

She packed the sandwiches she had promised Ruby, along with what was left of the cookies she and Janice had eaten the night before. She called the bus company, as Janice had needed the car, gathered her purse and tote bag, and left the house. As she waited outside for the bus to arrive, she reviewed what she could do to help Ruby confront her son. Confront? Any confronting, she knew, would have to come from her. Ruby, dear soul, was unable to confront anyone, certainly not her own son.

It was almost noon when Hannah arrived at *Sunset Manor.* Again, she made her way down the hall to Ruby's room without seeing anyone at the nurses' station. She did see the two staff women but, again, they seemed more interested in chatting with each other than dealing with patients who were trying to get their attention. The food cart was coming down the hall and many of the patients needed help getting back to their rooms where they would receive their lunches.

Ruby was sitting up in bed when Hannah entered. After the usual hugs, Hannah pushed aside the lunch tray that had just arrived and pulled out the sandwiches she had prepared from her tote bag. The two of them chatted while they ate. Thinking that it would look better if Harold saw that his mother was not bed-ridden, Hannah suggested that she help Ruby out of bed and into the chair by the window. With Ruby comfortably seated, Hannah pulled out a hairbrush from the small table near the bed and proceeded to help her spruce up. Lipstick was next offered, followed by some rouge. After five minutes, Ruby was the picture of a pleasant-looking, relatively healthy elderly woman—certainly not someone who needed around-the-clock care.

Harold arrived at 2:00. He was a tall man, with thinning gray hair, unusually full lips, and deep-set brown eyes. He wore brown slacks with an open-neck striped shirt under a tan blazer, which helped to hide the small bulge of his stomach. The appearance was of a confident, exuberant middle-aged man, a man in charge of his life—and perhaps the lives of others. Anyone other than Hannah would have described him as a good-looking middle-aged man. Hannah, however, couldn't see that. All she saw was a slick son-of-a-bitch out to hurt her friend.

"Harold, this is my friend, Hannah Lowenstein—remember, I told you about her?"

"Why, of course I remember. Pleased to meet you Mrs. Lowenstein. May I call you Hannah? I feel I know you. Mother has spoken so often of you. I want to thank you for all you've done for her. You know I can't get up here to visit her very often so it's nice to know that she has someone like you to help her."

He would have gone on talking if Hannah hadn't cut him short by saying, "Yes, I've heard a lot about you, too—and your lovely family—Mimi right? And Martin and Samuel?"

"Yes, that's right."

"Ruby talks so much about them. It's a pity that she can't see the boys more often. I know how important grandchildren are. I live with my daughter and her two children, you know. Wonderful person, my daughter. It's added years to my life just being able to live with her and her family. But, enough about me. Ruby tells me you have a car business in—Bloomfield, is it?"

"Bloomfield Hills, yes."

"It must be comforting, having your own business, not having to report to any boss. My husband, Leo Lowenstein—I lost him about four years ago—was a typesetter at one of the New York newspapers. He always had to work up to speed or his boss would be upset. But I guess being your own boss you can set your own goals."

"Well, it's not quite that simple. I have to sell enough cars each month to make payments—you know salaries, overhead, and, of course," he chuckled, "a little for me."

"Well, I'm sure that in an area like Bloomfield you have no problem selling enough cars. That's a fairly wealthy area, isn't it?"

"It's a nice area—good schools for the kids, and my wife loves the house and the neighborhood. And, yes, business is fine," he declared, as he unconsciously played with the diamond pinky ring he wore on his right hand.

"My goodness, I've talked more than I should have. I know you're here to make plans with your mother so I'll let you two talk. I hope you don't mind if I just sit here and knit. Ruby and I have plans for later this afternoon."

Harold looked at his mother, who nodded her agreement. "Oh, please stay," she said to Hannah.

Hannah retreated to the chair by the door, sat down, and picked up her knitting, hoping to give the impression of being engrossed in the scarf she was making for Madison rather than eavesdropping.

Harold drew his chair closer to Ruby and spoke in a quiet voice. "Mother," he said, "we need to make plans on where you'll go after you leave here. Of course, this place has more than rehabilitation services. They have very good live-in facilities which I think would work very well for you. It's quite reasonable and with your social security you could easily afford it."

"Harold, I hate it here." Ruby's voice trembled. "I don't want to stay here. I want to go home."

"You know that's not possible. It would cost too much to have the care you need at home. Do you know what it costs to pay for home-care? Why, at the least it's $15/hour and you'd need 24 hour care—that's $360 a day, or over $130,000 a year! You don't have that kind of money. There are other options, you know. There are other places, but they cost more than this place."

Ruby started to cry. "But I don't need that much care—just a little bit of help in the morning getting bathed and dressed. I'm okay on my own. I can get out of bed here by myself, and once my hip has completely healed— therapy is really helping—I'll be fine by myself."

Harold sighed. "But even if you needed less help, how are you going to pay for it? You only have that one $10,000 CD and your social security. Dad didn't exactly leave you much, you know."

"Don't say that!" Ruby exclaimed. "Your father did the best he could. It wasn't his fault that he didn't make a lot of money. He paid for your education, after all, and set you up in your business. Who knew he would drop dead at work in the prime of his life?"

Clearly this was a sore point for Ruby. Hannah, hearing all this, decided to get involved. She stood up and walked over to Ruby's side. "Why couldn't Ruby refinance her house?" she asked, all wide-eyed innocent. "That would give her enough money to pay for the help—and it just means that when she dies the house won't be worth as much."

Harold glowered at Hannah. "You don't understand. Refinancing has costs and it would give her a bad credit rating. It's all been taken care of. The house is listed, and it should be sold soon. It hasn't been maintained very well, so it probably won't bring in top dollar, though."

Hannah's suspicions were on high alert. Bad credit rating? What would Ruby need a credit rating for, anyway? She's going to buy a new condo? And her house was in excellent shape, and in a good part of town. Hannah was convinced that Harold was up to something.

"Look, I have to get back to work. Think about it, Mother, it's either stay here or we'll look around for another place. But going home just isn't an option."

He looked at his watch, declared that he was late for a meeting, gave Ruby a peck on the cheek, nodded to Hannah, and left.

Hannah bent down and gave Ruby a hug. "Don't worry, we'll figure something out. No way are you staying in this place. Even if he sells the house, you should be able to use that money—after all, he didn't pay anything for it. But let's not go there, now. We need to figure out how to get you out of here. What does the doctor say about releasing you?"

"What doctor? Did you see a doctor? Did you see a nurse? All I see is the woman who gets me bathed and dressed in the morning, and the young girl who brings my food. You could die here and they wouldn't know until the next morning when they came to bring your breakfast."

Hannah shook her head. "You've got to get out of here. Let me see what I can find out. I have an idea, but I need to check it out first. I'll be back tomorrow and we can make plans. Maybe you should rest now, okay?"

"Okay, but first help me into bed. I'm too exhausted to use the walker."

Hannah helped Ruby to the bed, fluffed the pillows and settled her in. Ruby closed her eyes, and Hannah tiptoed out.

. . . .

It was nearly 3:00 when the bus deposited Hannah at home. Meeting Harold had gone as she had anticipated—he was a son-of-a-bitch, although a dangerous son-of-a-bitch. All that smooth-talking her and then the way he treated his mother, as if she were a senile old woman who couldn't understand all he was doing for her. And what was he doing? As far as Hannah could see, he wasn't doing anything except selling her house! He never asked Ruby how she was doing, or what the doctor reported, or when she could be released from rehab. She had to find out what he was up to. Maybe David would have some ideas on how to get more information on his business—in a legal way, of course.

She made herself a cup of tea and settled down in the recliner. She was tired but couldn't relax. After a few minutes, she got up from the chair and took her cup of tea to the kitchen, where she pulled down her old recipe box from the shelf. "I know it's in here," she muttered. She hadn't made stuffed cabbage in quite a while and didn't trust her memory. "This is ridiculous," she said to herself, as she pulled out the card with the recipe on it.

"What's ridiculous, Grandma?"

"Maddie! I didn't hear you come in, darling. What's ridiculous is your old grandma has forgotten how to cook, that's what's ridiculous. Using a recipe for something I've been making for 50 years! Getting old isn't fun."

"Don't feel bad. Mom uses recipes all the time. What are you making?"

"I'm going to make stuffed cabbage. But don't worry. I'll make it so you can eat the filling without the cabbage—I know you don't like cabbage. Then I thought I'd use up the remaining squash we had last night, and then—ta da!—I'm going to bake a cake!"

"Why are you cooking so much?"

"Oh, it gets my mind off of other things." She handed the recipe to Madison. "Here, read this for me….I don't have my glasses handy."

By the time Janice came home from doing the weekly grocery shopping, the cake was cooling, dinner was ready, and Madison and Hannah were engaged in serious discussion at the kitchen table, Hannah drinking tea and Madison coke.

"What are you guys up to?" asked Janice.

"Mom, did you know that Grandma didn't date until she was twenty-one! Isn't that terrible?"

"What's so terrible?" responded Hannah. "I was busy with other things. Besides, then I met your grandfather and that was it. I was smitten—and never looked back."

"I think the grandpa part is so romantic," Madison sighed. "Just imagine, finding your true love at a diner. It's just like those people in *South Pacific,* you know, where they look across a crowded room and— zap, they're in love!"

"Well, honey, zap yourself upstairs and do some homework before dinner. Tomorrow's Sunday and you know you'll want to do something with Becky and Suzanne. And then you'll be too tired to do the homework for Monday."

Madison groaned, but rose and went upstairs. "Dinner will be in about a half hour," Janice called after her. She turned to Hannah and asked, "Is that a cake I smell? You've been busy. Is everything okay?"

Hannah grinned. "You know me too well. I couldn't settle down after I got back from visiting Ruby so I cooked—we're having stuffed cabbage, okay? I met her son. What a piece of work! I know he's up to something, but I don't know what. I know, I know I shouldn't get involved. But I'm not doing anything—I can't do anything. But you'd feel the same way if you met him.

He looks perfectly fine, and he knows how to charm old ladies, but he doesn't really care about his mother. He never even asked her how she was doing or what the doctor said. He just kept saying she needs around-the-clock care—I don't think the doctor said that!—and that he's selling the house so she has to either stay there or move into a more expensive nursing home, which she can't afford. She doesn't need all that care. She can pretty much take care of herself with just a little help, and she's getting stronger each time I see her. But she doesn't know where she's going to go. She doesn't want to stay in that place—and I don't blame her. I've never seen anyone come by to check on her."

"Have you checked out other places for her? How much money does she have? Can she pay for help if she lived on her own?"

"I think the house and her social security are all she has—oh, and a $10,000 CD, which Harold talked about. I don't think her husband was doing all that well—he doesn't seem to have left her with much besides the house and maybe a little savings. It's a good thing she has his social security coming in—I don't think she ever worked."

Janice went to the cupboard to take out the dinner dishes and Hannah, continuing to regale Janice with impressions of Harold, got up to help set the table for dinner.

"Maddie," Janice called. "Dinner's ready."

"Where's David?" asked Hannah.

"Where he always is—at Billy's. Billy's mom called earlier and asked if he could have dinner there. They're having pizza, and you know that's his favorite food. Works out fine for us—we don't have to listen to him complain about stuffed cabbage."

Dinner went without event, but when they were finishing dessert Madison broached the sleepover issue again. She had clearly prepared her arguments and spoke calmly, in a somewhat pedantic manner, listing all her reasons, and answering any potential objections Janice was likely to raise. When she finished, she sat back, cheeks flushed, and waited for Janice's reply.

Hannah remained quiet, also waiting for Janice's reply.

"Oh, God, I've raised a Clarence Darrow. I'll tell you what. If the parents are going to be there—and I'll check on that!—then, yes you can go. But I want you back before noon on Sunday, okay?"

Madison leapt out of her chair and ran to Janice. With a big hug, she thanked her mother. "Thank you, thank you. You're the best mother in the whole world. You won't regret this, you'll see. Oh, thank you!" She then dashed upstairs to text the news to her best friend, Suzanne.

Hannah smiled at Janice. "That was nice," she said. Just then, David announced his arrival with a slam and a shout.

"I'm home!"

"How was the pizza?" Hannah asked.

"Not as good as the ones we get from *Pizza Piazza*. They had ham and pineapple on one of them. Weird!" He took off his jacket, put his backpack down, and eyed the cake on the table. Big blue eyes turned to Janice, he pleaded, "Can I have some? Please!"

"A small piece, after you hang up your coat. I don't want you getting up in the middle of the night with a stomach ache. How many slices of pizza did you have, anyway?

"Only four—I didn't like it that much."

He sat down at the table, cut himself a huge piece of cake, and proceeded to bring his mother and grandmother up to speed on his latest success with *Killzone 2*, his latest video game. Not knowing what he was talking about, Janice and Hannah just listened, pleased that he was so happy, but concerned about the violence in the game.

Later that evening, while Janice was in her study working on her monthly report to the superintendent, David came over to Hannah, who was watching a rerun of *ER*.

"I've been working on that 'case.' I found the website for his business—that's a dorky name for a business: *Bernie's Bloomfield Buys*. Anyway, that's just his advertising place. But I found another site, one that lists discounts and stuff like that. He's listing a lot of discounts for his cars. Maybe that means he's selling hot cars?"

"No, darling, I don't think so. I think it means he's having trouble selling the cars at the full price. I wish we could find out if his business is in trouble. How can we get that information—legally?"

David pondered that for a while, but could come up with no answer. He would love to try to hack into that guy's financial records but Hannah had said "legally" so hacking was out of the question. Of course, since Hannah knew nothing about computers she wouldn't have to know how he got the information. He didn't say anything, but simply shook his head. "I don't know, but I'll speak to one of the tech guys at school and see if he has any suggestions." David didn't mention that the tech guy at school was a kid two grades ahead of him who had no qualms about hacking.

At 10:00, both children were asleep, Janice was still working on her report, and Hannah was falling asleep in her recliner. She woke with a start when a commercial, at full blast, came on. She stopped in to say goodnight to Janice, turned off the TV and went to bed. She was asleep before her head hit the pillow.

Chapter 7

THE FOLLOWING MONDAY, JANICE was able to serve breakfast to Madison and David, check that they had their respective belongings, and herd them out to the car without waking Hannah, who was sleeping unusually soundly. Janice was concerned about her mother. She was getting too involved in Ruby's problems. While Hannah was a strong woman, both physically and emotionally, she was, after all, seventy-eight.

It was at times like this that Janice realized how much she depended upon her mother. Not for what she did, but for who she was. Janice could get along without the social security check Hannah insisted on handing over every month, the help around the house, the cooking and baking that made coming home each evening such a treat. No, she could do without those things. It was Hannah's presence that made the difference in her life—in all their lives. To an outsider it might appear that Hannah was simply the background, the wallpaper, in the house. But to anyone who knew the family, they knew she was much more than that. She made the house a home.

Janice vowed to be more patient with Hannah. Most of her frustrations came from jumping to conclusions about Hannah's motives, which, when she calmed down and considered them, turned out to be simply Hannah's attempts to help. She knew her mother didn't have a mean streak in her—although she was always up for a fight if she thought someone was being treated unfairly. So why did she always attribute the worst to Hannah's comments? Was it simply a continuation of her childhood rebellion for independence, to show how different she was from her mother? She hoped not; that was childish!

All of this was going through her mind as she drove to school, with Madison and David in the back seat. They were unusually quiet, so much so that Janice feared she had scared them with her concerns for Hannah.

She laughed and said, "Well, I wonder if Grandma is up yet? She's sure a sleepyhead this morning. I'll let her sleep a while longer and then I'll call to wake her up. You watch, when we tease her about sleeping so long she'll deny she was sleeping: 'just resting my eyes' she'll say."

David hooted. "Yeah, she always says that when she's sleeping and the TV is on."

Hannah was awake when Janice called. "Oh, I heard you and the kids this morning, but just wanted to rest my eyes a bit longer. I'm going to see Ruby later today. I'll bring her some lunch— they serve terrible food at that place. It's a nice day so I can stop off at the market and get something for dinner. How about meatloaf? We haven't had that for a while? Or would you rather I should get some fish?"

"Probably the meatloaf—David doesn't like fish. Oh, and I won't be home for dinner. I'm seeing Paul tonight, so you and the kids go ahead without me."

"So how is Paul? He hasn't been around for some time now."

"He's fine, busy, like the rest of us. We'll talk tonight. I have to run now—the superintendent's coming for his monthly inquisition. I'll see you later."

Well, that went well, thought Janice. Maybe I'm growing up!

. . . .

Hannah was watching *The View* when the phone ran. It was Charlie Bernardi, who wanted to visit Ruby but didn't want to go alone. Would Hannah go with him?

What a silly man, she thought. Afraid to visit Ruby alone! What was he afraid of? Well, at least she wouldn't have to take the bus today; but she would have to make more sandwiches.

"Of course. I was just getting ready to take her some lunch. Why don't you have lunch with us? I'm making chicken salad sandwiches, okay?"

"Oh, that'll be nice. I can't eat onions, though."

"No onions, just celery in my chicken salad. Why don't you pick me up in about half an hour. That way we'll get there before they serve lunch—such terrible food."

"Fine, I'll be there."

Charlie arrived in his green 2003 Mercury Grand Marquis. A man in his late seventies, he was still attractive, keeping trim by daily visits to the gym. He wore his usual outfit of brown slacks, brightly colored Henley shirt, green plaid sports jacket and topped it off with white tasseled loafers. With his full head of gray hair, slicked back with pomade, he looked like the stereotype of a used car dealer, which he was or, more correctly, used to be before he retired.

....

Ruby was sitting up in the chair by the window when they arrived. "Charlie, how nice to see you. How have you been?"

"Fine, fine. But how are you? You look wonderful. You'd never know you were sick."

"Well, I'm not really sick—just a broken hip. But it's mending." She turned to Hannah and said, "I got out of bed this morning all by myself. I'm really getting stronger. Even the physical therapist thinks so. And I'm hungry for whatever you brought me. Last night's dinner was a dried up hamburger with fried potatoes. You could die from the food they serve here."

Hannah opened up her basket and brought out the sandwiches, an apple for Ruby, and the rest of last night's cake. Charlie's eyes grew larger when he saw the cake. It was obvious that he didn't get many homemade treats.

"See what she does for me! Every day she brings me lunch. And such a lunch! It's like having my own personal cook. I don't know what I'd do without her."

Hannah waved her hand, dismissing Ruby's compliments. "Enough, let's eat."

At that moment, the young woman with the food tray entered. Today she was wearing a t-shirt with "THEY'RE REAL" on the front. Hannah waved her away. "We've got real food here, dear," she said. "We don't need that stuff. Just leave the coffee—decaf, I hope."

The young woman shrugged her shoulders as she set the coffee on the table next to the bed, said "Whatever," and left the room.

The conversation flowed freely, with Charlie bringing Ruby and Hannah up to date on the events at the Senior Center. "The Hermans have a new Winnebago," he grinned. "They're heading to Florida for the winter and everyone is placing bets on whether they'll make it. You know Henry has such bad cataracts, which he refuses to do anything about, and Mrs. Herman—I think her name is Glenda, Gwen, something like that—doesn't even drive."

"But that's dangerous," exclaimed Ruby. "You ought to stop them. They could get into an accident."

Charlie stared at her in amazement. "How could I stop him: he's got a license. If they think he can see well enough to give him a license, who am I to disagree?"

"Well," Ruby replied, "when I see some of the people on the roads today I wonder if you have to do anything but be able to breathe to get a license these days. In my day, you had to…"

Charlie interrupted her. 'Yeah, but the point is that he does have a license and there's nothing we can do about that. Anyway, as I was about to say," he smiled at Ruby, "they miss you at the bridge games. I guess you're one of the few people who can give anyone a challenge."

After an hour, Ruby turned the conversation to the missing Mrs. Johnson. "She's still listed as a patient, but I haven't seen her for over a week. The therapist just shrugs when I ask about her, and I never see anyone else—you can never get a staff person's attention here unless you're dying."

Hannah listened, murmured what could be interpreted as shared concern, and then turned the talk to a criticism of the staff. Charlie then regaled them with tales of his ninety-five-year-old brother's "sexual" experiences at a nursing home in Florida, which made both women laugh and forget their concerns.

On the drive home, Hannah thanked Charlie for visiting Ruby. He looked uncomfortable with the compliment. "Well, she's a nice woman," he replied.

Hannah smiled. It had taken Charlie a lot to work himself up for the visit, even though once there he seemed to relax and enjoy himself. Such a strange man!

"Charlie," she said, "you used to sell cars, right?"

"Yeah, for 40 years, in Detroit first and then right here in town."

"How can you tell if a place is doing well—financially, I mean?"

"Oh, you can tell. You check the inventory: are new cars selling or are they still on the lot? Why are you asking?"

"Don't say anything to Ruby. I don't want I should upset her. But I'm trying to check up on her son. He's selling her house—don't ask—and I think he's up to something, but I can't prove it. He has a dealership in Bloomfield Hills and I'd like to know if he's in financial troubles, if that's why he's selling her house. He owns it, you see. He's forcing her out of her own home saying she needs twenty-four hour care when it's clear she can get along fine on her own, maybe with a little help until she's back on her feet."

"Selling her house? Where would she live?"

"That's just it. He wants her to stay where she is or move to some assisted living place or another nursing home."

"And you think he's hiding something?"

"Well, I wonder if he's trying to pull something. I guess legally he can do what he wants with the house, since he owns it. But the deal was that she would live in it. I don't understand why he's so anxious to sell it. He's the only one who thinks she needs that much care."

They had reached Hannah's house. Charlie, an old-world gentleman, got out of the car and went around to open the door for Hannah, who was already out of the car.

"Let me see what I can find out," Charlie proposed. "I know some people downstate who might know something. What's the name of his place?"

"*Bernie's Bloomfield Buys*," replied Hannah, with a smile. "Quite a name, huh?"

Chuckling, Charlie waved goodbye, got into the car, and drove off.

The house was quiet when Hannah opened the door. Remembering that Janice wouldn't be home for dinner, and that the children would enjoy the treat of pizza for dinner, rather than meatloaf, she removed her jacket and shoes and sat down in the recliner. She turned on the TV, put on last night's rerun of *Walker*, and promptly fell asleep—which was how Madison and David found her when they came in.

"Do you think she's sleeping or resting her eyes?" asked David.

"Sleeping," replied Madison.

"Resting my eyes," said Hannah, who awoke when she heard the door slam.

The children laughed.

"What would you rather have for dinner—meatloaf or pizza?" Hannah asked, knowing what their response would be.

"Pizza, pizza," yelled David. "Pepperoni and mushrooms. Get a big one. I'm real hungry."

"Where's Mom?" asked Madison.

"Your mother is having dinner with Paul. She'll be home later."

Hannah tried to resist, but curiosity got the best of her. She hated herself for succumbing, but before she could remind herself that it was none of her business she found herself blurting out, "What do you guys think of Paul?"

David shrugged his shoulders. "I don't know. He's okay, I guess."

Madison gave her response more consideration. She sat down on the sofa next to Hannah's recliner, indicating that she was prepared to engage in a discussion of the pros and cons of Paul. David took this opportunity to dash upstairs to get in a few minutes on *Killzone* before dinner.

Hannah looked at Madison. "Darling, what is it? Don't you like him?"

"No, that's not it. He's really nice—treats Mom well and I know she likes him. It's just that if she marries him there's no way she'll ever get back with Dad."

"Oh, Maddie darling, there's no way your Mom and Dad are ever going to get back together. I know you love your father, and he'll always be your father—that never changes. But don't expect them to get back together. They were very young when they married and they've grown into different people.

They live different lives now. They want different things in their lives. They both have moved on and you have to, too."

"But I miss Dad. I never get to see him anymore."

Hannah resisted the urge to point out that that was his choice. But you don't tell a seventeen year old that her father doesn't really care about her! Hannah got up and gave Madison a big hug. "Let's order that pizza before David raids the refrigerator and spoils his appetite."

That evening Hannah waited up until Janice came home. It was past her bedtime, but she wanted to talk to Janice before the usual daily activities took over their lives and the conversation with Madison was pushed to the back of her mind.

"So, how was dinner?" she asked, as Janice hung up her coat.

"Fine. We went to La Patisse… you know, that French restaurant on Highland Road."

"So, how is Paul?"

"Fine. Anything else you want to know?"

Hannah laughed. "Am I that transparent?—don't answer. I wanted to talk to you about Maddie, though. She's concerned that if you get serious about Paul—if you marry him—you won't get back with Jim. I know, I know. I told her that that wasn't going to happen, that you and Jim were over. But you know children. I think she needs reassurance from you."

"Oh for heaven's sake! Kids! Paul and I aren't even close to discussing marriage. And I'm not sure I ever want to get married again. But how do I tell her that her father is a bastard? He was a lousy father even when he was here. Now? He does nothing for the kids. Oh, he'll remember their birthdays— usually a week or so late—and occasionally he'll call and invite them out for something and then cancel at the last minute. Damn, I didn't realize she was still fantasizing about our getting back together."

"Well, she's at that age when fathers are important for girls—you know, role models and protectors. I think she's afraid to discuss this with you—she doesn't want to hurt your feelings. So maybe if you, you know, let her know it's okay to talk."

"Okay, I'll try. How is David about all this?"

"Who knows with that one. I think they both like Paul: David thinks he's 'okay' and Maddie thinks he's 'nice'—so I don't think Paul's the problem."

"Okay, I'll talk with Maddie." Janice got up, stretched, and smiled at her mother. "It's been a long day. I'm going to turn in. You should, too, you look tired. Are you okay?"

"Everything's fine. Charlie came by and we went to visit Ruby. I'll tell you about it tomorrow. Get some sleep."

Chapter 8

THE DOOR TO JANICE's office was closed. The conference with the members of the English department, who were concerned about parents wanting to have more control over the books the students were reading for class, had ended on an encouraging note. The issue had arisen over the 11th grade class assignment, *Rainbow Boys*, which some parents found offensive because it dealt with homosexuality. The teachers had met with the parents and were upset because the parents had not even read the book, but had condemned it simply on the grounds that it presented a sympathetic portrait of gay teens. The fact that it had received numerous literary awards seemed irrelevant to them.

Janice had listened to their concerns and ended up suggesting that they retain the book as required reading for the class, but allow a substitution for those students whose parents objected, so long as the parents signed a note indicating that they objected. While not a perfect solution, the teachers agreed. Janice felt bad about the compromise—giving into ignorance and prejudice rankled her—but compromises were what kept the lid on the ugliness that lurked just under the surface. What was needed was education for the parents, but she hadn't yet come up with a way to accomplish that.

Janice leaned back in her chair and thought about Hannah's comments last night. She knew she had to have a talk with the kids. She had been putting it off, thinking that ignoring the issue would make it go away. Well, that hadn't worked. But why hadn't Madison talked with her? Why did she go to Hannah? It hurt to realize that her daughter felt more comfortable sharing her concerns with her grandmother than with her own mother—although she had to admit that Hannah's presence in their lives had allowed her to devote more time to her job and to herself. Maybe too much! She needed to do something about that.

She remembered her own childhood. Even though Janice was an only child, Hannah was a stay-at-home mom throughout most of her childhood, working part-time at a department store only once Janice was in high school. Being a stay-at-home mother didn't mean that Hannah wasn't busy; it just meant that she didn't get paid for what she did! Janice had mixed feelings, even at this date, about Hannah's involvement in community affairs. An avowed socialist, Hannah canvassed the neighborhood with flyers each election, attended organizational meetings, picketed the newspaper where her husband worked when the company wouldn't agree to union demands, and staged protests outside the mayor's house for…well, Janice didn't know what for! All of this was embarrassing to a young girl, whose friends' mothers stayed home and baked cookies.

And Hannah's childrearing was embarrassing, too. To her, dressing Janice in jeans and t-shirts was the height of fashion at the time—which it was, although her jeans weren't the fashionable ones that other girls her age wore. And her hair! Even today, Janice laughed about that. Hannah's method for getting the snarls out of Janice's long hair in the morning was to use peanut butter. It worked, but it left a peanut butter smell that Janice carried around all day. And, Janice had to admit, Hannah was too lenient with her. With Hannah's lack of concern for neatness in the house, Janice could just drop her clothes and books wherever she was and Hannah never complained. In fact, sometimes the items stayed where she dropped them until her father came home. He was a typesetter for one of the big New York papers, and he worked long hours, often not getting home until after Janice was asleep. He never criticized Janice or Hannah, but simply picked up the discarded items and put them away, after giving both of them a big hug and kiss.

But Hannah was always there when Janice came home from school. And there was always a home cooked dinner awaiting her father when he came home from work. More importantly, she remembered the fun times: picking out books at the library and then running home to have Hannah read them to her, going on their "nature walks" where the most exotic thing they would observe would be a pigeon pooping, and walking to the local school playground where Hannah would push her on the swings.

The embarrassment faded as Janice got older, but memories of the good times remained.

. . . .

It had rained all morning, abating for a brief moment only to be followed by an even heavier downpour. Hannah had planned on visiting Ruby but, not having the car, couldn't motivate herself to face going out in this weather. She called Ruby and explained that she wouldn't be seeing her today. They talked for a while, Ruby going on about the missing Mrs. Johnson, Hannah trying to be sympathetic, but anxious to change the topic. She was surprised to find herself reacting with impatience to Ruby's concerns, convinced that her friend was becoming obsessed with Mrs. Johnson out of boredom. It seemed obvious to Hannah that Mrs. Johnson had gone home, and the staff had forgotten to remove her name from the list of patients. From what Hannah had observed, it was not a very efficient staff, so it was not surprising that something as trivial as keeping the list of patients up-to-date would not rank very high on their to-do lists.

By the time she finished her call to Ruby, tidied up the breakfast dishes, showered and dressed, it was time for a midmorning snack. Her breakfast of oatmeal, usually sufficient to keep her going until lunch, seemed inadequate this morning. She opened the refrigerator, intending to take out a yogurt cup, but ended up grabbing a piece of last night's pizza. She could never understand why people threw away leftover pizza; it was good, even cold!

Determining that there was nothing that had to be done around the house, Hannah sat down in her recliner and opened the novel she was reading. It was on Oprah's book list, but Hannah was having trouble maintaining any interest. She would give it another fifty pages, though, before giving up. There had been a time when she thought that not finishing a book was unforgivable—a sign of intellectual sloth. But that was when she was trying to make up for the lack of a college education. Now she read what she wanted, when she wanted and, not needing to prove anything, put down books she didn't enjoy.

The day passed pleasantly: a little reading, a little lunch, a little nap. Before she knew it, the children were home from school, shedding their wet clothing on their way to the kitchen.

"Maddie, David—come hang up your wet clothes. You know your mother will have a fit if she finds them on the floor."

"In a minute," called out David. "I have to pee."

When the clothes were hung up, David went into the kitchen and returned with a piece of cold pizza in his hand. "Ugh, that's so gross," exclaimed Madison.

"What? It's pizza, what's your problem? I'm hungry."

Madison glared at her brother and contented herself with a yogurt cup before going up to her room to most likely text her friends, whom she had just seen at school.

David came over to Hannah, pizza in hand. "Grandma, I found something out about that guy. We got into his books—you know, where they list things about money? I don't know what it means, but we printed it out. I'll get it for you—it's in my backpack."

When he returned with the papers, Hannah asked, "Who's 'we'?"

"The tech guy at school. He knows how to do this."

"Is that what's called 'hacking'? Is this all legal? Remember, I told you nothing illegal."

David looked down at his feet and muttered something about the tech guy doing this all the time. "Who is this tech guy?" Hannah finally inquired.

David, seeming extremely uncomfortable, replied "His name's Brian."

"So, what does this Brian do besides hacking into other people's private affairs?"

"He's a senior at school—but he's real bright and he's going to be a computer technician when he graduates."

"If he doesn't go to jail, first! David, I'm disappointed with you. Not only is what you did probably illegal and could get you in trouble; more importantly, it violates someone's privacy."

"No, it's not private. This is the stuff the guy sends to the tax people. Brian told me all about how businesses have to pay taxes and that's all open to the public—if you know how to get it. He told me you could actually ask for it, and they'd have to give it to you, but that would take a lot of time. This way was faster."

Hannah looked at her young grandson, pride in his intelligence and initiative mixed with concern for his naiveté. "Okay, what's done is done. But don't do it again."

Looking somewhat abashed, David asked, "Do you want to see what we found out?"

Hannah smiled. "Sure," she said.

. . . .

After dinner, Hannah excused herself and retired to her sitting room to call Charlie. She had looked at the papers that David had downloaded, but couldn't make much sense out of them. It seemed that Harold's business was doing okay, but she didn't know what some of the numbers were about. She thought that Charlie might be able to help.

Charlie didn't know if he would be able to help, but he certainly wanted to! They made plans to meet the next day when he would go over the papers. He would do anything he could to help Ruby and, if her son was up to something, Hannah knew he'd do his best to find out.

Chapter 9

CHARLIE RANG THE DOORBELL at 8:30 the next morning, anxious to get down to work. Seated at the kitchen table with coffee and Hannah's freshly made cinnamon rolls, he spread out the papers and started to read.

"This here column shows how many cars they sold, and this one how much money they brought in. These other columns are about their costs—you know, the price the dealership pays for the cars, salaries, overhead, things like that. It's not clear how many salesmen they have—I can't tell if they've let anyone go. And I can't tell how this year compares to previous years. That information's not here."

Hannah was leaning over his shoulder, watching where he pointed. The numbers didn't mean anything to her. "Numbers, schnumbers," she said, "what does it all mean? Is he cooking the books?"

Charlie looked up at her. "Where'd you hear that expression?"

"I watch TV. I know these things."

"Well, I can't tell that from these numbers. All I can say is that, from what's here, they're keeping their head above water—but just barely."

"So what do we do? I was hoping he was having money problems and that was why he was selling Ruby's house. How can we find out?"

Charlie took another cinnamon roll. Hannah was still standing over him, clearly frustrated. He looked up at her and said, "Hannah, sit down. You're making me nervous."

She sat down, with a loud sigh. Charlie, having finished his second cinnamon roll, got up for another cup of coffee and returned to the table. "I'll tell you what. I know some guys in the Detroit area—different dealerships, but they always know what's going on in the other shops. I'll see if they know anything about this guy's business."

Hannah brightened up at this suggestion. "That's great," she said. "How soon can you find out?"

"I'll call today. In the meantime, can we go visit Ruby?"

Hannah shook her head. What a strange man! A smart man, with a head on his shoulders. But when it came to women he was a little boy! She washed the dishes, got her coat and purse, and together they left to visit Ruby.

. . . .

Ruby wasn't in her room when they arrived. She was in the lounge, engaged in animated conversation with another woman. When she saw Hannah and Charlie, she beckoned them over. "This is Mrs. Bradshaw. Mary, these are my friends, Hannah and Charlie. Tell them what you just told me." She turned to Hannah and said, "Listen to this—it's like I was telling you the other day."

Hannah sat down next to Mary, a frail woman, at least in her late 80s. "Like I told Ruby, this place loses people," Mary Bradshaw began. "Mrs. Johnson is missing and so is Mrs. Greeley. Mrs. Greeley has been missing for a few months now. They say that she went home, but I don't believe it. She would have said goodbye to me. I've been here for almost a year and she was my friend. She wouldn't have gone home without saying goodbye to me."

"See, I told you there was something strange going on here," Ruby interrupted. "I didn't know Mrs. Greeley, but I'm sure that Mrs. Johnson didn't go home. She could barely walk even with a walker. And they still have her listed as a patient!"

Charlie stared at Hannah, clearly confused by the conversation. Hannah waved her hand at him, indicating that she would explain later. Now he should just sit there and be quiet.

"Does Mrs. Greeley have any family?" Hannah asked Mary.

"She has a son in California. He came to visit when she was first here, but I haven't seen him since then."

"Do you know how to get in touch with him? His address or phone number?"

"No, all I know is the town he lives in—Fall something, Fall River or Fall Springs—no, Fall Brook, that's it—in California."

"Well, if you know his first name—I assume he has the same last name as his mother—we might be able to get his phone number and call him. If she went home, he'd know about it, wouldn't he?"

Mary thought for a while. "I know his name, let me think. It starts with an 'R' – Richard, Roger, no—no, that's not it. Oh, I just can't remember!"

"Don't worry, it'll come to you. The same thing happens to me with names. I can't remember and then all of a sudden, when I'm doing something completely different it'll hit me."

"Matthew! That's it," cried Mary. "Matthew Greeley in Fall Brook, California!"

With that announcement, Mary sank back in her chair, having expended all her energy.

Hannah thanked her and motioned to Ruby and Charlie that it was time to leave the lounge. They went into Ruby's room and shut the door.

Ruby looked triumphant. "See? I'm not imagining things. Something strange is going on here."

Hannah wasn't convinced but agreed to look into Mrs. Greeley's situation. "But we don't have proof. I'll call this Greeley guy and ask to speak to his mother. I hope he doesn't have an unlisted number. Anyway, if he knows where she is that'll settle the question. I don't want to call from here, though. If there is hanky panky going on, they might have the phones bugged."

Charlie looked lost. "Hanky panky" obviously had a meaning for him that didn't seem to apply in this situation—whatever that was. He started to say something, but Hannah shot him a look which clearly meant, "Not now." He settled back in his chair, hoping that eventually someone would explain to him what was going on.

On the way home, Hannah brought Charlie up to speed on the case of the missing women. He listened, a frown on his face clearly indicating that he thought Ruby was jumping to conclusions. Hannah was so involved in trying to present a coherent picture for him that she failed to notice his skepticism. When they arrived at her house, he got out of the car intending to open the door for her only to find that she had already left the car and was on her way up the walkway.

"Thanks, Charlie. I'll let you know what I find out about the son in California. Call your friends in Detroit to find out about Ruby's son and let me know what they say."

Charlie, looking more skeptical with each passing moment, nodded and took off, shaking his head once he was out of Hannah's sight.

It was now 3:00 and Hannah hadn't eaten anything since the cinnamon roll that morning. She hung up her coat and headed for the kitchen, searching for something to nosh on that wouldn't spoil her appetite for dinner. All she could find was some cheese and crackers, which she put on a tray and carried to her recliner. It was too early to try to contact Mrs. Greeley's son—he probably worked in the daytime. She decided to wait until after dinner to call.

She tried to watch that morning's session of *The View*, but found she couldn't concentrate. She finished her cheese and crackers, closed her eyes to think more clearly, and promptly fell asleep until she heard Janice and the children come in the front door.

That evening, after the children had gone to bed, Hannah told Janice about the missing women. She tried to present it as matter-of-factly as possible, aware that Janice would jump on any hyperbole as unjustified. Janice listened, asked a few questions about the operation of *Sunset Manor*—some of which Hannah knew the answer to—and agreed with Hannah that something was strange. It wasn't clear, however, that they had done something to the women. It could be just poor management. Perhaps the women had been released and returned to their homes. The fact that Mrs. Johnson, for example, was still on the patient list might just be a matter of poor bookkeeping.

Well, Hannah had promised to find out about Mrs. Greeley. Looking at the clock and subtracting three hours for the time difference, she determined that it was 6:00 in California, a good time to make the phone call.

Fortunately, there was a listed number for a Matthew Greeley in Fallbrook—one word, not two—and, even more fortunately, he was home when the call went through. Janice leaned over Hannah's shoulder, trying to hear the other side of the conversation, but Hannah waved her away. When she hung up, Hannah looked at Janice and said, "He thinks she's still at the nursing home!"

The two women looked at each other, neither saying a word. Hannah muttered, "Hanky-panky, indeed!"

Chapter 10

Thursday morning Hannah awoke early. She was impatient to hear what Charlie had found out about the Detroit dealership and to tell Ruby the news about Mrs. Greeley. But calling at 6:00 a.m. was clearly not a good idea. Instead she showered, dressed, and went into the kitchen to make some pancakes for breakfast. Usually, pancakes were reserved for weekends, but she needed something to do until she could make her phone calls. Preparing a special breakfast for the family would serve to keep her occupied and would be a treat for the children.

Madison refused a second pancake, explaining that she needed to lose a pound before the homecoming dance in two days. David offered to eat her second pancake, along with his third. Janice drank her coffee, stealing looks at her mother. It was unusual for Hannah to be up and dressed so early in the morning. Janice remembered last night's discussion about Mrs. Greeley and was concerned that her mother was on another of her missions, which often ended up with Hannah getting in over her head. She wanted to tell her to leave things alone or, if she had to do something, simply report the missing Mrs. Greeley to the administrator of the nursing center. This evening, she promised herself, they would have a long talk.

Janice off to work, children to school, dishes all washed and put away, Hannah made her phone calls. First, to Charlie, who had talked to one of his friends in Detroit, and then to Ruby, arranging to bring lunch at noon. She didn't want to tell Ruby about the phone call to California over the phone. "Someone could be listening in, you know," she explained.

Charlie's information was interesting. *"Bernie's Bloomfield Buys,"* he reported, "has been downsizing for over two years. Now, the decline in the market for large cars and the recent economic recession are probably partly responsible, but the word is that Harold had been taking more out of the business than was necessary for years. It seems he lives the good life: membership in the country club, private schools for his kids, shopping trips to New York for his wife, and one of the guys told me that he had a fantastic collection of art works, and lots of expensive wine, which he talked about all the time." Charlie was obviously not able to see Harold's bank or credit card accounts, but he guessed that Harold was running up quite a debt.

Hannah concluded from all this that Harold wanted to sell the house and put Ruby in a cheap nursing home so that he could use the extra money to either pay off his debts, or continue his high living. She would have to be careful how she discussed this with Ruby—who wouldn't relish hearing that her son was cheating her.

Hannah packed up some cold turkey sandwiches—with mayo and cold slaw on multigrain buns—and called for the bus.

Comfortably seated in a corner of the lounge, eating their sandwiches, Hannah told Ruby about Mrs. Greeley's son's thinking that his mother was still at *Sunset Manor.*

Ruby leaned forward. "What did he say when you told him she wasn't here?"

"I didn't tell him. Why worry him before we are absolutely sure what happened. Now we have to find out what happened. How do we do that? Who would know?"

"I don't know who to ask. I don't know who to trust around here."

"Okay, I'll pretend to be an old friend of Mrs. Greeley—what's her first name?"

"Oh, let me think. Alice. That's it!"

"Okay, I'll pretend to be an old friend of Alice. And I'll ask to see her. Let's see what they say. Then we can go from there. But the more important thing is to get you out of here—before you, too, go missing!"

Hannah wheeled Ruby back to her room. She helped her into bed and went out into the hallway to wait for the young aide to come back to pick up the lunch tray, with the uneaten tasteless food and daily doses of lumpy rice pudding.

"Hello, dear," she said. "Would you know which room Alice Greeley is in? I just learned that she's here. I haven't seen her in years."

"Mrs. Greeley?" replied the young woman, who today was wearing a t-shirt with the words "CUPCAKE" on the front. "I don't know a Mrs. Greeley. That was probably before I started working here."

"Well, thank you anyway. Who would know how I could get in touch with her?" asked Hannah, with a smile.

"I don't know—probably one of the nurses?"

"Good idea. Thank you, dear."

As "Cupcake" picked up Ruby's tray, Hannah went down the hall in search of a nurse. Never having seen one in the building, she didn't know where to look. There appeared to be a nurses' station, but no one was ever there. She asked one of the staff women if they knew where Mrs. Greeley was, but they just shook their heads and returned to their cell phones. Well, she would just wander up and down the hall until she found someone. There had to be a nurse in a nursing home, no?

She checked all the rooms on the floor, and then took the stairs to the second floor. That seemed to be where they put the patients with Alzheimer's and other forms of dementia. But here she could find no nurse—no aide, no janitor, no one!

Getting more determined by the minute, she went to another deserted nurses' station and rang the bell that was sitting on the top of the desk. She rang it four, five times before someone finally came running down the hall.

"Please, you're disturbing the patients," a plump woman in a white nurse's uniform protested. "What do you want?"

"Oh, I'm so sorry," replied Hannah, with a saccharine-sweet smile on her face. "I was looking for someone to help me find my friend—Alice Greeley. I was told by her son that she was here and I thought I'd visit and cheer her up. She's such a dear, and I haven't seen her for many years—I've only just moved to town, you know and it's so good to find someone you know." Hannah rambled on, giving a very good impression of a dotty old woman. The nurse feigned interest, anxious to get back to her interrupted lunch.

"I don't think Mrs. Greeley is here any more—she was released a while ago. Perhaps you could visit her at home."

The nurse started to leave. Hannah grabbed her arm and, with the same saccharine-sweet smile, said, "Oh, that's too bad. I did so want to see her. Perhaps you could get me her home address?"

The nurse sighed, clearly annoyed at the inconvenience Hannah was causing. "I wouldn't have that. You should go to the administration office for that."

"And where would that be, dear?"

"It's on the first floor—near the entrance."

"Thank you so much. You've been so helpful." This was uttered with the same smile, but with much less kindly thoughts in Hannah's head.

She went down to the first floor, to the administrative office near the entrance. No one was at the front desk so she knocked on the closed door; as usual, no one was there. Convinced, however, that there had to be someone, somewhere in the place, she "yoo-hooed" in a loud voice. After three yells, a woman opened the door. She was fortyish, dressed in a dark blue business suit, mauve blouse with a bow at the neckline, and killer heels. Clearly dressed for success! She wore more make-up than Hannah had expected to find in a nursing home administrator and her jet black hair was cut short in an asymmetrical bob, which Hannah assumed to be the latest style.

The woman smiled at Hannah. "May I help you?"

"Yes, dear," Hannah started, saccharine-sweet smile back on her face. "I'm trying to find my old friend, Alice Greeley. I've only just moved to town and I haven't seen her in such a long time. Her son told me she was here, but the nurse upstairs said that she is no longer here, but that you would know where she is living so that I could visit her. It would be so nice to see her again after all these years."

Hannah was starting to get worried at how easy it was for her to appear dotty. But it was working. The woman looked at her with something close to sympathy and said, "I'm so sorry, but we can't give out that information. Client confidentiality, you know."

"But surely it's not a secret where she is. When was she released from here? How was she released—that is, did she drive herself, did she use a taxi, did someone from here drive her? I know her son didn't, as he thinks she's still here! Are you sure she's not still here, hidden away someplace? You seem to lose some of your patients!"

Hannah had lost her patience. More convinced than ever that something was amiss, she persisted in her questions. The woman, not to be outdone in stubbornness, just replied, in a tone that indicated closure, "I'm sorry, I can't help you," and stepped back into the office and closed the door.

Well, thought Hannah, the plot thickens! She returned to Ruby's room to report on her conversation with the administrator only to find Ruby fast asleep. Leaving a note that she would be back the next day, Hannah quietly tiptoed out, letting her friend sleep.

. . . .

Later that evening, Hannah shared her information with Janice. For once, Janice took her concern seriously. "You've got to tell her son that she's not there. You can't do anything, but he certainly can."

"I'm going to call him tonight—it's too early now, he's probably still at work. But I'm also worried about Ruby. What if she turns up missing next time I go to visit her? She's got to get out of that place."

"What's happening with her house? Has her son sold it yet? Perhaps she could live there until he sells it."

"Then where would she go?"

"Well, maybe the house won't sell. The housing market isn't doing very well these days and it is an old house. A lot of the houses on her block are being sold to fraternities, so it's no longer a very desirable neighborhood. She could end up living in her own house for the rest of her life!"

Hannah conceded the possibility, although with less confidence than she felt. She still believed Harold was up to no-good, although she didn't know what form it would take.

. . . .

Hannah got off the phone with Mrs. Greeley's son. It had been a short call, but a productive one. As she related the conversation she had with him, Janice's already large eyes opened still wider. An expression of frightened disbelief spread over her face.

"Why, that's … I don't know, horrendous. I can't imagine how he must feel."

"Not only doesn't he know what happened to his mother, he's still paying for her at *Sunset Manor*! He sends a monthly check to pay for her nursing care as well as an additional amount for her other living expenses. And it's not a small amount—it comes to over $4,000 a month. But he was more concerned about her than about the money—now that's a good son. He's going to fly here tomorrow to find out what's going on. I gave him our number so he can get in touch with me. I also told him about the missing Mrs. Johnson. She doesn't seem to have any relatives, so I don't know how to check on her—if she's still alive."

"You don't think they actually killed those women, do you? Why that's the most frightening thing I've heard. I can't believe that."

"I don't know. But maybe we could at least find out who was paying for Mrs. Johnson. There must be a way to do that."

"I don't know. Do you mind if I run this by Paul? He deals with estates and that sort of thing. Perhaps there's a way of checking."

"No, of course ask him. That's why it's good to have a lawyer as a friend," Hannah replied, emphasizing the word "friend."

Janice shot her a look which clearly said, "Don't go there," and Hannah nodded her acquiescence. Not a time to discuss Janice's love life; this was time to find missing women and protect Ruby.

Chapter 11

THE NEXT DAY HANNAH called Ruby to say she wouldn't be able to visit her until later in the afternoon as she wanted to stay home in case Matthew Greeley called. She related the conversation she had had with Greeley the night before, but cautioned Ruby not to say anything to anyone. No sense sending up warning signs.

The morning went slowly. Every phone call was answered quickly with anticipation only to find a solicitor on the other end. How many charities that deal with the environment could there be? Wouldn't more get done if they somehow combined their funds and worked together instead of one for the polar bears, one for the whales, and many others for the general environment? After explaining that she didn't make pledges over the phone, Hannah vowed to just hang up at the sign of another solicitor.

Filled with nervous energy, she needed something to keep her occupied. Watching TV was too passive, reading required too much concentration—cooking was the answer. She would do the preparations for dinner, maybe even do some baking. The baking part was easy—there were always enough ingredients around for cookies or cakes. But dinner was another matter. The weather was cool and a nice pot roast would be perfect. But she didn't have the roast. Reluctant to run to the store and perhaps miss Greeley's call, she turned to her recipe collection, hoping to get inspiration for a nice chicken dish—there was always chicken in the freezer.

She was still perusing her recipes when the phone rang. It was Janice, who wondered if she had heard from Greeley. The call was brief, with Hannah promising to call Janice back as soon as she heard from him. Hannah returned to her recipes, remembering the occasions on which she had prepared some of these dishes. Memories of family dinners, special occasions, and holidays flooded her mind. Leo was what she called a "good eater," which meant that he had a hearty appetite and enjoyed her cooking. It was almost embarrassing to hear his praises when she had prepared a dinner for special occasions. But beneath her modest protestations was a deep appreciation of his appreciation. Many of her friends had husbands who didn't seem to realize that their wives had actually prepared the food they were eating!

When she had finally decided on a chicken and mushroom dish, she took the chicken out to thaw and checked that the other ingredients were in the pantry. Assured that everything needed was handy, she started in on the dessert. Knowing that both Madison and David—and Janice—loved chocolate, she decided to make her famous "Death by Chocolate" cake: chocolate cake with fudge filling and chocolate frosting—a recipe from her mother-in-law who, while not a great cook, was a fantastic baker. While she was gathering the ingredients, the phone rang again. Expecting another solicitation call, she picked up the receiver prepared to hang up. It was Matthew Greeley this time.

"Mrs. Lowenstein? It's Matt Greeley. I'm at the airport, on my way to the nursing home. I was wondering if you would be available to come with me. I've only been there once and you seem to know your way around the place. If it's not inconvenient…"

Hannah interrupted him. "Oh, of course. I'd be glad to, no problem. Let me give you directions to my house."

She hung up the phone, quickly put away the cake ingredients, and gathered her coat and purse. When he arrived forty minutes later she was sitting by the door, ready to go.

Matthew Greeley was a tall lanky man in his late 60s. His curly dark hair was tinged with gray at the temples—why do men look so distinguished with gray hair, wondered Hannah—and his face was California-tanned. A handsome man, he wore khaki trousers, a light brown shirt, and brown bombardier jacket. He reminded Hannah of Clark Gable in his earlier movies.

After the appropriate introductions, they drove to the nursing home. On the way, Hannah filled him in on the events leading up to the discovery that his mother was missing. His already tight jaw was clenched even tighter as he listened to Hannah. By the time they arrived, Hannah could tell that he was ready for a fight.

The administration office was open, although there was no one at the front desk. After a few of Hannah's "yoo-hoos," the same woman as yesterday appeared. This time her dress-for-success outfit was a beige suit, with navy blouse, and 4-inch heeled beige shoes.

Smiling at Matthew Greeley, the woman took his extended hand between both of hers and, holding on longer than Hannah thought necessary, asked, "What can I do for you, sir?"

Greeley glared at her, extracted his hand and said, "You can find my mother!"

The woman stepped back, clearly surprised. "Excuse me. I don't understand."

"My mother, Alice Greeley, was a patient here—*is* a patient here, since I'm still paying for her care. This woman, Mrs. Lowenstein, tells me that my mother is no longer here, that she was released. I want to know where she is, and why I wasn't notified that she had been released."

"I'm sure I don't know anything about a Mrs. Greeley. I'll have to check the files. I'm sure there's been some misunderstanding…"

Hannah was not content to let her off the hook that easily. "Yesterday, you knew who she was but couldn't give me any information—'client confidentiality,' you said. Today you don't know anything about her?"

"You misunderstood me, I'm afraid. I didn't know whom you were referring to. My response was just general policy. *If* she had been a patient here, I couldn't give you any information about her. Now if you'll come back tomorrow, I'm sure I'll have this all cleared up."

"Well, confidentiality doesn't apply here," Greeley interrupted. "I'm her son, I have durable power of attorney, and I want to know where she is—NOW. If I don't get satisfaction here, I will go to the police. Do you understand?"

Greeley was clearly furious, his voice raised slightly, his jaw clenched even more tightly. Hannah thought that one more delay on the part of the woman and Greeley would resort to violence! Hoping to de-escalate the situation, she suggested that the woman examine her files and give him the necessary information.

The woman nodded nervously and quickly went into the office. After ten minutes had passed, Hannah "yoo-hooed" again. Greeley was at the end of his patience, threatening to go to the police, and Hannah was ready to join him. Just then a man came striding toward them, a large smile on his face, hand extended in greeting. He introduced himself as the Director of *Sunset Manor* and asked what the problem was. Hearing his voice, the woman came out of the office, and handed him a folder.

"This is Mrs. Greeley's son. There seems to be some confusion as to Mrs. Greeley's whereabouts. The records—as you can see—show that she was released about three months ago, but unfortunately no one notified Mr. Greeley, who has continued to pay for her care."

"I'm terribly sorry about that, sir. We will certainly reimburse you for your payments. Helen, make a note of that, will you?"

"The hell with the payments. Where is my mother?" stormed Greeley.

The director, clearly flustered, looked more carefully at the records. "There doesn't seem to be an address here. Terribly sloppy work. But we will get to the bottom of this, sir. Let me check with the other attendants and I'm sure we'll be able to locate your mother. I'm sure it's just a bureaucratic mix-up."

"And check on Mrs. Johnson—she's missing, too," added Hannah. "She's supposed to be in room 115, but it's been empty for the last week or so."

The director looked at the woman in the beige suit, who nodded. He turned to Greeley and repeated that they were terribly sorry and would clear things up as soon as possible. "How can we contact you, sir?" he asked.

"I'll be staying at the Holiday Inn in town. I expect to hear from you by this afternoon. Otherwise, I'm going to the police."

With that he turned and left the building, Hannah following close behind. When they were outside, Hannah asked, "Would you want to talk to any of the patients who knew your mother? Maybe they can tell you something."

He paced back and forth. He was a powerfully built man and seemed to be near the limit of restraining himself from striking out—at anything. Hannah used all of her charm to convince him to talk to Ruby and Mary Bradshaw, the woman who had first mentioned Alice Greeley's disappearance. Succumbing to Hannah's appeals, Greeley agreed and they re-entered the building. To neither one's surprise, the door to the administration office was closed and, again, no one was at the front desk.

They found Ruby and Mary in the lounge where Hannah introduced Matthew Greeley to them. Tears flowing down her face, Mary started talking. "Your mother was a good friend—we spent a lot of time together—she liked to talk, you know, even though her hearing wasn't so good. She was so proud of you—she had me read your letters over and over. I just can't believe she left without saying goodbye to me."

"When was the last time you saw her?" he asked.

"It's hard for me to remember, but it seems at least a month, maybe more. You know, one day is just like another in a place like this."

Hannah and Greeley left the two women with a promise to tell Mary where Alice was as soon as they found out.

"It doesn't look good, does it?" said Greeley. "It wouldn't be so bad if she had died a natural death—after all, she was eighty-seven and in poor health—that's why she was at that damn place! But not knowing is what's eating me up. What if she's in trouble? What if she's ill and not being taken care of? I should have insisted she come to California. There are nursing homes there, nice ones, and I could visit her when I'm in town. I travel a lot for my job, but that would have been better than this. But she was stubborn, didn't want to be a burden, and all that crap. Damn, I need to find out what happened. "

Hannah didn't know how to pose the next question. It was clear that Greeley was genuinely concerned about his mother, that he had taken responsibility about her care. But why hadn't he wondered why he hadn't heard from her for over three months?

"When was the last time you spoke to your mother?" she asked.

"We didn't talk on the phone—she's legally deaf, you know. We used to write, but that got to be too difficult, too—she's nearly blind and has severe arthritis. So I'd write letters to her, she'd have someone read them to her and kind of dictate responses to me. I think it was one of the staff, or maybe another patient, who did that. I'd get a response about every two weeks, and that continued." Reaching into his breast pocket, he pulled out a letter. "In fact, I received this letter just last week. That's why when you first called, I wasn't concerned; I assumed she was still here."

He extended the letter to Hannah, who read it through without comment. According to the letter, Alice Greeley was alive and doing well. She was enjoying playing bingo and spent many hours with her friend, Mary Bradshaw. Her blood pressure was under control and she hadn't had any dizzy spells for over a month. She missed Matthew and was looking forward to his visit at Christmas. It was dated two weeks ago.

"We need to find out who was writing this stuff. This is a clear attempt to cover up something."

"I'm not waiting. I'm going to the police now. I don't want to give those bastards time to do any more cover-ups."

Greeley drove Hannah home and headed to the police department to file his complaint. Before getting out of the car, however, Hannah got a promise from him that he would keep her informed. After all, she reminded him, his mother wasn't the only woman who had gone missing from *Sunset*.

. . . .

That evening the conversation at the dinner table revolved around the missing women. Even David remained at the table, finding the conversation more riveting than his latest video game. The remains of the chicken and mushroom dish, prepared by Hannah when she had returned home, were put in the refrigerator and everyone sat around the table eating store-bought cookies—no Death by Chocolate cake—and offering their versions of what had probably happened to the women.

David piped up, "I bet they were killed and then they sold their body parts to hospitals. I saw a movie about that," he exclaimed, convincing Janice that he was watching too many gory movies.

Madison suggested that perhaps the women had died and their bodies had gone missing. Hannah thanked them for their suggestions but reminded David that these women were in their eighties and not likely to have any body parts worth transplanting, which caused David to respond, "Then they're toast."

Janice was unusually quiet. After the children went upstairs, Hannah asked, "What's the matter? You're too quiet."

"I find this really frightening," she replied. "And I worry about you. If these people are doing what you think they're doing, you could be in danger by exposing them. Leave it to the police. Stay out of it, Mom."

"Darling, I'm not going to do anything more. Mr. Greeley is making the official complaint—and the police will deal with it. But I am worried about Ruby. She needs to get out of there—now. I'm going to see her tomorrow and find out what's happening with her house. If her son-of-a-bitch son hasn't sold it yet, she could move back in."

"What have you found out about him?"

"Well, all I know is what Charlie told me. He lives beyond his income. His business isn't doing too well—that may be because of the economy or it may be that he's taking too much money out of the business for his personal use. And he's let some of his salesmen go. I think, although I can't prove it, that he needs the money he'd get from Ruby's house. That's why he's so set on selling it. But that's all speculation. And even if it's true, it's not illegal. He owns the house and can do what he wants with it."

"What will Ruby do once he sells it? You know, he's going to sell it. It's just a matter of time."

"I know. I've been thinking about that." Hannah hesitated, wondering if this was the right time to raise the issue. She took a deep breath and asked, "How would you feel about Ruby moving in here?"

Just then Madison came into the room. "Mom, remember, you said I could get my nails done for homecoming?"

Janice looked at her mother and then turned to Madison. "I remember. How much do you need?"

"It's $15. I'm going to go with Suzanne—she's been there before."

"I have a $20 in my wallet. Take that."

Hannah resumed the discussion. "I know it's asking a lot—and it wouldn't be for long—just until things get settled for her. I've just got to get her out of there."

Madison put the wallet back and waved a $20 bill at her mother, who nodded. However, her curiosity was now aroused. "What are you talking about?"

The two women looked at each other. Hannah deferred to Janice to do the explaining. Janice hesitated, undecided whether or not to bring Madison into the conversation. Realizing that whatever decision she made, the children would be affected, she explained the situation to Madison.

"Do you remember Grandma's friend, the woman in the nursing home? Well, Grandma would like her to move in with us for a while."

"Why? Doesn't she have a home?"

Janice glanced at Hannah, indicting that it was now in her hands to explain.

"No, she doesn't have a home any more. And she's well enough to leave the nursing home so I asked your mother if she could come here until she finds a more permanent home."

"Where would she sleep?"

"We can worry about that later," Hannah replied. "The first question is whether she should move in. The decision is up to your mother. If she says no, it's no—no arguments. It's a lot to ask. It'll disrupt things having another person living here, so I want your mother should think it over before she says anything."

"That's a good idea," said Janice. "So, off to bed now. We'll talk about this tomorrow."

Madison waved at both of them with the $20 bill in her hand and went upstairs. Janice got up from the table and walked around to her mother. She gave her a hug and said, "Mom, I know how important this is for you. Let me think about it, okay? Let's get through Maddie's homecoming first!"

Hannah smiled and held Janice's hand. "Of course, darling. First things first. I'm sure Ruby will be safe so long as I'm visiting her every day."

Chapter 12

Saturday started with a bang—literally. David slammed the door as he went out to walk Max. Hannah was already up, relaxing in her sitting room with a cup of tea. She knew the day would be hectic with Madison getting ready for the homecoming dance, and she knew that her role would be to get out of the way unless they needed her help. She was also apprehensive about Ruby and wanted to spend some time with her. So many things were up in the air: Matthew Greeley's talk with the police; Harold Shapiro's selling Ruby's house; Janice's decision about Ruby coming to live with them. She wanted closure on something!

Hearing the door slam, she got up to prepare breakfast for the family. With that bang, everyone would be awake and downstairs soon. She entered the kitchen, surprised to see Janice there, hovering over the coffee pot, willing it to be ready. "I didn't hear you come down," Hannah said. "Did David wake you?"

"No, I was already up," Janice replied. "I didn't sleep well last night. But that boy! If I've told him once, I've told him a hundred times: some people like to sleep in on the weekends! There's no reason he has to slam doors."

"I know. But he's got so much energy he just forgets. And it is a nice morning. He'll give Max a good run, that's for sure."

Hannah started to crack the eggs for French toast. "So, why couldn't you sleep?" she asked.

"I don't know. There's so much to do today: help Maddie get ready, clean the house, finish some reports. Paul called yesterday. I thought we'd invite him over for dinner. Maddie will be out and David will probably want to stay over at Billy's. Is that okay with you?"

"Of course. Listen, I'll help with the cleaning—and with dinner, if you want. I think it'll be better if I stay out of Maddie's way—unless she should ask for my help. I'm just going to run up to see Ruby this morning. I'll be home the rest of the day."

"You can take the car; I won't need it. And Suzanne and Becky are picking Maddie up to get their nails done, so she won't need it either."

"Okay, that'll make it quicker than using the bus." Hannah didn't raise the issue of Ruby, just continued seasoning the egg mixture for the French toast.

Janice, however, asked. "So tell me…What's Ruby like? I mean, does she talk a lot? Is she loud? Is she fussy about what she eats? Does she need help getting around? Does she mind dogs? Children? You know…what's she like?"

Hannah stopped beating the eggs and, with whisk in hand, sat down across the table from Janice, who was sipping her coffee, steam rising as she blew to cool it.

"Ruby is one of the kindest people I've known. In fact, too kind in my opinion. She can't think ill of anyone, especially that son-of-a-bitch son of hers. But that's neither here nor there. She's rather timid. I've never heard her raise her voice, even when she's upset….She has to watch her salt, but other than that she eats everything. I've never asked her about dogs, but she's quite good with children. At the Senior Center, she helped to establish the 'Grandparents Club'—you know, old people who volunteer to spend time with youngsters. I think you'd like her and I really don't think she'd be a problem."

"Maybe I should go with you tomorrow—today's too busy—just to meet her. But don't say anything in case it doesn't work out. I'd hate to hurt her feelings." Janice looked at her mother, eyebrows raised. Hannah smiled. "That's a wonderful idea, darling. Just meet her and then whatever you should decide is okay."

Just then Madison came down. Long dark hair tousled, clad in polka-dotted blue pajamas and pink fuzzy slippers, she sat down at the table next to her mother and put her head on Janice's shoulder.

"Good morning, sleepyhead. I'm surprised you were able to sleep in this morning, with your brother banging the door and all you have to do," Janice said, as she hugged her daughter.

"I heard something, but then went back to sleep. I don't have much to do today. Suzanne's coming by about 11:00, and then after we get our nails done I'm going over to her house where some of us are going to do our hair. I should be back in plenty of time to get dressed. Kenny's not picking me up until 6:00."

"So when are you going to eat today?" This was a typical question for Hannah, always concerned that young people wouldn't eat well if not reminded by her.

"I'll have some of that French toast you're making, Grandma. And we're all going to go to dinner at that Mexican place before the dance. That reminds me, Mom, I'll need some money."

"Doesn't the boy pay for the dinner?" asked Hannah.

"Grandma, that's so old-fashioned."

"Well, he should at least offer," responded Hannah, as she poured the egg mixture over the bread.

Madison looked at her mother, who just shook her head and smiled. "Grandma remembers the days when boys came to the door to pick up their dates. Right, Mom?"

"Your grandfather would have had a fit if some boy honked his horn for your mother," Hannah said to Madison. "If they didn't come in, she didn't go out! And when they came in—oy, did he give them the third degree! Asked all sorts of questions, like: how were they doing in school, where were they going, who else would be there. And then telling them what time to bring her home. I ended up feeling sorry for the boys. Most of them were good boys. But your mother had an eye for the no-good-niks—the ones who smoked and wore leather jackets. She thinks I don't know how she used to meet them when she said she was going over to a friend's house. Your mother was no angel, you know."

"I didn't lie—I did go over to a friend's house. I just happened to run into someone along the way," Janice explained, looking at Madison. 'I never lied to my parents; that's unacceptable."

"I get the message, Mom. But, Grandma, I hope when Kenny comes in you don't ask him all those questions—he's shy."

"Me? You know I never interfere. What you do is between you and your mother."

"Yeah, sure," responded Madison, winking at her mother.

Just then David returned from his walk with Max. The dog immediately went to his water bowl, slopping water all over the floor. "You must have given him a good run," said Janice. "He's really thirsty."

"And sloppy," added Hannah.

"Umm, something smells good. Can I have some?" asked David, ignoring Hannah's comment.

"I'll set up a plate for you, but wash your hands first. You don't want dog stuff on your food."

"What's 'dog stuff'? I didn't even pet him," objected David.

"David, listen to Grandma. Wash your hands."

When David returned, with relatively clean hands, his plate was ready for him: two pieces of French toast and the bottle of syrup. By the time he left the table, the level of syrup in the bottle had decreased by about a third.

It was 10:00 by the time everyone left the table and the kitchen had been cleaned. Hannah showered and dressed, ready to visit Ruby. As she opened the door to leave, the phone rang. David picked it up and, looked at her. "Yeah, she's here," he said, and handed the phone to Hannah.

It was Matthew Greeley. He was staying in town a few more days, trying to track down his mother. His meeting with the police had gone well. They had taken his concerns seriously and were going to investigate the nursing home. But he still didn't know what happened to his mother. Hannah told him she was on her way to visit Ruby and, asking him to hold on for a minute, yelled up to Janice, "Do you mind if I invite Mr. Greeley for dinner tonight?" Fortunately, she had remembered to put her hand over the mouthpiece so her loud voice, which echoed throughout the house, was not heard by him.

"That's fine. Maybe Paul will have some suggestions for him."

"Mr. Greeley, would you care to come for dinner tonight? Nothing fancy, just plain food, but we could talk, and you wouldn't have to eat restaurant food again. There aren't many good restaurants in this town."

Greeley quickly accepted the invitation and was told that dinner would be at 7:00—leaving time for any unexpected hitch in Madison's 6:00 dinner plans.

. . . .

Ruby was in her room, sitting in the chair by the window. The room was dark, the blinds again closed. It was a glorious morning: sun shining, the gold and orange of the maple and oak trees providing a vivid palette against a blue sky. But in Ruby's room it was twilight: dark and somber. The light seeping in through the closed blinds managed to highlight the greenish-brown walls, making them even more bilious.

Hannah went over to the window, intending to open the blinds, when she noticed that Ruby's eyes were red. "What's happened? Are you all right?" she asked.

"I'm fine, just a silly old woman, that's all."

"Nonsense, you're not silly—you're old, but you're not silly."

Ruby smiled. "You don't sugarcoat things, do you, Hannah? I'm okay. I just had a call from Harold. He's sold the house and my things have to be out in two weeks. I don't know what to do. I told him I couldn't get my things out in that time, but he just said he'd get someone to put everything in storage. A whole houseful of furniture and all my things—in storage! I've lived in that house for almost thirty years, accumulated things, and he wants me to put it all in storage. And then, he said, it'll only cost me $200 a month for the storage!"

Ruby started to cry again. "My own son! I don't understand him any more. He never used to be like this. Oh, he was never one to show affection, but I assumed that he was like his father—didn't show emotion, but a good man. But this? I don't know why he was so anxious to sell the house. He knows I have nowhere to go—he certainly doesn't want me."

Hannah just listened. Torn between telling her friend that her son was probably in financial problems and needed the money from the sale of the house and wanting to protect her from the ugly truth that her son was a son-of-a-bitch, she kept silent.

After Ruby had calmed down, Hannah suggested that they go outside and sit in the sun. There would be few days of such mild weather left before the cold winds of winter appeared. She wrapped Ruby in a sweater and some blankets for her legs and wheeled her down the hallway out to the bench in front of the building. Comfortably seated, the two women lifted their faces to the sun. They sat that way for a few minutes, saying nothing, just letting the warmth reach their bones.

Ruby sighed. "I wish my husband were here. Bernie would know what to do."

"We'll figure something out, don't worry. You won't stay here, that's for sure. I don't want I should come visit one day and find you're missing."

"What's happening about that? Did they find Alice?"

"No, but her son went to the police and they're going to investigate. What about Mrs. Johnson? Any word about her?"

"No, but her name's not on the patient list any more. They took it off yesterday and closed the room."

"They're scared, that's what. They're covering their tracks; let's just hope it's not too late. Alice's son seems to be a good man. I don't think he'll give up until he finds out what happened to her. Did you know that she was practically deaf? That's why he never called her."

"I didn't know her. She was gone by the time I got here. Mary, Mrs. Bradshaw, knew her. She never said anything about it, but then she can't hear very well herself."

"Mr. Greeley's coming over for dinner tonight. I'll let you know what I find out. Oh, by the way, my daughter, Janice, would like to visit you tomorrow. What's a good time?'

"What, I have such a busy schedule you have to make an appointment? Any time is good. I'd love to meet her. I hope you realize how lucky you are to have a daughter like that. And grandchildren. I never hear from mine. I could die and they wouldn't care—or notice! It'd probably be an inconvenience to come to my funeral."

"Believe me, I know, I know," Hannah said, compassion for her friend apparent in her face. They sat for a while longer, two old women each with her own thoughts, until Hannah broke the silence. "Listen," she said, " I'm going to take you inside and then I've got to stop at the store. Tonight is the big homecoming thing for Maddie and I promised Janice I'd prepare dinner. Her 'friend' Paul is coming, and Mr. Greeley, too, so I want to make something special."

"So what's doing with Paul? Any prospects?"

"Who knows? These young people don't seem to know from marriage. They're all 'just friends.' Would it be so bad to make an engagement, to make some plans? But I don't interfere; what they do is their business. But I have my opinions, you know."

Ruby smiled. Of course, Hannah had her opinions—and usually found opportunities to express them.

....

Hannah arrived home, loaded down with bags from *Marty's*. The house was quiet: Madison was off getting hair and nails done, David was over at Billy's house, probably playing some new video game, and Janice was in the basement doing the laundry.

Hannah put away the groceries and called down to Janice. "Yoo-hoo, what do you want I should do? Have you vacuumed yet?"

Janice came up, carrying a basket of unsorted laundry. "You can help me sort these. I've changed the bed linens, but I haven't dusted or vacuumed. If you can do that, I'll do the bathrooms and floors."

"It's a deal." Taking the sheets from the basket, they talked while they folded.

"Well, Ruby told me that Harold sold her house and he's putting her things in storage, which he expects her to pay."

"No, you're not serious! Does she have any money besides her social security, which I assume is not very much?"

"Not as far as I know. She's really worried. I don't know how much he sold the house for, but I have the feeling that she's not going to get any of it, if he has his way. I don't understand what kind of an agreement they signed. You give away everything even while you're alive? What kind of a lawyer would write something like that? She said they had a lawyer draw up the papers, but I smell a rat. I bet it was a friend of Harold's—that son…"

"Yes, I know that 'son-of-a-bitch.' You know, Mom, if Dad were around to hear how you talk these days, he'd be very upset."

"I'm sorry, darling. I know I should watch my language around the children, but I get so angry at how he's treating his mother. I'll watch it, though. Anyway, I doubt that agreement is really legal—how can you can give up everything like that?"

"Well, we can ask Paul this evening. You do remember that he's coming for dinner, right?"

"How could I forget? I even stopped at the store to get things for dinner. I did the week's shopping, so we have enough for a chicken dish, a pot roast, or fish—I got a nice salmon. What would you like?"

"Wow, you bought all that? You must have gotten a raise in your social security" Janice joked. "How about a nice pot roast? We can call it 'boeuf bourgignon' and impress the men. See, I didn't forget that Mr. Greeley's coming, too."

Hannah laughed. "This promises to be an interesting evening. It'll certainly keep your mind off Maddie. Speaking of her, what time did you tell her to be home?"

"Remember, I told her she could go to that sleepover. I did check—the parents will be there, and they're responsible people. So I won't be waiting up for her. She has to be back by noon tomorrow, though. Do you have problems with this?"

"Problems? Of course I do. How could I not have problems about it? But times change, I know that. My ways aren't necessarily the best for today. And they're good children, so you must be doing something right," Hannah teased.

Janice smiled back. "Well, let me take this stuff upstairs and get to work on the bathrooms. The vacuum cleaner is in the living room. Don't carry it upstairs; I'll do that."

"Okay. Oh, by the way, I told Ruby that you'd be visiting tomorrow and she was pleased. She said any time would be fine."

"Okay, we can talk about it later."

. . . .

At 5:45 Maddie came down the stairs, dressed in a spaghetti strap magenta cocktail-length dress, with a form-fitting bodice and A-line skirt. Her long dark hair was pulled back into a flowing cascade of curls, with soft tendrils falling over her ears. She wore a simple crystal necklace with matching earrings, and on her feet were the black strap shoes with the 3-inch heels that Hannah had bought for her. Her practice walking in them had paid off—she was steady and walked with a grace she rarely showed. Looking at her, face flushed with anticipation, Hannah marveled at the transformation from a little girl to a beautiful young woman. Madison would be going off to college in the fall and things would change in the household. Hannah just hoped that everyone was prepared for what the future would bring.

David, however, was still a boy, not wasting the opportunity to tease his sister. "Boy, you look dorky," he laughed. "Kenny won't know who you are, all made up like that."

"Enough, David," scolded Janice. "This is a big night for your sister—and she looks lovely."

David smirked and sat down, anxiously waiting to see Kenny's reaction to Maddie's get-up. He got his answer as soon as Kenny arrived, who seemed tongue-tied when he saw Madison. Or maybe it was the line-up greeting him in the living room that rendered him speechless. He finally managed to say hello to Janice and Hannah, fist bump with David, and hand the corsage he had in his hand to Madison. Janice helped pin the flower to Madison's waist and, aware that Kenny was anxious to leave, went to get a shawl for Madison.

Hannah, however, wasn't ready for them to depart. "We need pictures. Where's the camera, David?"

David handed the digital camera to Hannah, who stared at it in puzzlement. "So what do I do?" she asked, as she fumbled with the camera.

"Here, give it to me," replied Janice, with impatience. "I've shown you how to use it: you just look through here and press this button." With that, she took two pictures of the young couple, after which Madison hugged her mother and grandmother, stuck her tongue out at her brother, and, with Kenny at her side, went out to join Suzanne and her date in the car.

Janice sighed and went to join Hannah in the kitchen to make the final preparations for the evening dinner. David, as planned, waved goodbye, slammed the front door and took off for his overnight at Billy's house.

· ·

Paul arrived early, dressed more formally than usual for what was supposed to be a casual dinner. A pleasant-looking man, he looked uncomfortable in his charcoal gray jacket, black slacks, white shirt and red striped tie. The gray strands scattered randomly throughout his dark hair and his horned-rim glasses gave the impression of a serious man, older than his 45 years.

The evening started out badly. Matthew Greeley was in a foul mood, having had no success in finding his mother and frustrated at what he was coming to consider a less-than-concerned approach by the police; Paul was nervous, trying too hard to impress Hannah that he was an appropriate suitor for Janice; Janice was tense, trying to get the conversation going and not having much success. Hannah realized that it was up to her to get the evening on the right track. She started with drinks. Not a drinker herself, she remembered how a little booze always helped her husband to relax after a tiring day—and it was even supposed to stimulate the appetite.

The men were on their second drinks, comfortably seated in the large upholstered chairs in front of the electric fireplace, which Janice had turned on hoping it would help to create a cozy atmosphere. Janice placed the salmon terrine appetizer on the coffee table in front of the fireplace, before she went into the kitchen to check on Hannah's "boeuf bourguignon" pot roast. Satisfying herself that everything was under control, she quickly returned to the men, not wanting to leave them alone in awkward silence.

Hannah joined them and reported that dinner would be ready in twenty minutes. Noticing the awkward pauses, she decided to just jump in. "Mr. Greeley, why don't you tell Paul about the situation with your mother. Paul is an attorney. Maybe he can give you some advice."

"Call me Matt, please. I don't want to spoil the evening talking about my troubles."

Hannah, thinking that nothing could be worse than the present situation, persisted. "Nonsense, we're all interested—and concerned—about what's going on at that place. Please."

"Well, in a nutshell, my mother's missing. She was in a nursing home, *Sunset Manor*. They claim she was released, but they don't know where she went. They've been accepting my checks for the last few months, even though she was no longer there. You have to realize, this is a nearly blind eighty-seven-year-old woman who is extremely hard of hearing, has heart problems, and arthritis so bad she can hardly walk. She can't take care of herself. Where is she going to go? And by herself? No doctor would sign a release form for her. I've been to the police who say they are looking into it, but I don't think they're doing very much. Anyway, that's where I am—trying to track down where she could be—or more likely, what happened to her?"

When he finished, Hannah jumped in. "Paul, I don't know what kind of cases you deal with, but maybe you know something Mr. Greeley—Matt—should be doing? His mother's not the only one that place has lost. There's another woman who's missing."

Paul's interest was clearly piqued. "The first thing I would advise is what you're already doing, getting the police involved. But you need to step it up. Have you filed an official missing person report? No? Well, I'd do that tomorrow morning. That puts more pressure on them. I don't know what your financial situation is, but sometimes getting a PI involved gets more results than the police. I could give you the name of the guy we use, if you want. But there's another angle to take: fraud. You say you've been paying for her care when she was no longer there. What kind of money are we talking about?"

"About $4-5,000 a month for about 2-3 months—I don't know when she was released. It seems to be at least two months ago, maybe longer."

"That might be enough to push it into Circuit Court. Look, one of the guys in my office handles those kinds of cases. Why don't you give me a call tomorrow and I'll set you up with him."

"Thanks, I'll do that."

The chill in the room having dissipated—partly due to the warmth of the fireplace, but also to the ensuing discussions of the lack of quality care for the elderly, the changes in child rearing, and the faults of the present administration in Washington—they sat down at the dining room table to indulge in Hannah's pot roast.

By the time Hannah's chocolate torte was served, Matt and Paul were comparing the merits of the coaching staffs at Ohio State University and the University of Michigan and placing imaginary bets on which team would make it to the finals.

At 11:00 Paul and Matt left, after arranging to meet the next day. Janice and Hannah looked at each other and laughed. "All in all, a successful evening—thanks to you, Mom."

"Women know how to talk to each other; men need a little help," replied Hannah. "You know, a lot of the credit goes to your Paul. He was really helpful to Mr. Greeley. That poor man. Not knowing is sometimes worse than knowing the worst."

"I know. I don't know what I would do if you came up missing. Do you think they moved her someplace and kept cashing his checks for the money?"

"I think she died—maybe they killed her, who knows? They're greedy bastards. What, the son's going to come in for frequent visits from California? And from what he said they were doing a good job of covering up. That last letter—maybe even more— was clearly not written by his mother—so someone at that place was writing them pretending to be his mother. It's sad how people look at us old people: when we're no longer useful, throw us away."

"Mom, you know that would never happen to you. Besides you're still useful!" Janice teased. "Well, it's almost midnight. Go to bed. So long as the food's put away the rest can be cleaned up tomorrow."

"It'll just take a few minutes to finish up here. I hate to wake up to a messy kitchen. Go, darling, go."

Janice smiled and left the room. Hannah cleaned up the remainder of the dinner dishes and went to her suite to prepare for bed. Exhausted physically, her mind was going full speed. She hadn't raised the issue of Ruby moving in, not wanting to pressure Janice, but she hoped that tomorrow's meeting would go well. All this talk about Mrs. Greeley—and the missing Mrs. Johnson—had strengthened her resolve to get Ruby out of *Sunset Manor.*

Chapter 13

Hannah slept late. She had finally fallen asleep around 2:00 a.m. and had slept soundly until 9:00. She thought it was unusually quiet for a Sunday morning—until she remembered that David was at his friend's house and Madison was at a sleepover.

She quietly started the coffee, not wanting to wake Janice. Sitting at the kitchen table, sipping coffee, she thought about the changes that were coming. Janice never talked about it, but Hannah could see that she and Paul were in love. As far as she knew, there were no long-term plans, but she could foresee the day when they would want to spend more time together—maybe even move in together. Where would that leave her? Oh, she knew Janice would never ask her to leave. But would she be in the way? Well, no sense worrying about that until the time came. In the meantime, she had to do something about Ruby.

At about 10:30, Janice came downstairs, eyes puffy from sleep, short hair standing on end, grunted "good morning" and headed for the coffee pot. Hannah smiled at her. "You look like something the dog dragged in," she teased.

"Oh, shit—Max! He has to be walked."

"Not to worry. I let him out in the backyard. He did his business and came right in when I called. I think he was hungry."

"Thanks." Running her fingers through her hair, Janice shook her head. "I don't know why I slept so late. It always makes me feel groggy, and I've got a headache, too. Is David back yet?"

"No, do you want I should call over there?"

"No, he's probably still sleeping. Those kids stay up all night playing their games and then sleep the morning away. Anyway, I can use the quiet now."

Hannah gazed at Janice. Even with her puffy eyes and porcupine hair, she thought her daughter was beautiful. Perhaps mothers always felt that way about their children, but Hannah believed she was unbiased. Even as a child, Janice received compliments on her looks. Reluctant to encourage what she considered an unhealthy emphasis on physical appearance, Hannah had focused her praise on Janice's behavior with friends and family and her performance in school, perhaps leaving Janice to underestimate her beauty.

"Do you think you'll be up to visiting Ruby today?" asked Hannah.

"Maybe this afternoon. I want to be here when Maddie gets home. She's supposed to be home by noon."

"That's fine. So, how about something to eat? Cereal, eggs, toast—what would you like I should make?"

"Maybe some toast. I'm not hungry, I'm still full from last night. That pot roast was really good, Mom. And the guys devoured it. I was hoping there'd be some left over for tonight, but it's almost all gone."

"What do you mean 'pot roast'? That was *boeuf bourguignon*," Hannah joked, poorly imitating a Julia Childs accent.

Just then, David dashed in, slamming the door behind him. "I'm home!"

Janice grimaced. "I know. I heard the door slam. So what time did you guys get to bed last night?" she asked.

"I don't know. Late, I guess. What's for lunch?"

"Lunch, didn't you just have breakfast?" Hannah replied.

"Yeah, but that was like an hour ago. I'm hungry."

"Okay, wash your hands and I'll make you some eggs."

"Aw, can't I have a sandwich? I had eggs at Billy's."

"Okay, okay, a tuna fish sandwich—no argument. Now go wash up."

David ran upstairs to put away his backpack and returned almost immediately to the kitchen. "So, you washed your hands? Let me see," ordered Hannah. With a chagrined look, David shrugged and went over to the sink to wash his hands.

Hannah opened the can of tuna fish, making note that it was the last one in the cupboard, added mayonnaise, and spread the mixture on a slice of bread. She started to add lettuce and tomato when David stopped her. "I want it plain," he said. Hannah put back the lettuce and tomato and handed him the sandwich and a glass of milk.

Within two minutes he had eaten the sandwich, drunk the milk, and left the room.

Janice looked up at Hannah. "Who was that strange person?"

Hannah laughed. "That was a hungry little boy, who will someday be a wonderful man—just be patient. So, what do you want to eat? Tuna fish?"

"Ugh, no; just the toast."

Hannah set the toast on the table and sat down across from Janice. "Darling, if you're not up to it, the visit to Ruby can wait. Another day won't make a difference. Maybe you should rest today."

Nibbling at her toast, Janice replied, "I'll be fine once I shower and let the aspirin do its job. I'm feeling better already. Besides, I've got a real busy week ahead and I don't think I could get free, so let's do it after Maddie gets home."

. . . .

Maddie arrived home shortly after noon, dressed in jeans and a sweatshirt, carefully carrying the magenta dress over her arm, black strap shoes dangling from her left hand. Her face showed no emotion, causing Janice to ask, "What's wrong?"

"Nothing's wrong, Mom. I'm just tired."

Knowing her daughter, Janice persisted. "Did you have a good time? Did you dance?"

"Yeah, I had a great time—with my girlfriends! I hate him! He danced one time with me and then spent the rest of the evening with Tiffany and her crowd. I never want to see him again." Tears were forming and Madison wiped them away with her free hand. Janice went to her, enfolding her daughter in her arms. They stood there, not saying anything, just holding each other.

Hannah sat quietly. Madison was upset and Janice was handling it. Her role was to be supportive. Other than that, just listen.

Madison grabbed a napkin and blew her nose. "I'm okay, Mom. I'm going to go upstairs and lie down for a while." Smiling shyly, she added, "We didn't sleep much last night. Suzanne and Becky kept me up telling me how lucky I was to be rid of Kenny, how he wasn't deserving of me—you know, all that crap to make me feel better."

"Well, they're good friends. Go take a nap, honey. We'll talk later."

. . . .

"See, I told you. You hardly ever see a nurse or anybody here—just patients. You wonder if anyone helps these people. Maybe it is easy to just 'lose' a patient— who would know?"

Hannah was talking to Janice as they marched down the hall to Ruby's room. "And these walls—have you ever seen anything so depressing?"

Ruby was in her room, sitting up in bed. On the table next to the bed was the food tray, with its uneaten food. Her face broke into a radiant smile when she saw Hannah and Janice.

"Oh, I'm so glad to see you—and you must be Janice. I've heard so much about you. Your mother thinks you're an angel, you know."

Janice laughed. "Well, not all the time! How are you feeling?"

"Oh, I'm ready to get out of here. They don't even take me for therapy any more, so I guess I'm ready to be released."

Hannah had lifted the cover off the food tray and sampled the soup. "Is this what they gave you for lunch? Janice, come look. The woman has high blood pressure and they give her salty soup and mushy food! Well, I brought you a tuna salad sandwich—salt-free tuna—and a banana, for the potassium, you know."

Ruby smiled. "I don't know what I'd do if it weren't for your mother. She's kept me going with her food and visits." Ruby turned away as her eyes misted over. "Ah, forgive me; I'm just a sentimental old woman."

Just then the young aide came in for the food tray. This time her t-shirt was blank. Hannah picked up the tray to give to her and said, "What? No writing on your chest, today?"

The young woman looked blankly at her, took the tray, and left.

The three women chatted about the weather, the conditions at the nursing home, and the problems raising teenagers. Ruby shared that she seldom saw her grandchildren, that she missed having young people around. The conversation stayed on neutral grounds until Janice asked about Ruby's plans.

"What are you planning to do when you leave this place? Where will you go?"

"I'm hoping that the people who bought my house—did Hannah tell you my son sold it?—will let me live there a while before they move in. But I don't know what arrangements my son has made with them….I haven't heard from him since he told me he sold the house. I don't know what I'm supposed to do with all my furniture. You know you accumulate a lot of stuff from almost thirty years in the same house. I may have to just stay here until things get sorted out."

"I don't mean to pry, but do you have any income other than social security? Any investments, things like that?"

"No, just my social security—and a CD."

"Will you be getting anything from the sale of the house?"

"I don't know. Stupid, right? I should know these things."

"No, not stupid. Just perhaps too trusting. Would you mind if I had a lawyer friend examine the papers you signed? To determine what your situation is. There may be a provision about selling the house before your death that would determine if you're entitled to any of the money."

"See, I told you she was smart as well as beautiful," interjected Hannah.

Ruby looked worried. "I don't want to cause any trouble. I can…"

Hannah interrupted her, causing Ruby to look away. "What trouble? Finding out what's rightly yours is trouble? You've got to face it, Ruby. If you don't get anything from the house, you're not going to have enough money to do anything but stay in a place like this—or worse. And, I'm going to say it: you need to look out for yourself; your son's not going to do it. As far as I can tell, he's looking out for himself."

Tears ran down Ruby's pale cheeks. Janice frowned at Hannah's insensitive remarks, but Hannah was relentless. She intentionally ignored Ruby's tears and Janice's frown, focusing on the dire consequences that would result if Ruby couldn't get any of the proceeds from the sale of the house.

"Ruby, you've got to stop this. If you don't do anything, you won't have money to do anything, not even get into a decent assisted living place. All we're talking about here is that you look at the agreement you signed. You can make your decisions on what you want to do after you know what your options are."

Hannah stopped short from sharing her suspicions that Harold was in financial trouble and needed all the money from the house in order to support his lavish life style. She didn't want to hurt an already vulnerable Ruby who seemed to need to believe she had a loving, attentive son.

Ruby reached for the box of tissues on the table and wiped her eyes and blew her nose. "Hannah, don't you think I know my son's no good? That he only thinks of himself? I've known that for years, even before my husband died. When Bernie was alive, Harold was a different person. Never very affectionate, but he did what his father expected of him. Bernie insisted that he respect me and so he did—when his father was there. I think he needed his father's approval. But with Bernie gone, there was nothing between us. Even as a child, he was difficult. Never listened to me, and when his father wasn't around he would criticize everything I did: the food wasn't seasoned right, I didn't know enough about politics—everything I did was wrong. But only when his father wasn't around. So I know what kind of a son he is. But I'm tired; I don't have the energy for a fight."

"You wouldn't have to do anything," Janice interrupted. "My friend would look at the papers you signed, and tell you your options. If you have any options, you would decide what you wanted to do. No one would force you to do anything you didn't want to do."

Hannah went over to Ruby and hugged her. "Here, eat," she ordered, as she handed Ruby the tuna salad sandwich. "You need to keep up your strength. And the banana... you need that, too."

While Ruby ate, Hannah entertained her with stories of Charlie. As fond as she was of him, she couldn't avoid caricaturing him as an Italian *nebbish*, a term Ruby hadn't heard in many years, but knew exactly what it meant. Not sure that Ruby would appreciate the background checking Charlie had done on Harold's business, Hannah left that out of her stories. Ruby blushed when Hannah told Janice of Charlie's crush on Ruby. "Oh, that's silly. What would he want with an old woman like me?"

"He's no spring chicken either. He probably wants what all men want—and it's not friendship!"

Janice was amused by this turn in the conversation. It had never entered her mind that women of her mother's age might still be interested in sex. Did her mother miss intimacy? Was she content with her life as it was? She seemed so content, so complete, but did she miss having someone special in her life?

The conversation continued, with Hannah and Ruby relating incidents from the Senior Center of ill-fated relationships. When they left, Ruby was more cheerful than when they had arrived.

. . . .

"David, Maddie, come down. We need a family conference." Hannah and Janice had arrived home at three-thirty. Maddie was resting and David was playing the latest game in his room. The children came down quickly; "family conferences" were usually about planning vacations, or buying a new TV—fun things like that.

When everyone was assembled around the kitchen table, drinking coffee or lemonade and eating the remainder of last night's chocolate torte, Janice told the children about Ruby and her situation. The children looked at her in anticipation. Maddie said, "That's so sad," and David said, "So?" Janice took a deep breath and asked, "So, what do you think about having Ruby come to stay with us for a while, until she figures out what she's going to do?"

Janice had not discussed this with Hannah, whose eyes were tearing up.

"Grandma, what's the matter?" asked Maddie, ever alert to other people's feelings.

"Nothing, darling, I just got something in my eye."

David seemed disappointed with the discussion. No vacation, no new high definition plasma TV. And who was Ruby, anyway? Janice turned to him and asked, "What do you think about having an old woman—sorry, Mom—coming to stay with us for a while? Would you mind that?"

David shrugged. "Where would she stay? I'm not giving up my room for her."

"Well, that's the generous little boy I love! No, you'll still have your room to yourself."

"Well, then, I don't care."

"Maddie, how about you? What do you think?"

"What's she like?"

"Well, Grandma knows her better than I do. But when I met her today she seemed to be a delightful woman. Quiet, friendly. She reminded me of Dora, our next door neighbor. You remember her, don't you? You stayed at her house after school until I got home."

"Oh, yeah. She always had cookies and milk for me. She was nice."

"Well, Ruby is nice, too."

"Where would she sleep? We don't have any extra bedrooms."

Hannah interrupted here. "We'll find a place. We could set up a bed in my sitting room. That way everyone could still have their own space."

"Do I hear 'okay' from everyone?" asked Janice. "David?"

"I don't care."

"Maddie?"

"Sure."

"Mom, I guess I don't have to ask you!"

Hannah smiled. "Darling, you've made two old women happy today. Now we have to see if Ruby agrees!"

David, clearly anxious to return to his game, looked at his mother for a sign that he could leave. Receiving one, he bounded up the stairs, slammed his door, and didn't appear again until called for dinner.

Hannah cleared the table and set about chopping the vegetables for the evening dinner. She chopped the onions first, using them to hide her tears of joy, so full of love was she for her family. She wiped her eyes and turned to Maddie, who seemed reluctant to leave the room. Hannah knew that sometimes she overstepped her boundaries, said the wrong things, asked the wrong questions, appeared to be too nosy. But, sometimes, one just had to ask!

"So, Maddie", she said. "Tell me about last night. It didn't go so good?"

Janice shot her mother a warning look, but Maddie seemed to welcome the question. She somehow had overcome her hurt feelings, most likely with the help of Suzanne and Becky, and was anxious to give her version of what had happened. This involved pointing out all of Kenny's faults, which at first caused Hannah to wonder what she had ever seen in him, but then remembered her own infatuations with men who had nothing to offer but their good looks. Thank God she met Leo before she had gotten too involved with those no-good-niks!

"But I did dance a lot, and everyone thought my dress was great…and those shoes! Everyone thought they were fabulous."

"Well, they are," chimed in Hannah.

"And Suzanne told me that Tiffany, the girl that Kenny spent most of the evening with, was a slut and that was the reason Kenny was interested in her."

Janice winced at the "slut" reference, but let it go this time. Feminist political correctness could wait. It was more important for Maddie to vent and get her self-esteem back.

By the time Maddie finished talking, she was laughing as she related some of the antics of the kids at the dance, which included a boy who had attempted to "break dance" and had had fallen on his head, and a largely-endowed girl whose spaghetti straps were insufficient to hold up her bodice. Maddie alternated between feeling sorry for the girl and laughing uncontrollably at the memory.

That evening, as Janice helped Hannah clean up after dinner, Hannah started to thank her. Janice stopped her, saying, "It was the only reasonable solution. I just had to make sure the kids were okay with it."

Hannah spent the rest of the evening watching a *Law and Order* rerun in her sitting room, while Janice viewed the latest production of Jane Austen's *Pride and Prejudice* on Masterpiece Theater in the living room, leaving Hannah to wonder what Janice was hoping to find in yet another version of the old story, ignoring the fact that she was once again watching, and enjoying, a rerun of an actual program she had already seen.

Chapter 14

Hannah greeted Monday morning with an excitement she hadn't felt in weeks. There was frost on the maple trees and holly bushes and, when the sun shone on them, they looked like luminescent crystal statues. The coming of winter usually depressed Hannah, but not today. Today she was going to get Ruby out of *Sunset Manor*.

She was singing an old Yiddish song she had learned as a child as she prepared breakfast for the family. Janice was the first one down. She smiled when she heard her mother singing. Janice was satisfied with the decision she had made regarding Ruby, but still had her reservations. She just hoped that Ruby wouldn't need too much special attention. Her mother, she knew, would do whatever needed to be done for Ruby, but she was herself elderly and not very strong. Janice worried about Hannah's health; sometimes Hannah took on more than she could handle.

This morning, though, Hannah was in fine form. Janice greeted Hannah with a hug, surprising Hannah—Janice was not one for public display of affection.

"What's the matter?" Hannah asked.

"Why should anything be the matter? Can't I give my mother a hug?"

"Of course you can. It's just unusual. I enjoy it—you should do it more often," Hannah smiled. "Here, have some coffee. Do you want any breakfast? You know, you should have something in the morning—breakfast is the most important meal of the day."

"Yes, I know. You've told me that a few times. No, I just want coffee. I've got to get to school early this morning. The maintenance people are complaining about their hours and I want to talk to them before things get too busy."

"They have a union, no? You should deal with the union."

"Mom, I am dealing with the union. Jeez, I'm not going to violate their rights! We just need to deal with the issue of their hours."

Janice found her anger rising and fought back any further response. It still galled her that her mother thought she had to be reminded about workers' rights. To avoid any escalation she went to the stairs and yelled to the children to get up. Knowing that it would take at least two attempts to wake David, she yelled again. Hearing a grumbling, "Okay, okay, I'm up," from him, she returned to the kitchen to finish her coffee.

As Janice was preparing to leave, Madison entered the kitchen. She, too, looked excited, anxious to face the new week. She had clearly erased Kenny from her heart and seemed to be basking in remembering the attention she had gotten at the dance. She had taken extra care with her hair this morning and her outfit was more coordinated than usual. She was ready to face the world again.

Hannah and Janice stared at her with raised eyebrows. "What?" Madison asked. "What are you looking at?"

"Nothing, darling.," replied Hannah. "What? We can't look at you? It's just you seem so happy—it's nice to see," said Hannah. "So what do you want for breakfast? I could make eggs, or you could have cereal."

"I'll have Cheerios, and orange juice."

"Cheerios coming up."

Janice shook her head, waved goodbye, and yelled once again at David to get up as she walked out the door.

David eventually came down, quickly ate a bowl of Cheerios, and left with Madison for school. Hannah was clearing the table when the phone rang. It was Matthew Greeley.

"Mrs. Lowenstein, I want to thank you for all your help. I'm leaving for California this morning. There's nothing more I can do here. I met with that PI that Paul recommended and we found out that my mother was dead. It appears that she had died a natural death but that the nursing home records had made a mistake and reported her released. The police were satisfied that it was simply a mistake and since the nursing home has returned the money owed to me there's nothing more to be done. She was cremated so I can't even have a proper burial for her, although that's the least of my concerns. No one took seriously the letters that were written after her death—they think that there had probably been a delay in mailing. Anyway, as I said, there's nothing more for me to do here."

Hannah listened to him, hearing the sorrow and frustration in his voice. "I'm sorry it turned out that way, Matt, but you can be sure what you found out about your mother will help us in tracking down the other women who seem to be missing."

"Thanks again—and let me know if you find anything out."

Hannah hung up the phone. She wasn't satisfied, but he was probably right—there wasn't anything more for him to do. But perhaps there was something she could still do. After all, Mrs. Greeley wasn't the only missing woman.

She showered, dressed, ate a quick breakfast of coffee and Cheerios, and called for the bus, which arrived on time, depositing Hannah at *Sunset Manor* by 9:30. The halls were empty, except for an old woman in a pink chenille bathrobe wandering up and down the hallway, stopping at each room, asking if anyone had seen Henry. Hannah had no idea who Henry was, but neither had any of the other patients.

Ruby was in bed, breakfast tray on the table, still covered. Hannah expressed her concern that Ruby wasn't eating enough, that she should at least eat the toast, which she suspected was on the tray.

"I can't eat. I'm so worried. Yesterday I went to the lounge. I usually meet Mary, Mrs. Bradshaw, in the afternoons. She wasn't there. I don't know where she is. I've asked around and no one has seen her since Saturday. It's like what happened to Mrs. Johnson. She's just disappeared!"

Hannah sat down. She looked at her friend, determination in her eyes. "We're getting you out of here today. We can deal with the missing women once you're safe and out of here.'

"Where am I going to go? Harold says the house is already sold and the people are moving in next week."

"You're going home with me. It's all set. You must have made a good impression on Janice. She raised the issue with the children and everyone agreed that you should move in with us. It's all set. All we have to do is get you out of here before you, too, disappear."

Tears rolled down Ruby's cheeks. Unable to speak, she just reached out for Hannah's hand. With her free hand, Hannah passed the box of tissues across to Ruby and took one for herself.

"Now I'm going to get Charlie over here to help. He'll do anything for you, you know. And then I'm going to deal with the office down the hall—if anyone's there."

Hannah used her cell phone to call Charlie, who, as expected, was eager to help. He suggested using his van to transport Ruby's wheelchair, which caught Hannah off-guard. Was the wheelchair Ruby's property? If not, would it be considered stealing? But Ruby did need the wheelchair. She was using the walker more often, but she did use the wheelchair at times, especially when she was tired. Well, let *Sunset Manor* sue them!

Charlie arrived within 30 minutes, carrying a cardboard box for Ruby's personal items. After everything was boxed up, he helped Ruby into the wheelchair and pushed her down the hall to the front door. Hannah stopped at the reception desk where, after many yoo-hoos, the woman with the jet black hair appeared. Hannah explained they were taking Ruby home and started to leave.

"Wait, you can't do that. Mr. Shapiro hasn't given his permission for her to leave."

Hannah stopped at the door and turned around to face the woman. "What the hell does Mr. Shapiro have to say about this? She's a grown woman, in perfect control of her faculties. She wants to leave—preferably before she 'disappears' like the other women in here—and that's that! You can tell Mr. Shapiro that his mother will be living with my family and that if he wants to see her he can call me—Hannah Lowenstein." Hannah gave the woman her phone number and walked to the door where Charlie was waiting. "And you can charge the wheelchair to Mr. Shapiro," Hannah yelled.

She was shaking with anger as she helped Charlie settle Ruby into the van, stashing the wheelchair in the back. Charlie noticed that something had upset her, but didn't ask any questions. Ruby's face was flushed, whether from excitement or apprehension was not clear. Charlie started the van, looked at both women, and took off. In less than twenty minutes, they were at the house, beginning the process of settling in Ruby. Wheelchair removed, Charlie pushed Ruby to the front door, lifted the wheelchair over the front step, and helped her get seated on the sofa in the living room. Hannah carried the cardboard box with Ruby's personal items and put them in her sitting room.

Once she realized that they had acted more quickly than anticipated, Hannah set about finding a bed for Ruby. Surprisingly, Charlie had the solution. He phoned a friend in the used furniture business, who promised delivery of a bed within the day. Hannah suggested that he stay with Ruby while she went out to get a new mattress.

By the time Hannah returned from *Bellaire's*, the local furniture store, Charlie was busy assembling the bed. Nothing spectacular, just a bed, but it appeared to be solid and was easy to put together. *Bellaire's* had promised to deliver the mattress before five that evening, so there was nothing to do but wait. Hannah used the time to rearrange her sitting room and move a small dresser and table from her bedroom into the room. The only problem encountered was the wheelchair. It wouldn't fit through the door! Ruby resolved that issue by announcing that she could get around with her walker so it wasn't necessary for her to use the wheelchair. She suggested that they return it to *Sunset Manor*, but Hannah wasn't buying that. They might need the wheelchair when they wanted to go someplace. Besides, the only way she would be going back there would be with the police, she thought.

So the three of them sat drinking coffee and eating some of Hannah's cookies while they waited. Charlie again entertained them with stories from his past as a young sailor. Hannah was becoming very fond of him. She hoped that once he got over being smitten by Ruby he would relax and let her see that he was truly a charming man. But right now, when not telling stories, he was tongue-tied around Ruby, who looked at him as one might a cute puppy.

The children had stayed after school for their respective club activities and arrived home with Janice at six. The wheelchair had been stored in a hall closet, the sitting room had been transformed into a bedroom, complete with mattress, pillows, and a brightly colored comforter that Hannah never used, and dinner was warming in the oven. Hannah had invited Charlie to join them for dinner, an invitation he quickly accepted. Introductions were made, hands were washed, and everyone sat down to dinner. Charlie inquired about David's latest video games and the two of them engaged in a two-way discussion about the merits of various games. Ruby, tearing up again, thanked Janice for her hospitality, promising that she wouldn't interfere with the family's life, that she was just so grateful to be out of that horrible place, which led to Madison asking about that horrible place. Conversation flowed, and Hannah and Janice just sat back and smiled. Perhaps this was going to work after all.

Chapter 15

R<small>UBY SLEPT LATE</small>. H<small>ANNAH</small> was on her second cup of coffee when the phone rang. She rushed to pick up the receiver before it woke Ruby and managed to bang her shin on the coffee table. She uttered a quiet "shit" and picked up the receiver. "Hello?"

A man's voice, gruff and angry, barked, "Is this Hannah Lowenstein?"

"Yes. And to whom am I speaking, please?"

"This is Harold Shapiro. I want to speak to my mother."

"She's sleeping right now. I don't want to wake her. Perhaps you could call back later."

"I want to speak to her NOW," he demanded. "Get her on the phone."

Politeness no longer a possibility for Hannah, she barked back, "Hold on, sonny boy. You're not talking to your mother now, so watch your tone. I'm NOT waking her. I'm not sure she would even want to speak to you, such a rotten son you turned out to be. Do you know how she was treated there? Do you know they 'lose' patients there? And selling her house from under her? You should be ashamed! No, I'm not waking her to talk to you. She'll call you—if she wants to."

"Don't think that I'm going to pay you for taking her in. You won't get a nickel from me."

"Keep your damn nickels, you son-of-a-bitch. You wouldn't know a friend if he bit you in the *tuchis*."

With that, Hannah slammed the receiver down, shaking with anger. She hadn't lost her temper like that for many years. When she married Leo, she would cuss like the proverbial sailor, but when he quickly let it be known that he didn't approve, she had made a sincere effort to watch her language. And she had succeeded—but the words were still there to be called upon when necessary. And today it had been necessary—for her. She was still shaking, but she felt good!

Ruby, with her excellent hearing, had heard the whole exchange from Hannah's side. It was not difficult to piece together the other side of the conversation. She called to Hannah, who made an effort to calm herself before going into the room.

Ruby, in typical fashion, apologized for her son's behavior. She started to defend him: she hadn't been a good mother; he was unhappy in his marriage; he was under a lot of pressure in his work. She would have gone on, but Hannah stopped her.

"Ruby, stop defending him. He's not a little boy who needs his mother's apron to hide behind. He's a grown man—and, believe me, he knows how to look out for himself."

"I know, I know. But I can't help it. He's my only child. It kills me that we're not close, that I never see the grandchildren, that he'd sell my house without even asking me. But what can I do? He's my son."

"You don't have to do anything different. He can still call you, visit you. Just don't let him take advantage of you—like with the house. I don't know what kind of a deal you made with him, but surely you should get some money from the house. How did he expect you to live?"

Hannah hadn't prodded Ruby about the particulars in the agreement and didn't know if now was a good time to raise the issue. But her anger was just below the surface and if she didn't say something she was afraid it would boil over—and that would really frighten Ruby. So she plunged ahead.

"Remember, Janice told you about a lawyer—he's her boyfriend….I think they're serious, but who knows with young people these days….Anyway, he'd be willing to look at the agreement you made with Harold about the house to see if there is anything for you once the house is sold. Do you mind if she calls him? He could look at the agreement and tell you what's what. He's a good lawyer—good-looking, too; a *mensch*—you'd like him." She looked at Ruby, compassion mixed with frustration on her face.

As expected, Ruby teared up again. Hannah was getting tired of seeing her friend cry. What good did crying do? She needed to get a backbone!

Ruby composed herself, again apologizing. "I don't remember what I signed."

"No problem. We just show the papers to Paul—that's her boyfriend—and he'll tell you what you signed. Where do you keep the papers?"

Ruby glanced away, avoiding eye contact with Hannah. "I don't know," she said in a small voice. "I think Harold has the papers."

"You don't have a copy?" asked Hanna, trying to keep the disbelief out of her voice. "Who made up the agreement? You must have had a lawyer, no?"

"Yes, I know who the lawyer was. He's a friend of Harold's."

"Figures!" blurted out Hannah. "Well, Paul can handle that. Don't worry. He'll know how to get a copy. Let's get you up and dressed. Do you need help?"

"Just a little. I just need help getting on my socks and shoes—the rest I can handle."

"Okay, when you're ready for help, just yell. I'll be in the kitchen, getting some breakfast for you." Hannah helped Ruby out of bed, gave her the walker, and watched as she slowly walked to the bathroom. Assured that Ruby could get along with the walker, Hannah went into the kitchen, the room where she felt most at home. Janice often worried that she was taking advantage of Hannah, who did most of the cooking. Hannah had quickly convinced her that it was what she loved doing—cooking for her family.

It was almost 11:00 when Ruby finally joined Hannah in the kitchen where she found a luscious omelet waiting for her. Hannah watched her friend attack the omelet as if she were starved. Ruby looked at her and smiled. "This is the best breakfast I've had since I was in the hospital. I'm going to get fat if I keep eating like this."

"Fat? You're wasting away, you're so thin. Men prefer a little meat on their women, you know."

"At my age, I don't think about men. Who wants an old woman, anyway?"

"Charlie, that's who! Why do you think he knocks himself out for you? The guy's crazy about you. You could do worse, you know. He's a nice looking man, he's handy fixing things, and he treats you like a princess. What more could you want?"

"He is sweet, isn't he? But I never know what to say to him."

"He'll get better. He's shy, not used to being around women, I think. But the women at the Center all think he's a good catch, so you'd better make up your mind before that Phyllis Parkins snatches him up—you know how pushy she is."

Ruby laughed. "Is she still flirting with all the men? I can't imagine that gets her very far."

Hannah nodded. "All it gets her is laughs. A seventy-five-year-old woman, dressing like she was eighteen! She looks ridiculous. But we shouldn't be catty. She's probably lonely since her husband died. Some women don't know how to live without a man. Me, I don't even think about another man. I'm spoiled; no one can compare to my Leo—he was one of a kind."

"I wish I felt that way about Bernie. Oh, he was a good man, but he didn't talk to me very much. I guess he didn't think I would understand what he was talking about. Anyway, I'll be nice to Charlie—because he's a nice man, nothing more."

"Well, that's good to hear because I invited him to dinner again tonight. He's been a big help and he doesn't get to eat home cooked meals very often so..."

"You don't need to explain," interrupted Ruby. "I think it's fine that he's coming to dinner. So what are you making?"

. . . .

Madison and David arrived home to find two old women sitting in front of the TV, fast asleep. Madison whispered to David to be quiet, not to wake them, when Ruby, with her x-ray hearing, woke saying, "It's all right, I wasn't sleeping, just resting my eyes."

David snorted. "That's what Grandma says all the time!" At which point, Hannah woke and asked, "What do I say all the time?"

"You never sleep—you just rest your eyes."

"Never mind, funny boy. Eyes get tired when you get old. All those years of seeing uses up the eye muscles."

David turned to Madison, clearly wondering if that was true. Could one use up one's eye muscles? Madison gave him a "how can you be so silly?" look and, wanting to change the topic, asked, "Is there anything for snacks?"

"There's some fruit and cheese in the kitchen," replied Hannah. "But don't eat too much. You don't want you should spoil your appetite for dinner."

David made a beeline for the kitchen, more sedately followed by Madison.

Hannah looked at Ruby and shook her head. "They're always hungry when they get home, especially David. If he had his way there would be two dinners every night: one when he got home from school and the other before he went to bed."

"It's nice seeing children with good appetites," replied Ruby.

By the time Janice returned home at 6:00, dinner was ready and Charlie had joined them. Halfway through dinner, Ruby turned to Janice and said, "Hannah tells me that your friend might be willing to check on that agreement I made with my son. I'm embarrassed to say that I don't have a copy of it and I don't really know what it was I agreed to. Do you think he could find out?"

Janice looked at Hannah, but spoke to Ruby. "Well, it's a legal document which means it has to be registered somewhere. I'm sure Paul will know what to do. I'll call him after dinner and ask him."

Ruby started to say something, but Hannah quickly diverted the conversation by turning to Charlie to ask what he had been up to all day.

The next half hour was spent listening to Charlie's activities: lunch and poker at the Senior Center where he won $50—under the table, as gambling was officially prohibited there. David was noticeably interested in the profitability of poker, so much so that Janice suggested that he leave the table and go upstairs to play his games. With the possibility of on-line poker, she didn't want to have to monitor any more of his computer activities.

While Hannah cleaned up after dinner, with Charlie and Ruby keeping her company, Janice phoned Paul. She returned to report that he would start tracking down the papers that Ruby had signed. All he needed were the names—which Janice provided—and the approximate date on which the agreement was signed. Ruby had to think about that. She knew it was at least five years ago, but couldn't get more specific. When Janice reported that to Paul, he sighed, but agreed to do his best.

Chapter 16

A T 11:45 CHARLIE RANG the doorbell. Ruby called out to Hannah, "Should I get that?" Hannah, wiping her hands on her apron, responded by going to the door. "Charlie, what a nice surprise! Come on in. We're just getting ready for a light lunch."

Charlie, looking sheepish, wiped his feet on the door mat, removed his coat, and walked into the living room, where Ruby was seated in her wheelchair.

"I don't want to intrude," he insisted. "You go ahead with your lunch. I thought you might need some help with things—you know, use my van, things like that."

"How thoughtful! Yes, we have to make plans. But, come, join us for lunch—there's plenty. Why don't you and Ruby make some plans while I get lunch ready?"

As Hannah set about preparing the soup and turkey sandwiches, Charlie and Ruby talked. Ruby was unable to focus on what needed to be done, but Charlie had come prepared. He had a list of questions: When were the new owners going to be moving in? What things did she want brought over from her house? What was she going to do with the rest of the furniture?

Ruby's eyes filled with tears ready to spill over. Seeing this, Charlie looked appalled. "I'm sorry, Ruby," he said, "I didn't mean to upset you. We can do this later, when you're up to it." Hannah didn't mention that Ruby teared up at almost everything, but chose instead to announce that lunch was ready. The three of them sat down to eat.

"Okay," Hannah said, "this isn't the time for tears, Ruby. This is the time for action. We don't know what the agreement about the house was, but we know that it's sold and the new owners are going to be moving in soon. That's done. What we have to do is get your stuff out of there. So, answer Charlie's questions. First, how much time do we have to get your stuff out of there?"

Ruby used her napkin to wipe her eyes. "He told me they're moving in this weekend. He's putting my stuff in a storage place. That's all I know."

"Well, then, let's get over there today. Charlie, is your van available?"

"Sure is. I emptied it out so we'd have more room for Ruby's stuff. But," he said to Ruby, "when is your son moving your stuff to the storage unit?"

"I don't know....I'm so useless. I don't know anything," she cried.

"Well, we'll go over after lunch and see what's what," said Hannah. "Sorry to say this, Ruby, but I don't trust your son. Are we sure the house is really sold? You know, he could be lying to get you out of there."

Charlie jumped at the chance to do something. "We can check that at the county office," he said. "Why don't I run down there now while you two get ready." Charlie got up, put his dishes in the sink, thanked Hannah for lunch, and took off.

Hannah cleared the table, ignoring Ruby's tears. After she was done, she went over to Ruby and gave her a hug. "Don't worry, we'll work this out," she said. "Now, let's get ready. Charlie should be back soon."

Charlie returned within the hour and the three of them set off for Ruby's house. As Harold had reported, the house had been sold and the new owners were taking possession that weekend.

"I stopped at the moving company—I know a guy there," he explained. "He told me that they're planning on moving the furniture to *Stash Away* tomorrow. It's good that we're going over today. Tomorrow would be too late to take what you want from there, Ruby."

When they arrived at the house, Charlie removed the wheelchair from the van and helped Ruby into the house. Hannah was grateful that Charlie, while old, was still strong! She knew she couldn't have handled the wheelchair as adroitly as he had.

The house stood on a large plot of land in a neighborhood of old Victorian homes. Most of the yard was devoted to flowering trees and bushes with two large beds in the back of the house—one for flowers and one for vegetables. The rooms were as Ruby had left them when she fell. Fortunately, Ruby was a fastidious housekeeper and, except for a few magazines lying on the floor in the living room, everything was in order.

Hannah realized that Ruby was not going to be much help, so she turned to Charlie. "I think we need to find out first what she wants to take to my house. It can't be anything big—we don't have much room—but personal things are okay."

Armed with pen and paper, Hannah followed Charlie pushing Ruby into the various rooms. It was a large two story house, with an attic that had been converted into a craft room that Ruby had used before she had broken her hip. As Charlie pushed her around her house, she grew quieter as they entered each room. "I have too many things," she murmured. "How am I going to decide what to take?"

Hannah took charge. "You just have to decide what you'll need for now. The rest can go into storage and you can decide what you should do with them later when you have more time." In each room, Hannah asked, "Do you want to take anything in here?"

It took only an hour for the list to be finished: clothes, photo albums, jewelry, a few personal items, and a favorite tea cup—in addition to the car, which they would pick up the next day. When Ruby looked worried, Hannah reminded her that the rest of the items were going to be safe, and when they decided what she was going to do she could get them all back. Ruby nodded, blew her nose, and inquired, "How are they going to pack everything up? Do they empty the drawers? Will they pack up the dishes? How will I find anything?"

"I'm sure they know how to do this. After all, they do this all the time," Charlie said, exhibiting more confidence than was justified. Usually quite a modest man, he obviously thought it best to exaggerate his knowledge this time. "I think they even label the contents of the boxes," he continued.

Blowing her nose again, Ruby looked at Charlie and nodded.

"I think I'll go out to the garden and pick the zucchinis and tomatoes that are ripe", she said. "We can make zucchini bread, okay?" Hannah had never eaten zucchini bread, but she just nodded and together they went out to the garden.

It took three hours for them to pack Ruby's things into the van, including the three bags of zucchinis, and one bag of tomatoes gathered from the garden. Hannah wondered how much zucchini bread she could convince the children to eat!

They were all set to leave when Hannah asked, "Do you have any place where you keep important papers? You know, like insurance, tax records, banking accounts, bills, letters—things like that?"

Ruby thought a moment and smiled. "Of course! I keep those things in a file box in the kitchen, under the sink."

Charlie raised his eyebrows. Under the sink? Maybe women really were different than men! Without voicing his amazement, he went into the kitchen and retrieved the file box. When he joined Hannah and Ruby, they were engaged in an argument on how to deal with the garden. Ruby wanted to remove some of her precious trees and shrubs—especially her rose bushes—but Hannah wasn't sure they could do that. It wasn't a problem to transplant them at Janice's house—there was plenty of room there, as Janice never planted anything. But it wasn't clear that they could remove things without the new owners' permission. And those trees were big! How would they ever move them?

Charlie came to the rescue. He found a shovel in the garage and proceeded to dig up some of the smaller bushes, turning to Ruby for approval each time. When he finished, the roses, rhododendrons, and azaleas were put in the back of the van. He had vetoed Ruby's request to remove the lilac bushes as they were the size of small trees.

Everything packed away, they set off, the three of them in the front seat with the back seat filled with bushes, vegetables, clothes, and the rest of Ruby's belongings.

It was after 6:00 when they arrived at the house, and Janice and the children were already home. Janice came out to greet them, frustration showing on her face. "Where were you? You didn't leave a note or anything. I was worried."

"Darling, I'm sorry. We didn't think we'd be gone that long. We had to move Ruby's things today as they're taking her stuff into storage tomorrow. Have you had dinner, yet? Maybe we should order pizza?"

Janice sighed. "The kids were just about to order pizza; I'll tell them to get more. But let's get some of this stuff in the house before it arrives."

Janice called Madison and David to help unload the van, and by the time the pizza was delivered, all of Ruby's belongings were in the house. The plants were going to remain in the van until the next day when they would be planted in the back yard. There was no problem with Ruby's photo albums, jewelry, or teacup—but where to put her clothes, when there was no closet, presented a problem. It was solved by piling it in the living room, after Hannah promised they would buy a portable clothes rack the next day. Janice raised an eyebrow at the three bags of zucchini, but said nothing. Hannah could deal with that.

They had just finished dinner—pizza, a huge salad, and a cheesecake Janice had picked up at the store—when the doorbell rang. David ran to answer it, expecting Billy, but it was Paul who entered. Refusing Hannah's invitation to the last slice of pizza, he pulled up a chair and sat down, eyeing the cheesecake until Hannah brought him a large slice.

"Well," he reported, after taking a big bite of the cake, "we found the agreement you signed, Ruby. Contrary to what you thought, or what you were told, you have some rights. The proceeds of the sale of the house were to go to your son—*if* you died before him. If you were still alive when the house was sold, the proceeds were to be used to accommodate your new living conditions. In other words, only after your death does your son receive the full amount of the sale."

Ruby seemed puzzled. "So I don't have to sell the house?" she asked.

"No, the house belongs to Harold and he can do what he wants with it. But you're entitled to some of the money that he receives. How much, depends on what it sold for and what you will need."

"I can check on what it sold for—that's public information," interrupted Charlie. "I'll do that first thing in the morning."

"Well, that's the first good news we've heard," said Hannah, as she rose to clear the dinner table.

David had already gone upstairs, but Madison was taking in every word. When the conversation seemed to have come to a close, she asked, "Does that mean that Ruby doesn't have to go to one of those assisted living places?"

"Darling, we don't know yet what Ruby will do," Hannah answered. "She needs time to decide. But at least we know she's not going to be tossed out on the streets, like her son-of-a-bitch son was going to do."

"Mother!" cried Janice, looking at Ruby. "That's uncalled for. He is her son."

Ruby smiled. "It's okay, Janice. I'm beginning to see things differently. There's just so much you can ignore. Your mother may use language that I don't use, but she sees things more clearly than I do."

Chapter 17

CHARLIE ARRIVED AT 10:00 the next morning, apologetic for being so late. He explained that the county office hadn't opened until 9:00 and then it had taken a while to get the information he needed. Accepting Hannah's offer of coffee and a bagel, he proceeded to take a paper out of his jacket pocket and described the details. "The house was sold to a fraternity—or maybe a sorority, I can't figure out these Greek names: Theta Eta Beta—for $375,000. I also drove by Ruby's house to check if the moving van was there. Yep, it was. They had most of the big stuff out already and were busy boxing up dishes and the small stuff. I asked if they had taken the stuff out of the dresser drawers and they said, no, that it's easier to keep everything as it is. They just box up the loose things."

Just then the phone rang. It was Harold, asking to speak to his mother. Hannah turned to Ruby and asked if she wanted to speak to him. Ruby gestured for Hannah to bring her the phone.

"Hello? Slow down, I can't understand you. Yes, I know they're moving the furniture today....Yes, I know they're moving in tomorrow. I went yesterday to take what I needed. We're going to pick up the car today and the rest, I know, is going to storage."

Hannah kept her eyes on Ruby, ready to take over if she started to cry. But Ruby didn't cry. Her voice trembled, but she seemed in control.

"Well, I'm sorry you feel that way. But what did you expect me to do? Stay in that horrible place? I don't know what I'm going to do yet; but when I decide I'll let you know. I may get an apartment, who knows? What?...Well, I'll have some money— some of the money from the house....No, my lawyer told me that....Well, of course, I have a lawyer—doesn't everyone? Anyway, when I know what I'm doing, I'll let you know. For now I'm staying with my friend's family. They're taking good care of me."

When Ruby hung up the phone, Hannah had tears in her eyes as she went over to hug her. "I'm so proud of you," she said.

"What? You thought maybe I was too old to change?" smiled Ruby. "Let's clear this place up and go pick up my car—and buy a clothes rack."

Charlie, not sure what had happened, was only too glad to take the women shopping. Ruby seemed different to him this morning. He didn't know if he liked her this way or not. The old Ruby seemed to need him; he wasn't sure about this new one.

. . . .

Clothing rack assembled, clothes put away, Ruby's car in front of the house, where Hannah had parked it after driving it back, the three of them sat down at the kitchen table. Hannah, as usual, offered lunch, but since no one was really hungry they just sipped the freshly brewed coffee.

"Well, I think I'll be moseying along," announced Charlie. "There's a game at the Center this afternoon and I'm feeling lucky."

After he left, Ruby and Hannah looked at each other and burst out laughing. "He moseys," said Hannah, with a shrug of her shoulder. "What, he's a cowboy? Do other people mosey?"

Ruby just laughed. "He is a dear man, though, isn't he?"

"A real Italian *mensch*," replied Hannah. "You could do worse, you know?"

Ruby didn't respond, just shot her a warning look. "Not to change the subject, but what do we have to do today? I don't want to be a nuisance, you know. I want to contribute."

"Contribute? What's to contribute? The house is clean, the kids are at school, the clothes are out of the living room. We can plan dinner—you can contribute to that. But the rest of the day is open. Do you want a rest?"

"Rest? All I've been doing is resting. I don't know, I feel there's something I should be doing, but I don't know what."

"Well, there are some things that we need to follow up on. But, first, we need to find out how to get the money that Harold owes you. I think we'll need Paul to help us on that. Then you'll know where you are, money-wise." She rose from the table and asked, "So, what should we make for dinner?"

They decided on roast chicken with matzo ball soup, a dish Hannah had not made since she arrived in Michigan. And, of course, they would make zucchini bread—lots of it! Hannah assigned the matzo ball soup preparation to Ruby, who was delighted to be asked. The two women talked while they worked and, by the time they were done, realized it was almost 4:00 and the children would be home soon. Hannah cleared the kitchen and together they went into the living room to watch last night's episode of *Walker, Texas Ranger.*

When the children arrived home, Hannah got up from her recliner to put the chicken in the oven, after she reminded David to hang up his coat, which he had dropped—along with his backpack—in the hallway. Ruby followed her, using the walker rather than the wheelchair. She was getting stronger each day, and her face was losing its pallor. Never a rosy-cheeked person, she now had the appearance of a healthy elderly woman, and she walked with what might even be called a bounce—if one could bounce with a walker.

David ran upstairs to text his friend Billy, whom he had just left, and Madison followed her grandmother into the kitchen. Seeing Ruby drop the matzo balls into the soup, she asked what they were. Hannah looked at Ruby and smiled. "They don't know much about being Jewish."

Madison objected. "I know I'm Jewish, because you're Jewish and if the mother is Jewish, the kids are. But we're not religious."

"I know. I'm not either. I'm what you'd call a 'cultural Jew'—I don't keep kosher, don't even go to the synagogue, but I still consider myself a Jew. It's hard to explain, darling, but it's important for me to remember I'm Jewish."

Ruby glanced at Hannah before saying to Madison, "You know, a lot of people have tried to get rid of Jews—not only the Nazis, but many others, too. We have our beliefs about God and how to live our lives, and that bothers some people because it's different from their beliefs. But it's better now than it was for my parents. They had to leave Germany when I was just a young girl. And when they came here they didn't have such an easy time, either. A lot of people here didn't like Jews either, but at least they weren't killing them."

Madison's eyes were opened wide as she listened to Ruby. "Were they being killed in Germany?" she asked.

Hannah and Ruby looked at each other. Hannah was the first to speak. "Darling, didn't you learn about the Holocaust in school?"

"No, I don't think so. We learned about the Second World War last year, about how we fought against the Germans and won. I think they said something about lots of people being arrested and put in camps, but I don't remember anything about a ... what did you call it?"

"Holocaust," replied Hannah. "Well, the 'camps' they sent these people to were concentration camps, places where they killed people. It wasn't only the Jews who were sent there— gypsies, gay people, even people who simply disagreed with the Nazis. But mostly the camps were filled with Jews. And it wasn't only in Germany; it was Austria, Poland, Ukraine—oh, lots of countries in Europe. Hitler—you've heard of him, right?— well, Hitler wanted to get rid of all the Jews and the others who he didn't think were the 'right kind of people'.…. And you didn't learn about this in school? What did you learn?"

"Not the way you're saying. We learned about Pearl Harbor and how the Japanese bombed us there, and how the president—Roosevelt—declared war and how we fought against Japan and Germany. Our teacher, Mr. Archer, told us his father was a soldier in the war and he told us how we beat the Germans and the Japanese."

"Did he tell you we dropped an atom bomb on Japan? That we killed hundreds of thousands of people, mostly civilians, and left many of them sick and dying from radiation?"

"But," interrupted Ruby, "that ended the war and saved so many American soldiers."

Hannah tried to hide her annoyance. She knew Ruby wasn't very political, but how could she be that naive? Clearly aware that the path of wisdom was to sidestep the issue for now, Hannah chose the other path!

"Well, yes, that was the argument at the time. But Japan was already beaten and ready to surrender. But we wanted an unconditional surrender and, Maddie, you need to know that this country considered the Japanese to be an inferior race—maybe like Hitler considered the Jews an inferior race. So killing them wasn't like killing a 'real' human being, not like an American. That's called racism and we were—and still are—a racist country."

Hannah would have continued, but at that moment Janice entered the kitchen. "What's going on? You all look so serious."

"Grandma was telling me about the Holocaust and bombing those poor people in Japan."

"How did that come up?" asked Janice, looking at her mother with raised eyebrows.

Madison then told her about their discussion about being Jewish and how Jews were treated and how terrible it was and how she hadn't heard any of this before. Her cheeks were flushed and her eyes were wide. "Mom, do you know that if we lived in Germany we would have been killed—just for being Jewish?"

"Well, that's not true today in Germany," replied Janice. "Things have changed."

"Yeah, changed," muttered Hannah.

"Mom," warned Janice, who did not want to get into a discussion of how anti-Semitism was alive and well.

Hannah turned to Madison. "How about helping set the table, darling?" She looked at Janice, nodding her agreement to change the topic, but said to Madison, "We'll continue this later, when we have more time."

The silence of the others at dinner was not noticed by David, who regaled them all with his success at reaching level five in his latest video game—a feat not yet achieved by his friend, Billy. In fact, if one believed him, only his tech friend at school had gone beyond that. The women feigned polite interest in his success, but after twenty minutes, Madison exploded. "Who cares about your stupid game, you twit? I'm going upstairs." She looked at her mother for permission to leave the table and, receiving it, left the room.

David was unfazed, continuing his saga of *how* he achieved his success. Finally, Janice had to stop him and suggest that he do his homework if he wanted to watch his current favorite TV program—*Dexter*—about a serial killer tracking down other serial killers. He gobbled down the last of his chicken, wiped his mouth on a napkin, and ran upstairs.

"I hope we didn't upset Madison earlier," said Ruby. "It started with the matzo balls, you know, explaining things about being Jewish. And then it went too far, I think."

"Too far?" exclaimed Hannah. "They don't even teach about one of the most horrendous wars in history any more. Not to even know about the Holocaust! I wonder if they teach them anything about slavery! Probably tell them that there were these black people who were such faithful servants that they never left the plantation!"

"Well, I just meant…"

"I know—I'm sorry. I shouldn't take it out on you. I just get so tired seeing the same things happening today. If these kids don't know what happened in the past, how will they recognize the signs that it's happening again? And it is. Just look at how the world ignores what's happening in the Congo—and what about the Sudan? Half a million people already dead in Darfur. If that were happening in England or France, you can be sure we would be doing something."

Janice sighed. She understood her mother's anger. But what was the point of getting upset about something you couldn't do anything about? Life had enough problems to deal with, problems that she hoped to find solutions for.

Changing the topic, Janice turned to Ruby and said, "Well, Ruby, I really enjoyed your matzo ball soup. Mom hasn't made that in many years. It took me back to my childhood. Now if the two of you would make some blintzes one of these days, I would be in heaven."

Hannah smiled at her and rose to clear the table. "Leave it, Mom," Janice said. I'll do the dishes tonight. You and Ruby go watch your programs; you worked enough today."

Chapter 18

THE NEXT MORNING, AS Hannah and Ruby were having their second cups of coffee, Hannah raised the question of Harold's phone call the previous day. "So, should we find out how much money you're getting? So you know what's what."

"How do I find out?"

"Well, Charlie told us how much the house sold for—$375,000, I think. Paul told you that you're entitled to enough to live on. So, that would mean what? Maybe all of it! Who knows how many years you have yet!"

"Oh, I couldn't take it all. After all, that was supposed to be his inheritance."

"Well, if he hadn't sold it, you would be living there, and he could inherit it when you died. Why are you concerned about him after what he's done? You need to look out for yourself."

"Oh, Hannah, I wish I could be more like you. I just never thought it would turn out this way."

"I know. It's all right. We'll talk to Paul, see what he advises."

The two women peered out the back window, trying to determine the best place to plant the bushes from Ruby's house. Hannah quickly deferred to Ruby's judgment about the proper amount of shade and the type of soil each bush needed. All Hannah knew about gardens was that you had to water them occasionally.

The day was gray, with the look of impending winter. Most of the trees were bare, except for the big old oak in the backyard which held on to its rust-colored leaves all winter. Ruby decided that the best place for the rhododendrons and azaleas was in a partially shaded area, protected from the wind. She knew that the best time to transplant them would have been in early spring, or at least early fall, but since that wasn't possible she would just have to give them extra care. A good acidic soil, lots of organic mulch, adequate watering and they should be fine.

The roses had similar needs. The acidic soil wasn't an issue, but they, like the rhododendrons and azaleas, needed five to six hours of sun, preferably in the morning, and good soil. Organic mulching was a must for all of them.

Ruby picked out the preferred sites and hoped that Janice would approve. "We're going to need help preparing the soil and carrying the bushes. I hope Charlie is available to help," she said. Hannah smiled. "It's handy having a man smitten with you, isn't it?"

Ruby blushed and changed the topic. "I'm really worried about my friend Mary—Mrs. Bradshaw. What do you think happened?"

"What do you mean?" asked Hannah.

"Well, she wasn't there the day I left *Sunset Manor*. Remember, I told you she usually went for therapy and then we would meet in the lounge. Well, she never showed up."

"Oh, I'm sorry—I forgot about that. Do you know if she had any family? Any visitors? We could go and ask around. Couldn't hurt."

. . . .

After much maneuvering with Ruby's walker, the two women boarded the bus. Hannah looked at her friend, concerned that this trip might be too taxing for her. Ruby was breathing hard and looked exhausted. What if her friend wasn't as healthy as she appeared? Was it their responsibility to check up on Mary? Hannah knew the answer to that question as soon as she asked it. Who else would check? She just didn't want to get Ruby involved in something she couldn't handle.

She looked over at Ruby. She seemed to be breathing easier and the color was coming back into her face. Hannah relaxed.

As usual, there was no one at the reception desk. Ruby wanted to wait, but Hannah took her by the arm and gently led her away. "We can get more information from the patients than we can from these people. Come."

They walked down the hall, peeking into the rooms, stopping to ask anyone they met if they had seen Mary recently. Having no success, they proceeded to the lounge where there were three elderly women watching *Oprah*. No success there, either. No one had seen her since the previous Saturday when she played Bingo in the lounge. In response to Hannah's questions, they all thought that Mary had seemed in good health, and good spirits. And, no, she had never spoken of any family and didn't have any visitors that they knew of.

They chatted a while longer, Ruby grateful for the opportunity to sit down. Hannah used the opportunity to learn more about the running of *Sunset Manor*. How many of the people were there for rehabilitation? How many were permanent residents? How often did they see a doctor or health care worker? Who paid their bills?

What she found out reinforced her suspicions of the place. She was convinced that the permanent residents were the most vulnerable. Many of them didn't have life threatening conditions but were unable to live alone. One of the women in the lounge had been at the place for five years. At first the proceeds from selling her house had paid for her care; now her social security checks went directly to *Sunset*. And, no, she never saw a doctor—except for when she fell in the hallway and sprained her ankle.

Once the women got talking, *Oprah* was forgotten, and they turned to voicing their complaints. Food was the main target. One of the women was a diabetic, and another had recently had a heart attack. They received the same food: high in sodium and fat, and tasteless. Their next target was the lack of personal care: bathing was limited to once a week and shampooing was only done at the "salon"—where they had to pay. A common problem at places like *Sunset* was the lack of privacy. Rooms had no locks and clothing and other items often went missing. Sometimes they would find another patient with an item that had come up missing, but sometimes they never saw it again, leading them to suspect the staff.

After forty-five minutes, Hannah stood up, indicating to Ruby that it was time for them to move on. They thanked the women for their help and started down the hallway. At the front door they were met by the Director, who had obviously been alerted of their presence.

"How nice to see you again, Mrs. Shapiro. I hope you're well. How can we help you?"

His smile grated on Hannah. How dare he smile at her that way, she thought. He doesn't care about any of these people. They're just meal tickets for him. But she kept these thoughts to herself.

Ruby, however, was flustered, not knowing how to respond. She turned to Hannah for help.

Hannah was the picture of innocence as she smiled the Director and said, "We were going to visit Mrs. Bradshaw, but couldn't find her. Can you check where she is? Perhaps she's in a different room?"

"I don't have access to that information at present, but I'll have Helen check and get back to you. Perhaps if you called tomorrow I could be more helpful." His smile grew more condescending as he spoke, his voice more unctuous. It took all of Hannah's control to keep from lashing out at him.

She turned to Ruby and said, "Let's go. We'll call her daughter. Maybe she knows where her mother is."

Once outside, Ruby looked at her. "She doesn't have a daughter."

"I know that. You know that. But I bet they don't know that. Let them worry. Let them try to track down a daughter. This place gives me the creeps! I can't shake the feeling that something's not right about it."

....

That evening Hannah took Janice aside and asked for her help. She knew she was out of her league, that she needed more than her gut feelings in order to get an investigation going. This was different from the other issues she had taken on in the past. In those cases, picketing, boycotting, letters to the editor—all those things were effective. But that was New York, where she knew whom to go to for support. This was Brewster, where she didn't know anyone in an official capacity. And people were so polite here in the Midwest, she was afraid her usual tactics would not be greeted with approval.

"I'm concerned, too, Mom, but I don't see how I can help."

"Well, maybe you could talk to some of the people at school—you know, ask around if they had any problems, or knew of someone who had problems, with that place. Could you do that?"

"I guess I could do that....Sure, I can. I can do that tomorrow."

After an hour of brainstorming they came up with a plan. Janice would ask around to find people whose family members were at *Sunset*; Hannah would do the same at the Senior Center. Together they might find others who were concerned

Before letting Janice get back to her work, Hannah reminded her to call Paul about the money that should be coming to Ruby. Janice replied that she was seeing him on Sunday and would ask him then. Hannah couldn't resist. "So, how are things going?"

"Mom, don't go there. I'm not interested in getting married again."

"Who said anything about marrying? A mother can't ask her daughter anything?"

Janice got up and looked at her mother. "I know you. You ask, but you're really making a point. And I don't want to discuss it."

"So you're a mind reader now? You know what I really mean when I ask a simple question? Such a talent you have! You should put up a sign: *Mind Reader Available.*"

Janice shot her mother a look, shook her head, and headed for her study. Hannah also shook her head and headed for the living room where Ruby was watching TV. She related the plans she and Janice had come up with and explained that they could use Charlie's help in driving them to the Senior Center the next day. To Hannah's surprise, Ruby jumped at the opportunity to call Charlie right then. Hannah brought her the phone, turned the sound down on the TV, and sat down in her recliner to listen to the conversation.

It was all set. Charlie would come over in the morning, help transplant the bushes, and take them to lunch at the Senior Center. Saturday was a busy day, as working spouses often joined the retirees for lunch before catching up on the various chores for the weekend. It would be a good time to talk to people about *Sunset*.

Ruby and Hannah settled back to watch *Ghost Whisperer*, about a woman who saw and talked to ghosts, spirits that had not "crossed over" because there was some unfinished business to deal with—like finding a murderer or apologizing to a loved one. Hannah commented that she didn't think the program was realistic: ghosts didn't really look like that. Ruby stared at her in amazement, saying, "You know what ghosts look like?" Hannah shrugged and went back to watching the program.

Chapter 19

Hannah was awakened by the phone. It was only 7:30, too early for anyone she knew to call on a Saturday. Being a light sleeper, she was able to pick up the extension in her bedroom after just one ring. When she heard Harold's voice, she was tempted to slam down the receiver. But his tone was pleasant as he asked to speak to Ruby. Maybe he won't cause problems, thought Hannah, as she brought the phone to Ruby, who also was a light sleeper.

Ruby's side of the conversation was minimal: "Yes," "No," "Okay," "Goodbye."

Hannah's curiosity was in full swing. "So, what did he say?"

"He says he'll give me half of what the house sold for: $75,000." Ruby looked devastated. "But Charlie told us that the house sold for $375,000—half of that's not $75,000. I don't understand."

Hannah sat down on the edge of the bed. The time had come to tell Ruby some more unpleasant truths about her son. When she finished telling her what Charlie had found out about Harold's business problems and how he seemed to be in financial trouble, Ruby started to cry.

"Why didn't he just tell me he needed money?" she sobbed. "He could have refinanced the house and used the money for himself. That way I could have stayed there and he could have had his money. Now it's too late for that. Oh, I have to help him. The poor boy, no wonder he's been so difficult lately."

Hannah looked at her in amazement. Her friend was hopeless. She was going to give Harold all the money! Well, not if Hannah had anything to do with it. Taking care of one's children had limits—and one of those limits was when the child was a greedy, sixty-year-old, son-of-a-bitch who was living beyond his means. But this was not the time to try to educate Ruby on reality. Better they should have breakfast first.

By the time Janice and the children came down to breakfast, the two women had showered and dressed. The table was set and the makings for omelets were ready for assembling. Zucchini bread was strategically placed on the table, with butter and cream cheese nearby, alongside a jug of orange juice. No toast or muffins were available in an attempt to coax the children to try the zucchini bread.

David was the first to ask for toast, after putting in his order for a cheese omelet. When told that there was no toast, but to try the "cake" on the table, he pulled the platter of zucchini bread towards him, and sniffed it.

Madison was appalled. "Mom, he's smelling the cake. His nose is almost touching it! He's disgusting. I'm not going to eat that."

"Maddie, he didn't touch it. David, behave yourself. Cut a piece and try it. If you don't like it, don't eat it. But stop playing with it."

Janice turned to Hannah and Ruby and asked, "What are you two up to today?"

"We're starting our investigation," Hannah replied. "We're going to have lunch at the Senior Center and ask about *Sunset*. Charlie's coming over later and he'll drive us. His van is better for Ruby than her car."

David was hooked. He looked up from his plate. "What investigation? Are you still checking up on that guy, Grandma?"

Hannah quickly diverted his attention away from their investigation of Harold's finances and explained, what she termed, "the case of the missing women," which kept David at the table longer than she thought him capable of sitting.

"Wow, just like that movie where they kill people to sell their parts. Do you think that's what they did to those ladies—killed them for their hearts and livers?"

"Mom, he's being gross again," exclaimed Madison.

"I'm simply asking a question; don't be such a sissy."

"Okay, you two," Janice interrupted. "Eat up and get upstairs and clean your rooms before you leave the house. David, remember you have soccer practice at noon. If you're going over to Billy's after that, I want you home for dinner—6:00, no later. Maddie, what are you doing today?"

"Suzanne's coming over after lunch and we're going to the mall."

Hannah looked at Janice, waiting for her response. Hearing none, she said, "What are you going to the mall for? You need something?"

"Grandma, you don't understand. You don't go to the mall just to buy something. Everyone's there. You hang out."

"On such a beautiful day, you hang out in a mall? Why not go for a walk, or … fishing?"

"Fishing? Grandma," Madison protested, "you don't understand."

"Obviously! Well, it's not my business—you know I don't like to interfere—but I'd think your mother would say something."

Janice ignored her mother and turned to Maddie. "Just be sure you get your homework done before tomorrow night. And be home for dinner at 6:00." She then got up from the table, cleared the dishes, and went upstairs to shower and dress.

Ruby and Hannah glanced at each other, raised their eyebrows and shrugged their shoulders, as much as to say: young kids, today—who can understand them?

. . . .

Charlie arrived promptly at noon, all decked out in a brown tweed jacket with a pale blue Henley shirt, open at the neck showing his gray chest hairs, non-pomaded hair gently blowing in the breeze, feet enclosed in an obviously new pair of dark brown wingtips.

Hannah whistled at him when he entered, causing him to blush, which made his already ruddy skin even redder. She winked at him, and said, "You look good, Charlie. Wait'll Ruby sees you."

Ruby came into the hallway in time to hear Hannah's comment, and blushed. Hannah muttered to herself, "My God, they're like two teenagers!"

Without offering any food to Charlie, Hannah hurried him and Ruby out the door, anxious to get to the Senior Center before lunch was served. Once people started eating, it was hard to divert them into talking. Ruby was using the walker more these days which made transporting her much easier. When they were all settled in Charlie's car, Hannah said, "I think maybe we should split up when we get there—you know, cover more territory. See if anyone knows anyone who's at *Sunset*, or was there, anything at all. We need names of people to talk to, find out if anyone else has gone missing."

Ruby seemed uncomfortable with the plan. She looked at Hannah saying, "I don't think I'll be any good at this. Maybe I should stay home."

Charlie, like a knight defending his lady, came to the rescue. "Nonsense, I'll be with you. We can do it together, right, Hannah?"

"Whatever!" Hannah didn't think she'd ever use that expression, one she chastised the children for using. Right now it seemed very appropriate.

The parking lot at the Center was half-filled, with cars pulling in as they arrived. "That one, that one there," said Hannah, pointing to a spot near the walkway. "That way Ruby won't have to walk so far." Turning to Ruby, she suggested, "You should get one of those stickers for parking—you know for handicapped people. Then we can park in those reserved spots—less walking for you."

Charlie obediently pulled into the spot, thinking that he was glad Hannah wasn't interested in him. He respected her, but found her too bossy. He preferred a woman like Ruby, one who depended on him. Getting out of the car, he ignored Hannah in the back seat on the driver's side, ran around to the other side of the car, and opened the door for Ruby. Hannah smiled to herself. So much for old-fashioned chivalry when the hormones were activated.

The cafeteria was filling up. People came up to Ruby to ask how she was doing, greeted Hannah warmly, and teased Charlie about escorting two "beautiful young women." Hannah, not amused at the phony flattery, commented that obviously their eyesight was failing. Ruby, on the other hand, clearly used to compliments, smiled sweetly. They separated, Hannah going to the big table in the center, Ruby and Charlie taking one of the small round ones by the window. Hannah had no confidence in Ruby's performance as an investigator, but she held out hopes for Charlie—if he could remember why he was here and not simply gawk at Ruby.

The lunch was a choice of macaroni and cheese or vegetarian lasagna, along with soup, salad, and brownies for dessert. Hannah satisfied herself with the soup and salad, but left room for dessert. She noticed that Charlie helped himself to both the macaroni and the lasagna, and two brownies. You would have thought he was filling up on carbohydrates before a marathon. Perhaps his "courtship" of Ruby was his marathon. Perhaps he was just hungry.

After slightly more than an hour, Hannah rose and motioned to Charlie and Ruby to follow her. They bid their goodbyes, with promises to come back, and left the Center. Once in the car, Hannah's curiosity was unleashed. "So, what did you find out?" she asked, leaning over the front seat in order to hear better.

Charlie responded. "Not much. Mrs. Flynn said her mother spent some time there after her hip replacement, but nothing unusual happened. That was about ten years ago, though. She didn't know anyone who was there more recently. And Jim, Jim Forbes, said his wife was there now. No complaints as far as he could tell."

"But," interrupted Ruby, "remember, he said that his wife had Alzheimer's and that she didn't seem to know what was going on. And since he visits her every day, it's not likely that she could 'disappear' without his knowing about it."

Hannah was impressed. Who knew that Ruby had a brain! Wanting to encourage Ruby's continued use of her brain, she said, "Good point, Ruby." She continued, "Well, I got some information. It seems that Martha Robinson visits some of the patients there, as a sort of good-will ambassador. You know, she doesn't have any family and the people at the Center are the only ones she really knows. So when someone's in the hospital, or the nursing home, she makes a point of visiting them. I think she makes the rounds every day— keeps her busy, I guess. Anyway, she remembered that every once in a while she would visit someone at *Sunset* one day and the next day they were gone. She didn't think much of it at first. When she asked about them, she was told that they had been released and gone to live with their family—usually out of town. But when they told her that about Edith—let me see" she said, checking the notes she had taken—"yes, here it is, Edith Swenson—she thought that was strange because she knew Edith didn't have any family. She didn't think any more about it, but when I raised the question, she got quite upset. I think she feels bad that she didn't follow up on Edith. So, that makes at least three women who have disappeared: Edith, Mary Bradshaw, and Mrs. Johnson. I think that's enough to go to the police. Remember, they know about Mrs. Greeley already—her son reported that."

Charlie was all for it, but Ruby didn't look convinced.

"I don't know about involving the police. What if there's a completely innocent explanation? Wouldn't we look foolish?"

Hannah ignored Ruby's concerns. But she did agree to discuss the matter with Janice that evening and talk to Paul before going to the police. It wasn't clear to her what the reasons were for these disappearances, but she was sure it had something to do with money. In her experience, it always had something to do with money.

When they arrived back at the house, Charlie took off his tweed jacket, exchanged his wing- tipped shoes for some sneakers he had in the back of the van, and set to work on the bushes. After two hours, his shirt soaked with sweat, he wiped his brow and declared that he was finished. When he refused Hannah's invitation to dinner, she knew he was "bushed!"

. . . .

That evening, Hannah spoke to Janice about what they had found out at the Senior Center. Janice listened patiently as Hannah peppered her report with vivid descriptions of their visit: what was served for lunch and what should have been served; who was wearing inappropriate clothing—women with skirts too short, men with shirts too tight; which couples were having problems; who was going in for cataract or hip surgery; and a lengthy report on the blossoming relationship between Ruby and Charlie. Finally, Hannah got around to Edith Swenson—the third missing woman.

"Don't you think it's time to go to the police about this?" suggested Hannah.

"Remind me who the others are," replied Janice.

"Well, there's Mrs. Greeley, who's no longer missing—she's dead, but she was missing until we found out she was dead. But the others are Mrs. Johnson—we don't know much about her—Mary Bradshaw, who Ruby knew and who seems to have just disappeared, and finally this Edith Swensen. Neither Mary nor Edith had families and so they didn't just go off to live with their children someplace. I'd like to know if *Sunset* is still getting money for them—you know, like getting their social security checks. Who would know if these women were still alive or not? The government keeps sending checks until they're notified, right? So if *Sunset* doesn't notify them, they could keep receiving the checks. So it's at least fraud, even if they're not being killed for parts."

"Forget the parts scenario! The question is how to prove fraud."

"That's where Paul could help. Ask him."

Janice sighed. There was so much to ask Paul about tomorrow she was afraid they wouldn't have time to talk about anything else. This was one of the few weekends that his daughter wasn't with him. Trying to juggle work and family, and a relationship with a man who was juggling work and family, sometimes seemed an impossible task. Having Hannah live with them had certainly made a difference in Janice's life. She did have more free time and felt less guilt, as the children certainly loved Hannah and didn't resent Janice's absence as much as in the past. But Paul lived alone, except when his daughter was there, and that was the problem. They could occasionally get together during the week, but with both their schedules so full, they were lucky to find time to have dinner together. Weekends were the only time both of them could relax, and that was only when Paul was free. But she couldn't fault him for that. He was a good father, something she appreciated after her experience with Jim. In fact, that was one of the things that attracted her to him, in addition to his good looks, intelligence, and sense of humor—and his performance in bed! She smiled as she remembered their last time together. They had behaved like teenagers: finished dinner quickly, headed back to Paul's apartment, and jumped into bed. And didn't leave bed until the next morning! She had been surprised, but grateful, that Hannah hadn't said anything about her arriving home the following morning. But Hannah had never been a prude. She had openly discussed sex with Janice when she was a young girl, and had made it clear that sexuality was a part of being human, so long as one used protection and loved the person.

But Janice agreed that something had to be done about the missing women. Did they have enough information to go to the police? Perhaps she would have something to add when she talked to her staff on Monday. Surely, the fraud issue would get the interest of the government!

Chapter 20

It seemed to Janice that the weather had turned from fall to winter overnight. She knew it was only temporary and that *real* winter was still a way off, but the gray sky and the dropping temperature led her to the closet to look for warmer clothes. She and Paul had planned on spending the day in Saugatuck, browsing among the galleries and boutiques, before dining at their favorite little café. If the weather didn't change, they might have to adjust their plans.

Dressed in layers, black slacks topped by a pale gold short-sleeved blouse, she was prepared for a full range of temperatures—from winter coat to light sweater to shirt sleeves. When Paul arrived, he laughed at the amount of clothes she had assembled. He wore a brown leather jacket over jeans and a black t-shirt and looked ready for whatever the day would bring.

After a cup of coffee with Hannah, and promises to call if they would be late in returning home, they left in Paul's bright red Mustang. Hannah waved to them as they drove away, smiling at how happy Janice seemed. She could tell, even if Janice couldn't, that her situation was about to change. Clearly a young couple didn't need a mother-in-law living under the same roof with them!

. . . .

Janice was reluctant to raise the issues regarding Ruby's money and the missing women. At least, not yet. That could come later; now was the time to enjoy being together. The drive to Saugatuck took almost two hours, during which time they caught up with each other's lives, relating the frustrations of their jobs and the concerns about their children. They made plans for which galleries they would visit and what they wanted to look for in the boutiques.

Janice used these trips to stock up for Christmas and birthdays, finding gifts that were not available in the stores in Brewster.

When they arrived in Saugatuck, the sun was starting to break through the gray sky, promising a warmer day than predicted. Janice removed her winter coat and threw it in the back seat of the Mustang.

The town was located between Lake Michigan and Kalamazoo Lake. A convenient distance between Chicago and Detroit, it was a magnet for tourists looking for a quaint village atmosphere where one could sail, golf, eat, and shop for art. As she and Paul strolled down the streets, looking in the windows of the shops, pointing out possible gifts, she felt lighter, as if she were a young girl again with no responsibilities other than for herself. She loved her family and her job, but just for now didn't want to think of either. No concerns about Hannah and what would happen as she got older and less able to take care of herself; no concerns about Maddie's growing into a young woman with all the changes that will bring; no concerns about David and how to keep him safe from the temptations waiting around the corner for young men; and no concerns about school budgets and parental expectations. No, today was a day for herself—and Paul.

After a light lunch at one of the outdoor cafés, they commenced their journey through the various galleries. They stopped first at Paul's favorite gallery, *Amazwi Contemporary Art,* specializing in African art, where they oohed and aahed over the current exhibit. Paul's interest was focused on three paintings but, deciding to buy only one, he chose Aswani's *Whispers,* showing three brightly clad abstract figures whispering. Too large to carry safely, he had it shipped to his home.

They stopped in *Czarina's Treasure,* where Janice bought a nested doll set for her secretary, and *Koorey Creations,* where she coveted a blue topaz pendant that would be perfect for Hannah if it hadn't cost $3,500!

After viewing tree sculptures at the *Ark Gallery* and laughing at some of the paintings at the *ThirdStone Gallery,* they ended up buying beaded bracelets for Paul's daughter, feather earrings that Janice thought Maddie would like, a graphic poster for David, hoping that he was still interested in that—it was difficult keeping up with David's interests which seemed to change more quickly than the weather—and some Italian pottery for Janice at *The Tuscan Pot.*

There were too many galleries to visit in one day, so they just window-shopped, entering only when they saw something of interest in the window. By the time they had finished their browsing they were exhausted. Next on their agenda was dinner at the *White House Bistro,* a charming, small restaurant with an outdoor patio. While still chilly, they chose to eat outdoors—after Paul made a trip to retrieve Janice's coat from the car.

Relaxing over a glass of wine, Janice decided it was time to raise Ruby's issues: how to find out how much money she was entitled to from the sale of the house, and what to do about the missing women.

Paul listened. After Janice finished, he replied, "The money issue is easy. All she has to do is work out a budget for her needs, you know: rent, utilities, food, things like that. She's guaranteed that by the agreement she signed. Maybe your mother could help her—I have a feeling Ruby isn't up to that. As for the missing women, you're going to need more evidence. You have to check to make sure that there aren't any relatives, even distant ones, who might have taken the women in; then you'll have to check death certificates to determine if anything was filed. The issue that will be the most difficult— well, not difficult, but time consuming—will be finding out if that place was still receiving government money for these women when they were no longer there. That's something that will get the attention of the feds."

"How can we find that out?" asked Janice.

Paul hesitated. Reluctant to get more involved without any official client, he examined the options. "Let me think," he said.

Janice was only too willing to let him think. She turned to her stuffed shells with arrabbiata sauce and devoted the next few minutes to savoring her dinner. When she glanced up, Paul was smiling at her. "You'd think you hadn't eaten in a week," he teased.

"I worked up an appetite coveting all those things I couldn't afford. Restraint takes effort, you know. Besides, this is excellent. Try some."

Paul took the shell off the fork Janice was waving at him, plopped it in his mouth, and proclaimed that, yes, it was good.

After some more wine, and a dessert which they shared, Paul sat back and said, "I have been thinking—I can eat and think, you know!—and here's what I suggest. Have Ruby hire me to file suit against that nursing home…. Yes, I know, there are no grounds for a suit yet, but let me finish. That way I have a client. It'll be *pro bono,* won't cost her a thing, but that allows me to use our PI to do some investigating. We'll have to think up something that we could sue them about. In fact, it never has to be actually filed. It's just so I can legitimately get involved. Do you think Ruby will go along?"

"I don't see why not. If she doesn't, I'm sure my mother will! We can speak to them tonight when we get back. Find out if there are any issues we can use."

Paul looked at Janice. "Are you sure you want to speak to them tonight? How about tomorrow, when you get home?"

Janice gave him a coy smile and said, "Why, sir, aren't you getting ahead of yourself. I haven't agreed to spend the night with you."

"Of course, how foolish of me. My dear, would you come home with me and spend the night in passionate lovemaking until the early hours of the morning?"

Janice laughed. "I don't know if we're both up to it, but I'd enjoy trying. I'd better call my mother—she worries, you know."

"That's what all my young girlfriends say," joked Paul, who received a kick under the table from Janice.

． ．

Hannah had just finished clearing the dinner table when David came into the kitchen. Maddie was in her room, preparing for a quiz in her French class the next day, and Ruby was watching TV in the living room. Hannah was surprised to see David—usually he rushed upstairs after dinner to his latest video game.

"Grandma, can I ask you a question?"

"Of course, darling. What is it? Is something wrong?"

"Why doesn't my dad like me?"

"Why would you think that? Of course he likes you. He loves you. But he's got his own problems and has trouble showing his feelings. What makes you think that?"

"I don't know. I was over at Billy's and, I don't know, his father is a real neat guy—talks to us, shoots baskets with us, you know, does things with Billy and me, when I'm there. Dad doesn't do anything with me, even when he does come by. He never asks what I'm doing, just takes me to places he wants to go. He never even smiles at me."

Hannah looked at her grandson, seeing in him the young man he would soon be. His short brown hair, which always looked uncombed, was so like his grandfather's, as was the way he furrowed his brow when he was thinking. While still a boy, she could see signs of his grandfather in him, which, to Hannah, was the highest praise.

Standing at the kitchen counter, Hannah put her arm around David's shoulder. "Listen to me, darling. I'm going to speak to you as an adult. I'm not going to sugarcoat what I say. Your mother may not approve of what I'm going to say, but I think you're old enough and smart enough to handle it.

"Your father didn't know how to be a good husband or a good father. That's why you mother divorced him. It wasn't easy for her to do that. After all, you and Maddie were very young and couldn't understand why your daddy went away. I know your father loved you and Maddie—and maybe even your mother—but he didn't know how to show that love. And he did some pretty bad things back then. He drank too much, he spent too much money, he couldn't keep a job, and he wasn't faithful to your mother. Maybe he was too young to be a good father, I don't know. But I do know that when he wasn't drinking, when things were going okay for him, he adored you kids. You probably were too young to remember, but he would carry you on his shoulders and pretend to be a horse you were riding, and when he was feeling well he would help you build things with those blocks you had—Legos, or something. It's just that when things started to go bad for him, he changed. I don't think he changed his love for you. It's just that he got messed up and couldn't think of anyone but himself. And that's where he is now. It's not that he doesn't like you—he doesn't like himself. Maybe one day he'll pull himself together and be able to be a father to you, but right now he just can't do that. It's not you he's angry with, it's himself."

David's large brown eyes were shining, tears held back by an act of will. Hannah gently embraced him. "I just wish your grandpa were here to see what a wonderful young man you've become. He'd be so proud of you."

David looked embarrassed, but replied, "I miss Grandpa. He was a neat guy."

Hannah replied, "You got that right, kiddo."

Just then, Ruby called out, "Hannah, come see this. That David Copperfield man is going to make the Empire State Building disappear."

Hannah sighed, David laughed, and they both left the kitchen, he to his video game and she to the disappearing building.

It was 10:00 when Janice called to report that she would see Hannah in the morning. Hannah didn't ask any questions, just smiled to herself.

Chapter 21

Janice returned home at 7:00 a.m. on Monday, kissed the children, and was out the door by 8:00, leaving no time to talk with Hannah about Ruby. It also saved her from any subtle questions from Hannah about Paul and his "intentions." She knew it was only a delay; questions would come later.

But today she had to find time in her busy schedule to interview her staff about their experiences at *Sunset Manor*. She was anxious to get whatever information she could to Paul in order to get the investigation underway. Her initial skepticism about the missing women had been replaced by a burning need to pursue the issue.

It wasn't until the lunch hour that she was able to corral people in the staff lounge to ask her questions. Most of the younger staff had no experience with nursing homes, but there were still some who remembered their former colleagues, who would be of an age to require nursing homes. One of these teachers remembered visiting a friend at *Sunset*. While she didn't think that her friend had received particularly good treatment there, she had no reason to think that anything was amiss at the place—just a shortage of personnel.

It wasn't until Janice returned to her office that she remembered the nested dolls she had bought for her secretary's collection. Rummaging in her briefcase, she found them and presented them to Gwen, who opened the package and exclaimed, "Oh, how lovely. I don't have these. Thank you so much."

She held them in her hand, turned to Janice and asked, "What was all the talking about in the lounge? Are there problems I should be prepared for?"

Janice laughed. "No, nothing like that. I was just trying to find out if anyone had any experience with someone in *Sunset Manor*, the nursing home. But most of them are too young to have anyone there."

"What are you asking about?"

"Basically, if they had any problems with the place."

"Well, my aunt was there until she moved in with my folks. That was about three years ago. She's since passed away, though."

Janice motioned to Gwen to sit down, and closed the door. "Do you remember," she asked, "if there were any problems while she was there?"

"Well, all I remember is that my folks were concerned enough about the care she was receiving there that they brought her to live with them, even though that was a big inconvenience for them. She was my mother's sister and, while they were very close, she needed more care than my mother could provide. They had to hire someone to come in and help out. But, I don't remember what the problems were at the nursing home. If it's important, I could check with my mother."

"Oh, that would be a great help. If you could get back to me with whatever your mother remembers, that would be great."

"Well, if you don't have anything pressing for me to do, I could give her a call now."

"Splendid. Yes, do it!"

Gwen left the office and returned fifteen minutes later, with raised eyebrows. As she reported, her mother had been concerned with the lack of nursing staff and the food that they served. Her aunt had serious diabetes and was consistently served food with a high sugar content. Her blood sugar was rarely monitored and one day they found her so disoriented that they feared for her life. Once she was home with them, she improved rapidly.

Janice asked if Gwen's mother had had any indication that people went missing. Gwen's eyebrows went even higher. "Missing?" she said. "You mean like disappearing?"

"That's exactly what I mean," replied Janice.

"Well, I didn't ask my mom about that, though I think she would have said something if that happened. Let me call her back."

Gwen returned after ten minutes, closed the door and sat down. "You're not going to believe this. My mother remembers that my aunt had a roommate who was released and sent home, although my aunt was upset because the roommate never said goodbye and never called her after she left. My mother just dismissed it as a friendship that wasn't strong enough to continue and tried to convince my aunt of that. She remembers that my aunt was never convinced, but stopped talking about it after a while. Do you think something happened to her?"

"I don't know, but there have been a few cases like that. The person is there one day and gone the next and no one knows where they went. Do you know the name of the woman?"

"Carol something. I'll get back to you tomorrow. I don't want to call my mom again—she's in the middle of a bridge game!"

"Thanks, this is helpful."

. . . .

Hannah and Ruby had just finished lunch, when Ruby suggested that she bake some cookies for the children. Hannah, worrying that it might require too much standing for Ruby, questioned if Ruby was up to it. Ruby smiled and said, "I feel so much better since I'm here, I think I could make a whole dinner. Let me make the cookies. I want to do something for the children."

"Okay, you're on, toots," Hannah replied, going to the cupboard to get the ingredients. "What kind of cookies? What'll you need?"

"How about cherry winks? Do you have maraschino cherries? And nuts?"

"No, but if you really want to make those I could run out to the store."

Hannah breathed a sigh of relief when Ruby changed to snickerdoodles and retrieved the necessary ingredients from the cupboard and refrigerator. Setting up a chair at the counter for Ruby to use, she sat down at the table to keep her company. She was delighted to see Ruby so happy—such a change from just a week ago.

By the time Madison and David were back from school, the kitchen was filled with the sweet aroma of the cinnamon and sugar cookies cooling on the counter.

"Smells good," declared Madison. "What kind are they?"

"Can I have some?" asked David.

Ruby nodded permission to David and replied, "They're snickerdoodles."

David guffawed. "Snicker whats? What a silly name."

"Well, forget about the name," said Hannah. "See if you like them. Maybe you won't and that'll leave more for the rest of us."

David frowned at Hannah, took a bite, and pronounced that they were "decent," which Madison had to translate for the women as high praise from him.

Hannah brought out the milk and juice for the children, and poured two cups of tea for Ruby and herself; all four sat down to eat snickerdoodles. They were engaged in listening to the events of the day as reported by Madison and David, when Janice entered the kitchen. "You were so busy in here you didn't even hear me come in. What's going on?"

"We're eating snickerdoodles," David shouted, giving emphasis to the last syllable. "Ruby made them and they're decent."

"Oh, God. I know language changes, but must it change every year. 'Decent' means what now?"

"It means really good, Mom," said Madison. "Only boys use it though; it's so dorky."

David started to respond, but was cut off by a glare from his mother. "Well, I think you've probably had enough cookies. How about doing some homework before dinner?"

Madison got up from the table, saying, "I don't have any homework, but I get the message."

David, grabbing another cookie from the platter, looked puzzled. "What message?"

"Just go and do your homework," sighed Janice. "So, what have you two been up to today?" she asked as David left the room.

"Nothing much," replied Hannah. "Ruby wanted to make something for the children—here, try one, they're decent," she laughed. "So, how was your date yesterday?"

Janice bit back the urge to deny it was a date. After all, what else could you call it? "We had a lovely time. I almost bought you a beautiful pendant, only it was $3,500—slightly more than I could afford."

Hannah laughed. "Oh, and I was wanting something special I should wear to lunch at the Senior Center."

Janice poured herself a cup of tea and sat down. Turning serious, she looked at Ruby and said, "Ruby, I spoke to Paul about your financial situation. You'll need to work up a budget—you know, how much you'll need each month for living expenses. Mom, maybe you could help Ruby with that? According to Paul, the agreement you signed entitles you to whatever you will need to live on."

"But Harold said that he only received $125,000 for the house and that he would give me $75,000. I don't know how long that will last me."

Hannah groaned. "You don't understand. The house sold for $375,000. Even half of that would be over $180,000, and you're entitled to more if you need it. Don't be foolish. You don't want you should end up in some place worse than *Sunset Manor*, do you?"

Ruby started to tear up, but caught herself when she saw Hannah's frown. "I know you're trying to help, but I just don't know."

Janice intervened. "Look, there's no hurry. Take your time. You and my mom, when you're ready, sit down and add up what your monthly expenses are going to be. Then you can deduct what you receive from social security, and anything else you're receiving, and the difference is what you should get from the sale of the house. From what Paul said, you can be guaranteed a certain monthly allocation for as long as you live."

Hannah rose and walked over to Ruby. "Don't worry; you can be fair to Harold. Just don't be a *schmo*. Look out for yourself, too." She gave Ruby a hug and then said, "Come, you have so much energy, give me suggestions on what I should make for dinner."

Seeing the effect the discussion had had on Ruby, Janice chose not to mention what she had learned from Gwen. Better to wait until she had more information about the possibility of another missing woman.

Chapter 22

HANNAH AWOKE ON TUESDAY morning to bright sunshine, highlighting the frost on the trees, turning the yard into a fairyland. Forgetting for a moment that this was the result of the weather turning cold and the approach of winter, she stood at the kitchen window taking in the beauty of the scene.

She was still there when Janice entered the kitchen and helped herself to a cup of coffee.

"Mom? What are you looking at?" she asked.

"Look. It's beautiful. Like that scene in *Dr. Zhivago*—you know, when everything is iced over."

Janice smiled. "Yes, it is beautiful—and cold. So if you and Ruby are going out today, dress warm."

"Thank you for that advice, darling!" laughed Hannah, sarcastically.

Janice looked out over the yard, trying to see it as her mother did. All she saw were barren trees and grass slowly turning brown. She looked forward to when the snow would cover the grass with a white blanket until spring. She wished she could view the world as Hannah did, looking beyond what was there in front of her to see what could be. Hannah's visions of what could be frustrated her: they seemed so full of hope when all she could see was the hopelessness of anything changing. But she knew that it was that hope that kept Hannah so vital, so full of life, even at the age of seventy-eight, when most of her friends were content to sit and watch life pass by.

Hannah broke into Janice's reverie. "I think I'll take Ruby to the Center for lunch today. We can use her car. When we get home, I'm going to try to get her to work on a budget. She'll come around, but it's not easy for her. It's hard for her to admit that her son is a son-of-a-bitch. But I think I can get her to focus on what she'll need and then we can try to convince her to get it."

Janice nodded. This was the other side of Hannah: her get-down-to-business side. It made living with her interesting; Janice never really knew what Hannah would get involved in next.

"Well, good luck," she said. "I might have some more information on another missing woman when I get home tonight. I didn't want to mention it last night—Ruby seemed upset enough without getting into that."

"Good. I'm getting anxious to do something about these women. It just doesn't feel right."

"Well, if Gwen, my secretary—remember you met her at the Christmas party last year?—well, if she's right, there's another woman who disappeared from that place. According to Paul, that might be enough to start an investigation. But don't tell Ruby, yet. Let me see what I find out and what Paul suggests."

Okay....What time will you be home tonight? More importantly, what do you want I should make for dinner?"

"The usual time. And anything you and Ruby cook up will be fine. See you later."

On her way out the door, Janice called to the kids to hurry up or they would miss their bus.

Madison and David ate a hurried breakfast, put on their coats and thirty minutes later left to catch the school bus, David dashing back to the house to grab the backpack he had left in the hallway.

After calm had settled in the house, Ruby joined Hannah for coffee and toast. Trying unsuccessfully to coax Ruby into eating something more substantial, Hannah gave up, planning to make sure she would eat a hearty lunch.

They were chatting about the weather, comparing it to the winters of their youth in New York, when the phone rang. Expecting another call from Harold, Ruby tensed, relaxing only when Hannah handed her the phone saying, "It's for you—your beau, Charlie."

Ruby blushed. "Good morning, Charlie. Why, yes that would be lovely. Let me check with Hannah." She turned to Hannah and asked, "He wants to take us to lunch at the Center. Would that be all right?" Receiving a nod from Hannah, she spoke into the phone, "Yes, that'll be fine....Okay. See you at 11:45."

'Now don't you start," she said to Hannah, who had a big grin on her face. "He's just lonely."

"Lonely, my *tuchis*. He's got the hots for you, kiddo. You'd better watch out—you know those hot-blooded Italians!" Hannah enjoyed teasing Ruby, who blushed so readily.

After tidying up the kitchen, the two women sat down to watch *The View* until Charlie came to pick them up. Today's "hot topic" was on the proposal to raise the tax on incomes over two million dollars. Ruby tsked, tsked, indicating her disapproval. Hannah stared at her in amazement. "What, you feel sorry for those people?" she asked.

"Well, I just don't think people should be penalized for being successful," Ruby replied. "Bernie always said that if the rich people continued to be taxed so much, they would stop being productive and then where would the country be?"

"You think the guy at the top who gets two million or more a year, should pay less taxes—with all the loopholes they have—than the guy who works for him for $50,000? Where would your 'successful' people be without the little guys who do the work? And, it seems to me, that rich people never have enough money, so if they get taxed, they'll just try to make it up by making more money and hiding it the way they do now.... And besides, where do you think the money for social security, and Medicare, comes from? If we don't increase taxes, people like you and me would be left high and dry."

Hannah was on a roll. It had been a long time since she had had to defend her political views, although she felt guilty taking it out on Ruby, who didn't seem to be able to respond except by saying, "Well, I don't know."

Fortunately for Ruby, Charlie rang the doorbell just as Hannah was about to expound on the importance of nationalized medical insurance, or "socialized medicine," as she preferred to call it.

They arrived at the Center just as the food was being brought out. Charlie's eyes opened wide at the brownies piled on the large tray, but Hannah reminded him that he had to eat his lunch before he had dessert, which caused him to look at her in amusement.

They joined some friends at the large table, and caught up on the gossip. Nothing really new: Phyllis Parkins had now set her claws for the new man who had joined the Center, a widower whom she thought needed comforting; and the Hermans had arrived safely in Florida, after a ten day trip, averaging less than two hundred miles a day. Ruby was pleased to be encouraged to return to the bridge table—people complained that they were getting sloppy without her there to challenge them. It was a pleasant lunch and, after Charlie had consumed three brownies—pointedly looking at Hannah as he put each one in his mouth—they bid their goodbyes, promising to return soon.

On the drive home, Hannah raised the issue of preparing a budget for Ruby. Charlie jumped at the chance to be of help, asking Ruby, "Do you mind if I work on that with you?"

Ruby smiled coyly. "Oh, I hate to bother you with that. You must have more important things to do."

Reassuring her that there was nothing more important in his life than helping her, Charlie suggested that they get to work on it as soon as they arrived home. Hannah, in the back seat, rolled her eyes at the two of them in the front seat.

The afternoon was spent brainstorming on what Ruby would need to live on her own. Charlie put himself in charge. "Well, clearly rent goes on the list, and so does heating and electricity. And, of course food, that goes without saying. But don't forget you'll need money for gas and car repairs…and what about your medical costs—things like insurance, medicines, doctors? You know you have to budget for those things, too."

Ruby nodded agreement and gazed up at him as if this was the wisest thing she had ever heard.

After an hour they had a list which included such things as personal items and entertainment. The last was contributed by Hannah, who thought that Ruby should be able to have dinner out occasionally, see a movie, or even travel—although she hoped that the budding romance between Ruby and Charlie would blossom and that Charlie would be entertaining Ruby.

"Well, the way it adds up is about \$\$3,000 a month," reported Charlie, checking his calculations.

"No, she'll need more than that. You have to allow for unexpected things—like something breaks and has to be fixed. And what if she can't find a place to rent for what you've listed? I'm sure if Ruby finds that she has more money than she needs she'll know what to do with it."

Hannah looked over at Ruby as she said this, and was rewarded with a nod. However, once Ruby realized that even at \$3,000 a month the full amount of the sale of the house would be used up in ten years, leaving nothing for Harold, she was uncomfortable. Hannah reminded her that she still had her social security so the full amount wouldn't have to come from the house. "Besides," she reminded her, "the money from the house was supposed to be an inheritance—for after you died, not before. If Harold hadn't gone and sold the house, you wouldn't be in this position. He just got greedy."

Ruby started to object, Charlie looked concerned, and Hannah apologized. "I'm sorry, that was uncalled for. It's just that I get so frustrated when you don't look out for yourself." She appealed to Charlie. "Maybe you can make her see reason here."

"I know you're trying to help," Ruby said. "And, believe me, I'm not so blind about my son any more. I just want to be fair. If he's doing this, he must be hurting, although I don't see how. He has a successful business."

Hannah looked at Charlie and raised her eyebrows. When Charlie didn't respond, she said, "Charlie, you know about the car business. What do you think?"

Finally Charlie got the hint. "Well, Ruby, you know the auto industry is hurting. A lot of people got caught up living like the good times would be forever. Perhaps your son was one of them, you know, caught in a life style he can't support any more. That wouldn't be surprising; it's happening to a lot of people. And, yeah, it's scary and people do strange things when that happens. But Hannah is right, you have to look out for yourself. Your son has options."

Hannah marveled at how Charlie had accomplished with a velvet glove what she would have used a hammer for. She was seeing more in Charlie than she had realized was there. Perhaps he would be just what Ruby needed. She invited him to stay for dinner and retreated to the kitchen to start the preparations, refusing help from Ruby. A little time to themselves might be just what was needed for those two, she thought.

. . . .

Dinner was quickly prepared: broiled salmon, broccoli, and Waldorf salad. David looked at the salmon and made a face. "Not to worry, my dumpling," said Hannah. "For you I have a special treat: a hamburger!"

Janice shook her head. "Mom, you're spoiling him. He has to learn to eat what we eat."

"Darling, he will. Just give him time. Remember those peanut butter sandwiches I used to slip you when we were invited out to dinner? You eventually learned to like new foods and so will he."

David looked at his mother. "You liked peanut butter?"

"Enough about food. Let's eat," said Janice, smiling at the memory.

"Well, David," asked Charlie, "what games are you playing now?"

"I want to get that new *Grand Theft Auto* game—you know, the *Chinatown Wars* one?—but Mom won't let me buy it, she thinks it's too violent. All the kids at school have it, though. I've played it at Billy's and it's awesome!"

"David, I told you I don't like you playing that game. The original one is bad enough, what with killing people and blowing up things. I'm surprised that Billy's mom let him buy it."

"Well, he didn't buy it," David volunteered reluctantly. "This guy at school had it and Billy copied it. But, Mom, we know it's only a game—we're not going to go out and shoot people. The game is just great fun. It's got the best graphics, and it's fast—really challenging."

Much to Hannah's relief, Charlie didn't get involved in the discussion between mother and son, reinforcing her newly emerging opinion of his potential. After a brief silence, Hannah turned to Madison, who had been unusually quiet throughout dinner. "So, darling, what's new?"

Madison looked up from her plate and replied, with her eyes blazing, "Can you believe it? Becky's dating Kenny! She knows how he treated me. How could she do that? Well, my friend, Suzanne," she said, emphasizing the word *friend*, "won't speak to Becky either. And Becky doesn't understand what the problem is—all she says is that I told her I wasn't interested in him any more. What a lame excuse to betray me!"

David, clearly not interested in the conversation, asked, and received, permission to leave the table, and the adults continued to listen sympathetically to Madison as she described how humiliated she felt. Various courses of action were proposed and rejected, leaving only the "grin and bear it: it's all a part of growing up" suggestion on the table. Madison wasn't happy with the results of the discussion, but did appreciate that the adults had taken her concerns seriously.

After the young people had left the room, Janice reported on her conversation with Gwen. Gwen's mother had remembered the woman's name: Carol Goodman, who might be another missing person from *Sunset Manor*. That made five cases: Mrs. Johnson, Mrs. Bradshaw, Edith Swenson, Carol Goodman, and, of course, Mrs. Greeley.

She shared Paul's suggestion that Ruby hire Paul to file suit against the nursing home—they could work up some charge which would allow his investigator to gather the necessary information. She pointed out that he would take it on a *pro bono* basis, and so wouldn't charge Ruby anything. All she had to do was hire him.

Ruby turned to Charlie, who nodded his agreement. "Sounds like a plan," he said.

"How do I hire him?" she asked.

Hannah started to say something, but was interrupted by Janice. "Here's his number. Call him tomorrow to set up an appointment. He could probably meet you here, if that's more convenient."

"No, I think she should go to his office," Hannah chimed in. "It makes it more official, more legitimate. Ruby, tomorrow morning you can phone Paul and make the appointment."

Charlie again nodded his agreement, which was all that Ruby needed. "Okay, tomorrow morning, I'll call."

With that, Charlie rose, thanked Janice for dinner, and left. Janice insisted on helping Hannah do the dishes, before going off to work on the revised maintenance schedule she was proposing to the union the next day. Hannah and Ruby settled in the living room, watching another rerun of *Walker, Texas Ranger*—"such a handsome man" they agreed, before turning in for the night.

Chapter 23

T HE FIRST THING THAT Hannah did in the morning, after Janice and the children had left, was to convince Ruby to contact Harold. At first Ruby was reluctant to do so, but when Hannah pointed out that it was only fair to let Harold know what she was going to do about the money, Ruby relented.

At Hannah's suggestion, Ruby called him at work, thus lessening the chance of his turning ballistic on the phone. When she got through to him, she calmly outlined the budget she had prepared the previous day, ending with the request that she would need a guaranteed monthly income of $3,500—yes, Hannah had been somewhat persuasive—and that she wanted to have a legal document prepared to that effect.

Obviously, Harold had no problem with bellowing in a public place—Hannah could hear him sputter from across the room. Seeing that Ruby was becoming upset, Hannah took the phone from her. "Harold, this is Hannah Lowenstein. Your mother has spoken to an attorney who assures her that the document she signed allows her enough money to live comfortably until her death. Then, and only then, you get to use whatever remains. Now you know your mother is not a spendthrift, that her request is quite reasonable, and that none of this would have happened if you had not sold the house under her. So, now, you listen. This is going to be done, with or without taking you to court. She's staying with my family now, but she'll be getting her own place soon. Unlike the predictions you made, she is completely capable of living alone and taking care of herself. We'll be looking for a nice place for her to rent—a *nice* place, not some dump. You should speak to your lawyer, or accountant, or whatever, to make sure that $42,000 a year—if my math is correct—is put into her bank account for her until her death, which I wouldn't expect to be very soon. So I guess that means you can't touch *any* of the money from the sale of the house yet!"

Hannah held the phone away from her ear, allowing Ruby to hear the profanity being uttered on the other end. She shrugged her shoulders and returned the phone to her ear. "Listen," she said, "now listen. I'm hanging up. If we don't hear from you that the money has been placed in her account by Friday, we're taking the matter to court. Bye." She slammed the phone down and tried to calm her pounding heart before facing Ruby.

Ruby's face was wet with tears. Hannah went over to her. "It's okay. He's just playing hard ball. When he speaks to his lawyer, he'll see that he has no choice."

"But if he's having money problems, why didn't he come to me? He knows I would have helped him," Ruby cried.

'My own view, and it's only my personal opinion, is that he's been living quite high and, now that business is slow, he's having trouble keeping up his standard of living. Remember, you told me all about the private schools for the boys, and his wife seems to enjoy a rather luxurious life style. I think he saw an easy way to get a few hundred thousand from you, something you wouldn't have been able to give him. So he sells the house, lies about how much he got for it, and pockets about $300,000. Of course, he's angry now. But he'll get over it. It's not as if a wonderful mother-son relationship is going to be ruined!"

"Oh, Hannah. It sounds so terrible the way you say it. I know you mean well, but I can't just forget that I have a son."

Hannah didn't see why not: who would want a son like that? But she didn't say anything. Instead, she suggested that they make an appointment with Paul to file suit on the missing women.

After spending the next thirty minutes searching for Paul's phone number—which was on the kitchen counter, under yesterday's newspaper—they managed to get an appointment to meet with him that afternoon.

The next hour was spent with both women taking extra care with their outfits, determined to give the impression of professional women seeking the services of a lawyer. They succeeded in giving the impression of two nicely dressed elderly women desperately seeking help.

Paul's office was on the third floor of a large downtown building. Hannah had driven Ruby's car, a large 1982 Lincoln, and found that parking was more of a problem than with Janice's 2001 Civic. Parallel parking was not one of her skills, and twenty minutes were spent looking for two contiguous parking spots so she could head, rather than back, into the space. Fortunately, they had left plenty of time to make the 1:30 appointment.

They entered the building, took the elevator to the third floor, and stepped out into a large reception area with an elegantly dressed young woman at the desk. She smiled and asked them to take a seat while she let Mr. Burrows know that they were there. They sat down on the lush brown leather chairs which picked up the rich color of the wood panels. Set against the warm ochre of the wall, large paintings were hung, paintings which seemed to Hannah to be masses of colors twirling and weaving, resembling nothing she had ever seen, but which she knew must be considered "fine art." She was about to comment on them to Ruby when they were ushered into Paul's office by the receptionist.

The meeting with Paul was short: contracts signed, explanations regarding the legal process given, handshakes all around, and they were out in less than 30 minutes. Ruby appeared bewildered, but Hannah was ecstatic. Now, maybe something would be done.

Having planned on spending at least an hour with Paul, the women decided to stop in for a "little something" at their favorite ice cream parlor. Worried about spoiling her appetite for dinner, Ruby ordered a small cone of chocolate ice cream; Hannah, with no such concern, opted for a double butter pecan waffle cone—with chocolate fudge on top. Laughing, she told Ruby she was glad the children weren't around to see her bad example.

When they arrived home, both women were in excellent spirits. The excitement at filing a lawsuit against *Sunset Manor,* combined with the ice cream snack, seemed to overcome any concerns they had about what they had initiated. Even Ruby, ever reluctant to cause trouble, was rambling on about "getting those SOBs"—she couldn't say "sons-of-bitches." When the children came home from school, they found two old ladies sitting in front of the TV, giggling like young girls.

David looked at Madison, clearly confused. He had never seen his grandmother giggling before! Madison walked over to the women and asked, "What's so funny, Grandma?"

Trying to gain her composure, Hannah responded, "Oh, we're just being silly, darling. We're celebrating the lawsuit we filed with Paul today. You know, the one against that nursing home? Well, maybe now we'll find out about the missing women."

"Oh."

"And, on that note, I'd better get going on dinner. Let's go, Ruby. You can peel the potatoes." Together they walked into the kitchen, still giggling, Ruby hanging on to Hannah's arm for support.

· ·

The conversation at dinner that evening revolved around the lawsuit.

Janice was pleased that Ruby had consented to be the initiating party. As Paul had pointed out to her, it had to be initiated by someone who had "standing", that is, someone who had a reason to claim that they had been harmed. He had convinced Ruby to claim she had been harmed because she had to leave *Sunset* before she had finished her therapy out of fear for her life. He didn't expect it to hold up in court, but that was not what they were aiming for. What they wanted were grounds for Paul to get the PI to investigate. Anything suspicious would be shared with the police, who would take it from there.

David was excited about the possibility that the women had been murdered and that he would get to be interviewed by the police, which possibility produced a guffaw from Maddie. "Why would they interview you? To hear your stupid opinions?"

"They're not stupid, bird-brain," he retorted, "I think they really were murdered. And then they sold whatever parts were good and threw the bodies away. That happens, you know!"

Before Madison could reply, Janice jumped in. "Enough, already. I don't want to hear any more about murder and selling parts. We don't know what happened, so let's not go off on wild speculations until we get some information. There may be a perfectly good explanation for what happened to those women."

David went back to eating his mashed potatoes, but not before he mumbled, "They're toast."

Chapter 24

THE NEXT FEW DAYS brought no news about the investigation. Hannah wanted to call Paul to find out what was happening, but Ruby convinced her to be patient. "Let's not bother him. He'll call when he has something to tell us."

Hannah reluctantly agreed. She had confidence in Paul, but was finding it difficult to control her impatience. Janice had made it clear that Paul was doing this as a favor to her and she didn't want Hannah interfering. Although why Janice should think Hannah would interfere was quite puzzling to Hannah, who considered herself to be a model of restraint.

Charlie had come by every morning that week in time for a cup of coffee, a roll, and an opportunity to see Ruby and invite her, and Hannah, to lunch at the Senior Center. Hannah was beginning to feel like the proverbial fifth wheel—unnecessary, but useful in an emergency, although she couldn't envision what kind of emergency might arise.

After three days of lunch with Ruby and Charlie, Hannah needed time alone. Claiming that she had work to do at home, and reminding Ruby of the afternoon bridge games and Charlie of the always available poker games, she easily convinced them to go without her.

With a sigh of relief as they drove off in Charlie's Grand Marquis, Hannah tidied up the kitchen and sat down with a third cup of coffee and the daily crossword puzzle. She was truly fond of Ruby, and glad that the family had so easily adjusted to her living with them. But she had gotten used to her time alone each day. If Ruby stayed much longer, she would have to figure out a way to set aside time for herself, without hurting Ruby's feelings. She saw in Charlie a possible solution.

. . . .

It was after 3:00 when Charlie and Ruby returned. Ruby was flushed with excitement, bubbling over with news from the Center. Charlie, too, was excited, having won $200 at poker. After refusing "a little something to eat" from Hannah, Charlie took off with promises to be back the next day to take them to the Center.

With Hannah seated in her recliner, Ruby on the sofa, the gossip was dispersed. At first Ruby brought Hannah up to date on the health of their various friends and who was on vacation; next came a description of who wore what, followed by an even more detailed description of the food that was served. Finally, she got to the exciting news: Phyllis Parkins was dating that new man! They had been seen having dinner together and, to go by their behavior at lunch, they were clearly beyond the "getting to know you" stage.

"You should have seen her, all decked-out in that short leather skirt she wears and a sweater that goes down to here," Ruby reported, pointing to the mid-point on her own chest. "She was all over him, feeding him as if he were incapable of lifting a spoon! And he just sits there. I don't think the poor man knows what hit him. It's like he's still in shock over losing his wife and Phyllis is moving in before he wakes up. If it weren't so sad it'd be funny."

"Well, she's tried that before," Hannah interrupted, "and most of the men have survived. Perhaps this one'll wake up in time to realize what's happening. Although you have to wonder about these old geezers. They sure seem vulnerable. It's as if they can't live without a woman—though usually they go for the young ones."

"Well, I don't see the young women coming around for these old men, unless, of course, they're rich."

Hannah smiled. Maybe Ruby wasn't so naïve after all! She wanted to ask how things were going with Charlie, but found herself reluctant to pry. Strange! That rarely happened to her.

They were still talking and laughing when David and Madison barged in, arguing as usual. This time it was David who was criticizing Madison.

"That's so lame," he shouted. "Who cares about why he got kicked out of Jefferson. He's a neat guy, really smart. So if I want to hang with him, that's my business, not yours."

"Oh, you're so simple," Madison shot back. "For all you know, he could be a drug dealer. What do you think Mom would say about that?

Hannah looked up with raised eyebrows, but didn't say a word. David ran upstairs, Madison waved and went into the kitchen. Seeing an opportunity to talk with Madison, Hannah got up and headed for the kitchen.

"What can I get you, darling?" she asked.

"I'm not hungry, Grandma, just thirsty," Madison replied, as she poured herself a glass of juice.

"Everything all right?"

"Yeah. It's just that he's so stupid. He could get into a lot of trouble. He doesn't know anything about that new kid—the one who just transferred over from Jefferson. And already he and Billy are hanging around with him as if they knew him their whole lives. I tried to talk to him, but he's so stubborn he won't even listen."

"Well, it's hard for him to take advice from his big sister. Do you know something about this new boy, something bad?"

"No. I just think that if someone gets kicked out of school, there's usually a good reason to stay away from them."

"Do you know why he was kicked out of school? In fact, do you know that he *was* kicked out? Maybe he transferred for some other reason."

"You don't understand, Grandma. No one transfers in the middle of a semester unless they were kicked out of their old school. And you have to be pretty bad to be kicked out."

"Well, I probably don't understand. But your mother will, so we'll leave it to her to talk to David, okay?"

Madison looked at her grandmother, nodded, finished her juice and headed upstairs to do her homework while listening to her latest *Kanye West* CD, at low volume so her mother wouldn't hear—she knew Janice wouldn't approve if she heard the lyrics.

Hannah returned to the living room, sat down next to Ruby, and shook her head. "I'm glad I didn't have to worry about drugs when Janice was in school. It's hard for kids today, too much trouble so easily available. Of course, marijuana was available in Janice's day, but that's not like these new drugs."

Ruby looked surprised at Hannah's acceptance of marijuana, but quickly changed the subject to plans for dinner.

Hannah jumped up. "Oh, damn—it's already 4:30. Janice will be home soon and I haven't even thought about what to do for dinner."

Ruby ignored Hannah's profanity and suggested that they go see what they could put together for a meal. Holding on to her walker, she followed Hannah into the kitchen, where they found the makings for crab cakes and rice. With a tossed salad and some of the snickerdoodle cookies they had frozen, dinner would be acceptable to everyone but David, for whom Hannah would make a grilled cheese sandwich.

. . . .

Dinner went smoothly. The only trouble spot was when the grilled cheese sandwich appeared on David's plate. Janice objected to what she considered coddling, saying that he was old enough to eat what the rest of the family was eating. How would he ever get used to a variety of foods if he only ate what he already liked?

David attacked the sandwich as if he were afraid that at any minute it might be removed from his plate. Janice laughed. "My God, David, slow down. I'm not going to take it away."

Madison turned to Ruby and asked in her best grown-up voice, "How are you feeling today?"

"Oh, much better, dear. I really don't need the wheelchair any more.... Hannah, perhaps we should return it to *Sunset?*...And I had a lovely day playing bridge at the Senior Center. So I'm almost as good as new."

"We're not returning anything to that place. Let them come get it if they want it."

"Doesn't it belong to Ruby?" Janice asked.

"We don't really know," replied Hannah. We just used it to take her out of that place. They didn't say anything at the time—I told them to put it on the bill, so I guess it does belong to Ruby."

Janice looked skeptically at her mother, but Hannah stared her down, silently defying her to make an issue of it. Janice got the message and turned the conversation to the impending lawsuit.

"Have you heard anything about the investigation?"

"No, not a word. I was thinking of calling Paul this morning, but didn't want to bother him. I know how busy he must be."

Ruby raised her eyebrows at this announcement. Seeing this, Hannah retracted. "Well, it was really Ruby who kept me from calling. She has more patience than I do."

Janice laughed, causing David to ask what was so funny. "Grandma isn't known for her patience—or her tact—when she's on a mission. And, believe me, she is on a mission."

"Oh, you mean with the disappearing ladies," he replied.

"They're not disappearing, stupid. They're missing. You make it sound like a magic trick," objected Madison.

"Okay, what is it with you two tonight? I could hear you arguing upstairs when I came home."

Madison looked at Hannah, who looked at David, who looked down at the table. Finally David spoke.

"She keeps bugging me about Vince, that new kid from Jefferson. I think he's neat and she keeps saying he's a drug dealer. He's not. He's smart, though and he knows a lot about computers, and he's fun. I like him. Anyway, it's none of her business who my friends are," David replied defiantly.

"Maddie? Do you know something about Vince or are you just circulating rumors?"

"Mom, that's not fair. I'm just trying to protect David. He's too trusting."

"That's very commendable; but if you start treating Vince as if he were a convicted drug dealer, that'll get around and others will start to believe it. Do you have any reason to believe that?"

"Well, no. But why else would he have been kicked out of Jefferson?" Madison sat back, with a look of triumph.

"Honey, do you know anything about Vince?" asked her mother.

Madison's moment of triumph faded. Looking uncomfortable, she turned to Hannah for support, who simply asked, "What have you heard about this Vince, darling?"

"Well, kids have been talking, you know. Loretta Marchand said her mother knew someone whose kid went to Jefferson and she told her that he'd been expelled. And you know they don't just expel kids for nothing."

Janice sighed. As principal of the high school, she knew the reason for Vince's transfer from Jefferson High, but was not about to breach confidentiality. However, she also knew this rumor would sprout wings and fly around the school if not put to rest.

"Look, I can't give you details. But let me assure you that Vince was not expelled; he was transferred at the request of his parents. He's not a drug dealer. He seems to be a very nice young man. And unless he does something unacceptable, I don't see any reason why he can't be David's friend. Case closed, okay?"

Madison murmured an "okay" and David, with an arm pump, shouted "Yes! I told you, jerko," to Madison.

"That's enough, David. I think it's time for homework. Upstairs. You, too, Maddie."

Both children left the room, David jubilant, Madison subdued.

Janice looked at Hannah and Ruby. "It's so hard to keep these rumors from spreading. And it's often the parents who are the main instigators, telling their kids things that the kids then pass on as gospel. This kid, Vince, is a basically good kid who got into trouble at his old school because he's gay, or at least he thinks he is. Once he announced it, he was the target of every goon in the school. His parents were concerned about his safety and asked to have him transferred. I don't know if he'll announce his sexual orientation here, but at least we don't have as many goons here as at Jefferson. And I've alerted the staff to be on the lookout for any problems before they spread."

Ruby was interested. "Do you have many gay students?" she wondered.

"We have a few who have come out. The other students seem to be okay with that. We haven't had any problems—except with some of the parents who think these kids should stay in the closet! These are the same parents who object to their children reading anything that strays outside their safety zone—nothing about gays, or race, or sex; nothing about anything but what they consider mainstream America."

"Mainstream America, my *tuchis*," exclaimed Hannah. "These small-minded people always claim that they represent the majority, when they're often just the loudest. If they had their way, everyone would be exactly like them—God forbid."

"You appealing to God—that's got to be a first," said Janice with a faked expression of shock on her face. "But, yes, you're right. They are typically close-minded, not wanting anything to shake up their well-established beliefs. But, unfortunately, those are the parents I have to deal with most of the time. But right now, I have work to do. So ladies, good night."

With that, they all got up, Janice to her study, and Hannah and Ruby to clear the table, put the dishes in the dishwasher, and head to the living room to watch another rerun of *Walker, Texas Ranger*. Even Ruby lusted after Walker!

Chapter 25

HANNAH AND RUBY WERE on their second cups of coffee. It had been a quiet morning— the children off to school, Janice off to work. They were quietly planning the day when the phone rang. It was Harold. Hannah handed the phone to Ruby and started to work on the daily crossword puzzle, not wanting to appear to be listening to the conversation that she was eagerly following.

"Hello, dear," said Ruby. "Oh, that's nice. Why, of course. I'd love to see you and the children….Tomorrow? Well, let me see if Hannah can drive me…. What? Oh, that would be lovely. Yes, tomorrow at 2:00. Wonderful. See you then."

Ruby was beaming when she hung up the phone. "He's going to pick me up tomorrow afternoon and I'll spend the day with him and the family. I haven't seen the children since last Christmas—why, that's almost a year. I think he's coming around, don't you?"

Hannah certainly didn't agree. In fact, she was worried that Harold would kidnap Ruby, put her in a place where she would never be found, and use the money from the house for himself. But how could she tell Ruby her fears? Oh, this was not good.

"Why, that's very nice. He's going to drive all the way up here—and back?" Hannah asked.

"That's what he said. When I mentioned checking with you to see if you could drive me, he said, oh, no, he would pick me up."

Hannah looked away. She hadn't seen her friend that happy since…well, she didn't know since when! But she just couldn't share her friend's happiness. She had to do something. But what?

Laundry! That's what she'd do. At least it would give her time to think— and the laundry had to be done, anyway.

· ·

That afternoon, while Ruby was napping, Hannah called Charlie. After describing Ruby's plans for the next day, expressing, even exaggerating, her fears for Ruby's safety, Charlie came up with his own plan: he and Hannah would go down to Detroit for some yet to be determined reason and deliver Ruby to Harold's home. Hannah was delighted with the plan and they spent the rest of the conversation thinking up plausible reasons for driving to Detroit. After Hannah rejected seeing a Lions game—Ruby would know that Hannah wouldn't drive a hundred miles for that!—they agreed that Charlie would be helping Hannah look for a "new" used car. With his knowledge of cars, he would be her technical advisor.

That sounded good to both of them. All that was left was for Hannah to raise the issue of wanting a car and getting Ruby to see that driving to Detroit, the car capital of the U. S., was reasonable. And, she would argue, it had the advantage of saving Harold the drive to pick up Ruby. Surely that would sound reasonable to Ruby.

And it did. Ruby, ever so eager to see the bright side of things, thought it was a marvelous idea—and so thoughtful!

· ·

"Grandma, tell me more about being Jewish." Madison had come downstairs in purple polka dotted pajamas and pink flowered robe and joined Hannah at the kitchen table. It was 6:30 in the morning, and the house was silent, the others still asleep.

"What are you doing up so early, darling? Are you okay?"

"I couldn't sleep."

"Is something wrong? Did something happen? Wait, let me get you something to eat—do you want juice? Or maybe some hot chocolate?"

"I'm not hungry."

Madison was a serious young woman. Today she looked even more serious. She took a deep breath and said, "Some kids were talking about a new boy at school. He's from New York and just moved here. They were like making fun of him—he dresses funny, wears a kind of cap on his head all the time, won't eat any of the cafeteria food. They said he was a Jew and that his people killed God. Did Jews kill God? I didn't think you could kill God."

Clearly perplexed, Madison looked to her grandmother for answers. Hannah realized that this was going to be a discussion requiring patience, tact, and, most of all, honesty. Fortifying herself with another cup of coffee, she responded, "No, you can't kill God—God is supposed to be a spirit, not something with a body that can be destroyed. What they're probably referring to is the killing of Jesus, who was a Jew—Yes, did you know that? The Christian religion was founded by a Jew— interesting, huh? And the history is complicated, too complicated to go into now, but there are books you should read to find out about the Romans and the Jews at that time.

"But your friends are probably simply repeating what they've heard from their parents. There aren't many Jewish people in this area, and what people aren't familiar with they fear. I hope the new boy isn't experiencing any troubles at school."

"Well, nobody talks to him—and they do kind of make jokes about his cap."

"Jewish men are supposed to have their heads covered—indoors as well as outdoors—to show respect to God. What, they should wear a cowboy hat? No, they wear a cap—it's called a *yarmulke,* very small, almost unnoticeable—except when they trim it with beads and other fancy things. And the food, well he probably comes from an orthodox family where they eat only kosher foods."

"What's 'kosher' mean?"

"Oy, darling, you're putting me through my paces this morning. You have to remember, your grandma is not religious. I never got into all the rules and regulations that religious Jews follow, so my answers are very simple. 'Kosher' means that the food is prepared in a certain way, blessed, sort of, by a rabbi— you know what that is, right?— and certain foods can't be eaten with other foods. Like meat can't be eaten with dairy—people who keep kosher homes have separate dishes for meat and dairy. Anyway, your new boy can't be sure the food at school is prepared the right way, so he brings his own food in."

"But you're Jewish and you eat meat and cheese—that's dairy, right?"

"Yes, but I'm not an orthodox Jew. They believe in all the restrictions that are listed in the Old Testament—well, not all, some are pretty silly. In fact, darling, your grandma is Jewish only in the sense that I was born and raised a Jew. I'm Jewish only in that sense; but when anti-Semitism—you remember, we talked about that?—raises its ugly head, then I announce that I'm Jewish—to sort of let them know they're talking to a Jew and they better be careful what they say. Otherwise, I'm what you might call an agnostic. Do you know what that means?"

"You don't believe in God?"

"Well, that's true. But atheists also don't believe in God. I'm not an atheist, because they claim they know there's no God. Me? I'm not that smart to know something like that. I just don't know, and I don't believe what I don't know. Besides, I think religion—Jewish, Christian, Muslim, all of them—makes people think that what they're doing is what God wants them to do, and they do terrible things. But that, too, is for another day. Anyway, where were we?"

"You don't believe in God. But aren't you afraid of dying? What if there is a God and a heaven—you won't be able to go there."

It was clear to Hannah that Madison was imagining her grandmother in hell! She spent the next half hour trying to explain her beliefs—or lack of belief. She explained how most Jews didn't stress believing in a hereafter, but were more concerned with how one lived one's life on earth. And that if there was a God like most people believe, it wouldn't be one that punished someone simply for not believing, if they had lived a good life, not hurting others, but, in fact, helping others.

It was at this part of the discussion that Janice entered the kitchen.

"How long have you two been up? And why so serious?"

"There's a new boy at school who's Jewish and the kids were teasing him. Grandma's been explaining Judaism to me. And, Mom, did you know that Grandma is a—what do you call it, Grandma?"

"Agnostic, darling."

"Yeah, an agnostic."

"Oh boy, you two have been serious. Well, it's too early for me to be serious—I need coffee and something to eat."

Fortifying herself with coffee and a piece of toast, Janice turned to Madison and asked, "What are your plans for today, honey?"

"I'm meeting Suzanne this afternoon. We're going to the mall—they're having a sale on shoes and she needs some."

"Well, you don't need shoes, do you?" asked Janice.

"No, I'm just going along. But, Mom, what do you think about Grandma's being an—agnostic—right, Grandma?"

"Right, darling."

"Well, that's up to Grandma, isn't it? We can't tell her what to believe."

"Are you an agnostic, too?"

'No. I believe in God. Grandma's skepticism didn't rub off on me."

"Well, I don't know what I believe," said Madison, clearly troubled by the awareness that one could actually decide whether to believe or not.

"Darling, it's not something you have to decide today," Hannah reassured her. "You have a lifetime to think about such things. And when you do decide, it's not as if you're stuck with that forever. Who knows? Maybe tomorrow I'll get a message from God that's so clear I'll become a believer! It's possible, no? Not likely, but possible."

Hannah was relieved to see Madison's slight nod of agreement. While she wanted Madison—and David—to learn to question what they were being taught, she didn't want them to worry unnecessarily. However, her relief lasted only a few minutes.

"But, Grandma, what if a person dies before they make up their mind? What happens to them, then?"

At this point, Janice interrupted. "I think that's enough about religion and dying for today. Let's talk about something else."

"No, Mom. It's important. I don't want Grandma to go to hell!"

"Darling," Hannah replied, "Jews don't believe in that kind of hell. At worst, I'll have to go to some kind of heavenly school where I'll be taught the truth. So don't worry about me. God, if there is a God, wouldn't be like those good-for-nothing church people on TV, talking about burning in hell if you don't send money to them—such rubbish. The God that I could believe in would be a loving God, who would want his children to love each other, and be good to each other. And, if someone couldn't believe because they didn't have enough evidence to believe, why God would supply the evidence— eventually. Remember what I said before—the God that Jews believe in is more concerned with how we live here on earth, than in just believing."

Hannah hoped that this simplified, and somewhat fanciful, view of Judaism would be enough to assuage Madison's concerns. She looked at Janice, raised her eyebrows, and nodded, indicating that she wouldn't attempt to impose her beliefs on the children—but also wouldn't lie about her beliefs— and got up to prepare breakfast for Madison.

By the time Ruby and David joined them in the kitchen, the conversation had turned to Hannah and Ruby's trip to Detroit, and to Hannah's newly acquired desire for a car of her own. Janice had her doubts; Hannah had never expressed an interest in having her own car. But she realized that something else was going on and that Hannah would explain later.

David had all sorts of advice about what kind of car to get. Nothing boring like a sedan—Hannah needed to update her image. A nice convertible, or sports car, or even an SUV—something that didn't say "Granny."

Everyone laughed at the picture of Hannah driving a convertible, which led Hannah to protest. "Why, that's an excellent idea, David. I hadn't thought of that…though I think a convertible isn't very practical in this part of the country. But I like the idea of a sports car. I think I'll look into that."

David beamed, pleased that his suggestion had taken roots; Madison looked amused; and Ruby, clearly focused on her meeting with Harold, seemed oblivious of the whole conversation.

Charlie arrived shortly after 11:00. He agreed to the cup of coffee and piece of Danish offered by Janice and started to sit at the table, only to be reminded by Hannah that they had to hurry. He gulped down the coffee, wrapped the Danish in a napkin, helped Ruby gather her walker and purse, and followed Hannah out the door.

David was the first one to speak. "Gee, Grandma can sure be bossy at times."

Janice laughed, "She sure can," she said.

....

The ride to Detroit was uneventful, with Ruby and Charlie in the front seat talking about the change in the weather and Charlie telling stories about his time in the Army, and Hannah in the back seat. Unable to hear the front-seat conversation, she pulled out the small paperback she always carried in her large purse and proceeded to read. The gentle rhythm of the car and the murmur of the conversation in the front seat resulted in Hannah dozing off after ten pages. When she awoke they were turning off the highway.

Ruby directed Charlie to Bloomfield Hills and Harold's house. It was a large, sprawling house, clearly designed to impress. With its combination of pseudo-Tudor elements, and large disproportionate colonial columns, it was an architectural monstrosity. The long circular driveway was surrounded by an expanse of well-manicured lawn. There were few trees, and no flowers that Hannah could see. To Hannah it was an ostentatious display of wealth, not taste. Ruby, however, was overflowing with pride, pointing out the many features that testified to Harold's success: six bedrooms, four bathrooms, a game room, two living rooms, a pool and tennis court in the back. Hearing this, Hannah was tempted to ask why they couldn't have used one of those bedrooms for Ruby!

Harold met them at the door, politely shook Charlie's hand, and gave Ruby a peck on the cheek. To Hannah, he just nodded. All that was visible from the doorway was a large living area which opened onto a patio overlooking what appeared to be a golf course. Except for the green of the outside grounds, everything was beige: beige walls, beige carpeting, beige furnishings, and an arrangement of beige flowers in a gold-colored vase! Without inviting them in, Harold told Charlie he would call when Ruby was ready to be picked up.

Realizing that they were being dismissed, Hannah and Charlie nodded and turned to go to the car. Hannah glanced back, concern apparent on her face. "What's the matter?" asked Charlie.

"I don't know. It's just a feeling. I'm worried about her."

"What could happen? She can't disappear from her own son's house."

"I know, but she could be persuaded to agree to something. You know, agree to give him all the money, or something like that. She's so anxious to believe he's a good son that I think he could convince her of anything—especially with the whole family there."

"Well, anything she agrees to would have to be witnessed by disinterested people and the family's certainly not disinterested. Besides, she could always claim she was coerced. I think she'll be okay. Let's find some place for lunch. I'm starved."

Not completely convinced by Charlie's unruffled demeanor, Hannah got into the car and reluctantly admitted that lunch was a good idea. She reminded him of a place she had seen on the way down where they could grab a late lunch. Charlie took off, spinning the tires, the Grand Marquis shooting down the driveway as if on a police chase. He was hungry.

It was now 1:30 and the lunch crowd had dispersed. They were seated in a booth near the window overlooking the traffic on Woodward Avenue. They ate in silence, talking only to request passing the ketchup for Charlie's fries or the pepper for Hannah's salad. When they were finished, Charlie, with a mischievous grin, asked Hannah what kind of car she was going to buy. He knew lots of used car dealers and could get her a deal. She just glared at him. "Don't be funny—I need a car like I need a heart attack. What are we going to do while we're waiting?"

"We could look at cars—okay, I can tell you don't want to do that. Well, then, do you want to do some shopping? There are malls around here."

"I don't know. I can't think of anything except Ruby. Do you think we could go pick her up before he calls?"

"Sure, but not now. She just got there! We'll give it until 4:00. That way we can say we need to get home before dark. But that gives us a few hours or so to do something."

"Look, if you want to look at cars, or visit some of your old friends, that's okay with me. It'll give us something to do."

"Sounds like a plan. One of the guys works nearby at a Subaru dealer. Let's go see what they have. Maybe you'll meet a car that you just can't resist," he said with a grin.

By the time they found the dealership, which was not quite where Charlie remembered, it was 3:00. Charlie and his friend immediately fell into talking about the newest models and what they could do. No "How've you been?" No "How's the family?"—just car talk. Hannah paced, alternating between concern for Ruby and dismay at the social skills of men. At 4:15 she interrupted the car talk and reminded Charlie that they had to pick up Ruby—now.

They arrived at the house, rang the doorbell, and waited. When Harold finally opened the door, his face was flushed and he was frowning. Whether something had happened to annoy him or whether their early arrival was the cause was not apparent. What was apparent was Harold's anger.

"Hi," said Hannah. "We thought we'd come by to pick Ruby up as we have to get back before dark. You know, Charlie's not so young any more. He can't drive in the dark."

Charlie frowned at Hannah, but said nothing.

Ruby came to the door. She had been crying, although that didn't alarm Hannah. Ruby could cry at the slightest offense. Hannah just wanted to get her out of there and find out what had happened.

"We need to get back, Ruby. Are you all finished here?" Hannah's attempt at innocence didn't fool Harold, who glared at her.

"Yes, I'm finished here. I'll get my purse. I'll just be a minute."

Harold stood there, continuing to glare at Hannah. When Ruby returned, he opened the door for her and said, "I'll be in touch." Ruby nodded and went to hug him, but he stood rigid as stone. She just patted his arm.

It took all of Hannah's resolve to keep from interrogating Ruby once they were in the car. They drove in silence, until Charlie turned to Ruby and asked if she was okay. She smiled at him and nodded. Taking a deep breath, she started to speak.

"I should have known it wasn't going to be a family gathering. Only Harold and Mimi were there—the boys were out someplace. We had lunch on the enclosed patio—beautiful yard, right on a golf course—and then we talked about the house. They wanted me to sign something agreeing that we could both use the money as we needed. That didn't sound so unreasonable..."

At this point, a yelp could be heard from the back seat, but Ruby continued. "Then Mimi started talking about how difficult it was going to be with both boys in college next year—Samuel is a senior in high school this year, and Martin is in his second year at Hillsdale—and how important it was for them to go to good schools and how expensive those schools were.

"I was all set to agree to Harold's proposal when the phone rang. Mimi answered it and came back to the patio just beaming. It seems their plans for a trip had been confirmed and they're going on a month cruise to the Greek Isles in the spring. When I asked how much that cost, Harold lost his temper; he said that he worked hard and deserved a vacation. Then I started looking around. Their house is filled with marble fixtures, Persian rugs, and genuine antiques—I can tell, I used to collect antiques, but nothing like what they have. And then I thought, why should I have to pinch my pennies so they can live like a Rockefeller! So I told them, I didn't think his idea was acceptable, but that I'd consult my lawyer for advice. Well, he really blew up at that. Said that family shouldn't need lawyers to settle their disagreements. And then you came. It was like in the movies, being rescued by the cowboys. So there you have it—how I spent the afternoon with my son."

Ruby took out a tissue and blew her nose. Hannah leaned forward and gave her friend a hug. "You did good, sweetie," she said. Charlie just drove, not commenting on the cowboys.

Chapter 26

Janice was anxious to hear how their day had gone. She had prepared a light meal for them, not knowing if they would have had time to stop for dinner, and was rewarded with a grateful Charlie, who looked about to faint from lack of food. When they were all seated at the table, Hannah turned to Ruby. "Tell Janice how things went," she prodded.

Ruby hesitated, but then quickly got to the point. She had not agreed to Harold's proposal, and was ready to go ahead with the plan Paul had arranged. And then she surprised everyone.

"And I think once that's settled, I need to start looking for a place of my own. There are some new apartments on Lincoln Road I've heard about. Mrs. Griswold—you know from the Center? Well, she said she knows some people who like it there. So I thought I'd look into them this week."

Hannah and Janice glanced at each other. It was Janice who spoke first. "You know you're welcome to stay here for as long as you want. You haven't been a burden at all. In fact, I think you're a good influence on my mother!"

"Thank you, darling!" Hannah responded, with a sarcastic grin. "But Janice is right, Ruby. You don't have to rush off into anything. Get your strength back first. Then you can think of moving."

"You've all been so kind to me—I just don't want to overstay my welcome."

And then Ruby started to tear up. Seeing Hannah's rising annoyance, Janice kicked her under the table. "You're no trouble at all," she said to Ruby, "so don't let that affect your decision."

Charlie alternated between eating and looking at each of the women as they spoke. He started to say something, but was cut short by Hannah's glare. He returned to eating.

The conversation moved on to the practical details of implementing Paul's financial plans for Ruby, which led Janice to report that Paul had invited them all to join him for brunch Sunday morning. His firm had just added *Justine*, a new restaurant in town, to its client list, and he wanted to check out the menu. Charlie was the first to respond. "I've heard good things about that place, although it's quite pricey."

"Well, then, this may be the only opportunity we get to eat there," laughed Janice.

"That's so lovely of him to include us," said Ruby. "Should we dress up?"

"How dressy could it be?" asked Hannah. "This is Brewster, where a clean t-shirt is considered dressing up."

Janice ignored Hannah's remark, and replied to Ruby, "I think any of your outfits would be fine. Nothing too fancy. So, Charlie, can you be here about 11:00 tomorrow? Paul will pick us up, but we'll probably need two cars. The kids, especially David, are really excited about this."

Plans made, Charlie finally out the door, the three women tidied up the kitchen before they headed off to their respective rooms, each with her own thoughts about the day's events.

. . . .

Charlie showed up fifteen minutes before 11:00. When Paul arrived shortly after, in his Mustang,

Charlie suggested they all go in his newly washed Grand Marquis, which could easily accommodate six people, seven if they squeezed four in the back seat. With Ruby and Paul in the front seat with Charlie and the others in the back, they took off.

They were seated close to the buffet tables, which were loaded with appetizers, breakfast and dinner foods, and a large array of desserts, which seemed to mesmerize David. After being warned by Janice that there would be no dessert until he had eaten a meal, David had to decide: breakfast or dinner? He wasn't up for such a decision, so he helped himself to something from everywhere. When he returned from his trip to the buffet tables, his plate was obscenely filled with food: waffles with strawberries, bacon and eggs, lasagna, chicken, mashed potatoes, and a thick slice of roast beef.

Madison looked at his plate and exclaimed, "That's so gross! You're a pig!" Her plate held some appetizers and a large salad.

Janice also looked at David's plate. "I don't see any green on that plate. How about some vegetables?"

David nodded, his mouth already full, indicating that he would go back for vegetables after he emptied his plate. He knew dessert wouldn't be forthcoming until he had something green on his plate.

Charlie's plate was almost as filled as David's, although he seem to have concentrated solely on the dinner dishes. Roast beef was a treat for him, so his plate was overflowing with two large slices of roast beef, a mountain of mashed potatoes with gravy, and a side of lasagna!

Ruby had trouble carrying her plate, as she was still somewhat unsteady on her feet. If Charlie had not been so interested in the food, he would have jumped at the chance to help her. But he missed his opportunity and Paul had come to the rescue. Walking with her down the buffet tables, he carried her plate as she chose the few items to eat. He reminded her that it was all one price so she should try as many things as she wanted but, even at eighty, Ruby was concerned about gaining weight. She returned to their table with a modest amount of salad, chicken and vegetables, claiming that she was saving room for dessert.

By the time they were ready for dessert, Paul had turned the conversation to Ruby's finances. It was all settled. Paul would send Harold an official letter notifying him that the money from the sale of the house was to be put into a special account at the bank. The money would be handled by the bank, as Trustee, and a monthly check would be deposited in Ruby's account until her death, at which time whatever was left over would go to Harold. This would all be accompanied by documentation from the court, which would include a deadline for the transfer of the money into this special account.

Everyone raised a glass to celebrate the occasion—some with iced tea, some with mimosas, and some with coke. Then they all hit the dessert table for further celebration.

David returned with another obscenely filled plate, which caused Janice to comment on the virtue of restraint and Madison to again call him a pig. Neither comment, however, deterred him from attacking the assortment of cakes, puddings, and ice cream assembled on the small plate.

Over coffee, Paul reminded them that the investigation of the missing women was underway and as soon as he had any information he would let them know. This reminder led Ruby to tear up, but a glare from Hannah, who was quickly tiring of Ruby's sensitivity, stopped the actual flow of tears.

....

That evening, while Ruby and the children were watching TV, Janice took Hannah aside. "Mom, you're being unfair to Ruby. I don't think she notices, but every time she starts to cry, you glare at her. She's not being phony, she just expresses herself by crying—whether it's good news or bad."

"I know she's not being phony, but, what...tears for everything? I don't have time to cater to her 'sensitive' nature. I know she's had a difficult time with her son, but enough already. Lots of people have worse problems and they don't cry all the time."

"You can't judge her by how you would handle things. You're a tough cookie; she isn't. I can't really imagine her living alone. Even when she's completely healed and can get around on her own, I think she'll need someone with her. Maybe she should go into some sort of assisted living arrangement."

"I don't want to raise that issue. I think she'll really cry if we suggest that. You know, what I'm hoping—I know it's going to sound far-fetched—I'm hoping that she and Charlie get together. I know he has the hots for her, and she's becoming more dependent on him, so, who knows, with a little finagling, maybe it's possible."

"Oh God, don't start playing matchmaker! Just be a little more patient with her."

"Okay, darling. I'll try. But it's not going to be easy. I have little tolerance for wimps."

Janice shook her head and smiled. Hannah was Hannah and Janice knew there was no changing her. But she also knew that her mother was a kind and caring person and wouldn't intentionally hurt Ruby's feelings. She'd have to leave it at that.

Chapter 27

IT RAINED ALL DAY Monday. A cold, bone-chilling rain. Ruby's plans to
go apartment hunting were put on hold. A phone call from Charlie was
handled by Hannah, who told him that, no, they weren't going to look for
apartments, but, yes, he could take Ruby to lunch at the Senior Center—and
maybe stay for bridge and poker?

Hannah had made these arrangements without consulting Ruby. Feeling
sheepish about making plans without Ruby's involvement, she went out of her
way to be patient with her. Ruby was worried about how Harold would react
when he received Paul's letter. Hannah's initial reaction was to say, "Who
cares?" But taking a deep breath, she allowed Ruby to fret a bit longer before
interrupting her, saying, "Let's watch *The View;* we've been so busy we haven't
seen it for a while. In fact, the TiVo recorded all of last week so we could watch
those, too. I keep forgetting about that. I still don't understand how it knows
what to record, or how it can go backwards and then catch up when you're
actually watching the real show. David tried to explain it to me, but it's still
a mystery to me. Anyway, we could catch today's show before Charlie picks
you up. Later this afternoon, we could watch the others, if you want."

Ruby agreed that it was a good idea. Having been reminded of the
possibilities of TiVo, she asked Hannah if she knew how to record her soap
operas. Hannah hated soap operas—all self-involved, rich people who wouldn't
last a day in the real world. And the problems they had! Who knew who was
whose father? And everyone all dressed up and then undressed, hopping into
bed with whoever was the flavor of the week. Such nonsense—and such a
bad influence on women who thought that kind of life was desirable. She
was tempted to go into her critique of how capitalism used soap operas to
brainwash and sedate women so that they wouldn't realize how they were

being manipulated into buying products they didn't need and trying to achieve a life they couldn't attain—and in her eyes, shouldn't even desire—and how it kept people, especially women from seeing the injustices around them, but, remembering Janice's talk the previous evening, she just smiled and said, "sure."

Charlie arrived shortly before noon and in response to Hannah's rather perfunctory offering of coffee and a Danish—he was going to lunch, why would he need a Danish?—he accepted. Hannah wondered if the man had any limits. He seemed to be able to eat, and eat heartily, at any time—and he wasn't fat!

He had brought a present for Ruby—an intricately carved ebony cane, topped by a pewter band. Ruby gushed about its beauty and how thoughtful the gift was. Hannah had to agree about its beauty and Charlie's thoughtfulness, but thought Ruby's gushing was a bit over the top. Charlie, however, seemed delighted at Ruby's effusive praises.

They left, Ruby with the cane in her right hand, and Charlie with Ruby on his right arm, making a quite attractive couple. Hannah smiled as Charlie opened an umbrella and placed it over Ruby with his left hand, which required him to bend awkwardly over her. Her matchmaking plans seemed to be working.

. . . .

Hannah sat down in her recliner, intending to read the book in her lap. After reading a few pages, she put the book down, unable to concentrate. Something was bothering her, but she couldn't think what it was. The morning had gone well. She thought back to yesterday, but found nothing had happened to disturb her. In fact, the day had been fine. What was wrong with her? Why was she near tears?

Well, that wouldn't do! No crying for her—especially since she didn't know why she felt like crying. She got up and went to the kitchen. Maybe she needed some lunch. Finding nothing of interest in the refrigerator, she resorted to heating up a can of soup from the cupboard. Fortunately she didn't have blood pressure problems, otherwise canned soup would be a no-no.

Sitting at the table, she tried to take stock of her feelings. She was in good health, the problems with Ruby were getting settled, and the investigation over the missing women was underway. Was she bored? Was she tired of worrying about Ruby? What was wrong with her? She was fortunate: she had a wonderful family, Janice had made a comfortable place for her, she felt she contributed to the family, taking over some of the responsibilities from

Janice's shoulders, being there for the children. She felt she belonged, she wasn't a burden.

But that was it! This couldn't continue! Seeing Janice and Paul yesterday, she realized that their relationship was serious. It wasn't simply a friendship, a dating situation; it was love! Surely, they would want to move on, and moving on typically meant living together—or, hopefully, in her eyes, getting married. She would be in the way. No new couple needs a mother, or mother-in-law, around all the time. She would have to find a place of her own. And she would have to raise the issue. Janice would never ask her to move out.

Sighing, with a heavy heart but no tears, Hannah got up, washed the dishes, and returned to the living room. Well, that was better. At least she knew what she had to do.

. . . .

It was almost 4:00 when Charlie and Ruby returned. Ruby was anxious to bring Hannah up-to-date about events at the Center, and Charlie was anxious to leave before she got into that. He bid goodbye to Hannah, kissed Ruby on the cheek, and took off.

The women chatted, Hannah laughing at some of the stories Ruby related. They were in the kitchen, Hannah preparing the Hungarian goulash they would have for dinner, and Ruby sitting at the table chopping the ingredients for a salad. After Ruby had finished her stories, Hannah raised the issue of apartments. "What are the rooms like, the ones at that place you were talking about?" she asked.

"I haven't seen them, but according to the brochure there are lots of options, you know, different number of bedrooms. The pictures show a nice-sized kitchen and living area." She got up to get the brochure from her purse. "We should go look at them."

"Are they expensive?"

"Well, it says here that the price ranges from $800 for what they call a studio apartment—which I wouldn't want—to about $1,500 for a three bedroom—which would be too big for me."

"We could go look at them tomorrow. I might be interested, too," Hannah said nonchalantly, browning the beef and onions.

Ruby looked up from the brochure to glance at her friend's face. "What are you talking about? What's wrong?"

"Nothing's wrong. Why should anything be wrong just because I might be interested in a change? You know, things don't last forever; the kids are getting older, Janice is getting more involved with Paul. It just may be time for me to move on, you know, get my own place—leave the kids their privacy."

Hannah said all this without looking at Ruby, spending more time fussing with the goulash than was necessary. The last thing she wanted was for Ruby to notice how upset she was; that would just push Ruby over the edge and Hannah wasn't in the mood to deal with Ruby's tears tonight.

Desperately trying to change the topic, she asked, "Where is everyone tonight? The kids should be home from school by now."

"Don't you remember? Janice said they would all be late—she had a meeting and the kids had something to do after school and they would come home with her."

"Oh, yeah, I forgot. Well, that works out good; dinner will be ready by the time they get home."

"Hannah, is something bothering you? I don't understand why you're thinking of moving. Has Janice said anything? Am I causing a problem here?"

Realizing that she was being unfair to her friend, Hannah sighed, washed her hands, and sat down next to Ruby at the table.

"I'm sorry I raised the issue. No, Janice hasn't said anything. But you saw them yesterday. Paul can't keep his eyes off of her, and she tries to appear aloof but you can see she adores him, too. What do they need an old woman around for? They should have a house to themselves."

"Now, who's being the foolish one! You don't even know if they are going to move in together, and you certainly don't know that they would want you to leave. Why don't you talk to Janice, tell her what you're thinking. Then you'll know where you stand."

"She'd never ask me to leave. I'd have to be the one to raise the issue. Even then, she wouldn't agree—she'd think she wasn't being a good daughter. No, I'd have to present it as a done deal—tell her I've decided to move out, have found a place…"

"But you don't even know if they're going to move in together! You're running on like a chicken with its head chopped off. I've never seen you like this. You're always the sensible one. You're making me seem sensible!"

Hannah smiled. "You're right; I am being foolish. But it's something I have to consider. Maybe I will talk to Janice, though. Put the bee in her bonnet, as they say. Come, let's catch a little of *Walker* while the goulash cooks. What do the kids call it? Eye candy?"

When Janice and the kids arrived home, they found two old ladies sitting in front of a blaring TV, sound asleep.

. . . .

Dinner conversation was dominated by Madison relating the recent adventures of Kenny, her former boyfriend, and Becky, her former girlfriend. David, after making some gagging gestures at his sister and receiving threatening signals from his mother, quickly ate his food and asked permission to leave the table. Permission was quickly granted.

"I don't know what I saw in him," Madison was saying. "He's not really that cute, and he's such a liar. Everyone knows he's cheating on Becky, but she thinks he's just perfect—she struts around as if she's won some prize. Yeah, he's a prize! Wait'll she finds out what a jerk he is. But it serves her right. She saw how he treated me—her best friend—and then she goes off with him! Everyone's laughing."

Hannah and Ruby just listened, not wanting to say the wrong thing—which they were likely to do. Janice, however, didn't have the luxury of just listening. This was her daughter and her responsibility.

"Well, honey, do you think that Becky really knew how you felt about Kenny? Remember, you kept saying he was just a friend. Maybe she didn't realize you would see her dating him as a betrayal."

"Mom, of course she knew. And even if she didn't, she could have asked me how I felt about her dating him."

"And what would you have said?"

Madison hesitated. "I guess I would have told her to go ahead, I don't care."

Janice smiled. "So why do you care now? Honey, Becky was a friend of yours, and I know you feel hurt. But, try to see it through her eyes. She's not a particularly pretty, or popular, girl. This guy—who is cute—asks her out. You told her you're not really interested. I know you were hurt at the dance—and he behaved badly even if you weren't serious about each other. But who knows what he told her. To her, this is her big chance to date a popular guy. You're right, he is a jerk, and she is going to be hurt by him. But she's going to need her friends even more when that happens."

"You expect me to be friends with her, again? No way!"

"I'm not saying you have to be best friends with her again. But you don't have to join the group laughing at her and making nasty remarks. I think you're better than that."

Madison started to object, looked around the table, and shrugged. "Yeah, okay," she responded.

Ruby, relieved that the conversation hadn't turned confrontational, suggested that they all share some of the brownies she had brought back from the Senior Center. She had taken them for Charlie, but forgot to give them to him. "This is better," she decided. "He doesn't really need any more sweets."

Somehow David heard the word "brownies" and was down the stairs in a flash, ready for his share. Janice rolled her eyes. "I don't know which is sharper on him—his nose or his ears!" she exclaimed.

Chapter 28

THE EARLY MORNING SKY was overcast when Hannah gazed out the kitchen window. The trees were bare, the grass still green in spots, but with a slight covering of frost. Winter would soon be here, she thought. She had lived in the north all her life and the cold didn't bother her; it was the barrenness of the landscape that depressed her. This was especially so in Michigan which, surrounded by lakes, was a contender for the state with the least number of sunny days. She would need some projects to keep her mind off her annual depression.

Thinking of projects, her mind went immediately to the missing women. She made a mental note to check on the status of the investigation. Surely, Paul's PI should have something to report by now.

Hearing stirrings throughout the house, she got up from the table and started to prepare breakfast for the family. Today was an oatmeal day—with cold cereal for David. Perhaps she was spoiling him by catering to his food preferences. But wasn't that what grandmas were for? He would be on his own soon enough.

The next hour was a flurry of activity: breakfast for Janice and the children, finding David's gym shoes, and getting everyone out the door on time. Ruby had wisely stayed in her room until everyone left.

Sitting at the table, drinking another coffee while Ruby ate her oatmeal, Hannah raised the issue of apartment hunting. She had circled some listings in the classified section of the newspaper and showed them to Ruby. Together they narrowed the list down to three possibilities—all within the city limits.

While Ruby showered and dressed, Hannah called Paul's office. She was surprised when she was put through to him immediately and started by apologizing for bothering him. After being assured it was no bother, she proceeded to ask about the investigation. Had they found anything out? Had they talked to the police? Did they find any of the recent missing women?

Paul had no new information, but promised to get back to her later that day after he met with the PI. Hannah thanked him, and was pleased when he quickly accepted her invitation for dinner that evening. She just hoped that Janice would be equally pleased, which led her to call Janice to find out!

Ruby emerged from her room, dressed in a navy blue skirt suit that Hannah had not seen before and which reminded her of what an attractive woman Ruby was. Smiling, Hannah pointed to the freshly brewed coffee on the counter and motioned for Ruby to join her at the table.

Carefully sitting so as to not crease her skirt, she suggested that perhaps they should call Charlie and have him come with them. "He knows so much about things like plumbing and electricity—things I don't know anything about. You know, Bernie took care of all of that and after he died I always just hired people. But Charlie really knows about these things—he's so smart."

Hannah didn't see why that would be necessary at this stage, but agreed to invite him along. After all, the more they saw each other, the more Ruby might realize the advantages of having him around. Hannah just hoped that Ruby didn't also see the disadvantages!

Charlie arrived within 30 minutes, giving the appearance of having been sitting by the phone waiting for a call from Ruby. He extended his arm to Ruby, who was leaning on her new cane, and they left the house, Hannah trailing behind. If she weren't so anxious for them to "bond" Hannah would have considered him rude.

They spent the morning looking at apartments. Most of those in Ruby's price range were in shoddily built housing for transient workers at the local Casino. Contrary to Hannah's initial reaction, she found Charlie quite helpful.

"You'd have a problem with the water pressure in this place," he reported at the first stop—"you can't flush the toilet and wash the dishes at the same time." At another place, he announced, "If you want toast with your coffee you're going to blow a fuse! This electrical system is way underpowered."

The last place they visited, the one in the brochure Ruby had showed Hannah, seemed ideal. Heating, water, and electrical systems were deemed adequate by Charlie; the rooms were spacious enough and, since the building was new, it was clean; the appliances, while not top-of-the-line, were certainly adequate. It was a real possibility.

All of a sudden, Ruby started to cry. Charlie, not sure what was happening, looked at Hannah, who said, "It's okay. She's just overwhelmed. She does this a lot." Then she turned to Ruby and said, "Stop crying! You don't have to make a decision today. Think about it; there's no rush. You can stay with us as long as you want." Which was not quite true. If Hannah considered herself a burden for a new couple, Hannah and Ruby combined would be even more so. But this was not the time to remind Ruby of that.

Ruby dried her tears and smiled sheepishly. "I know, I know. I'm a silly old woman. Just ignore me."

Charlie appeared anxious to avoid any more of Ruby's tears, so he suggested lunch at the Senior Center. Hannah refused his invitation and asked to be dropped off at home so she could make preparations for dinner. And once she mentioned dinner, she realized that she had to invite Charlie, too! The more the merrier, she thought, hoping that Janice would agree!

At home, she quickly went through her recipe collection, made a list for shopping, and, using Ruby's car, drove to *Marty's*.

. . . .

Paul arrived shortly after Charlie, who had appeared with a large bouquet of red carnations and white lilies for Janice, who thanked him and went to put them in water. Ruby couldn't stop praising him for his thoughtfulness. "What a lovely thing to do, Charlie," she cooed, which made Charlie blush even more.

In the kitchen, Hannah opened the oven to check the brisket they would have for dinner and looked up at Janice who was preparing a vase for the flowers. Their eyes locked and both women burst into laughter. "I think your matchmaking attempts have been successful, Mom. They're goofy about each other."

"Yes, they're smitten, and that's good. But why do they have to act like lovesick teenagers? What I have to go through when I'm with them, you shouldn't know. You'd think this was their first relationship—or beginning of one. After all, Ruby was married, and I'm sure Charlie has had women friends before. They act like *young* teenagers, not even as mature as Maddie! But I wish the best for them. A little companionship at their age is nothing to joke about."

Janice looked at her mother. "Do you ever miss that kind of companionship, Mom? I mean since Dad's gone?"

"You know, darling, I was spoiled by your father. I can't imagine being with anyone else. Oh, it might be nice to go out to dinner or a movie with someone. But I'm afraid I'm too impatient. Men my age still seem to think that women need protection, that we're dainty little things that need a big strong man around, and that drives me up a wall. So I'm better off the way things are…. Of course, maybe I should try some young men—maybe I'd find them more compatible," Hannah suggested, with a wink at Janice.

Janice just shook her head and laughed. "I doubt it," she said.

....

Dinner was proclaimed a success by Charlie, who had helped himself to two portions of everything and was waiting for dessert, which Ruby had hinted was something special. When the dessert appeared—a three-tier chocolate cake with cream filling between each layer, and a shiny chocolate glaze on the top that Ruby had baked and which was served with a raspberry sauce—Charlie was speechless, looking at Ruby with such devotion, it brought a smile to Hannah's lips. This was surely a testament to the truth of the adage that the way to a man's heart was through his stomach.

David also was speechless, or almost so. "Wow," he gushed. "That's the biggest cake I've ever seen."

Ruby blushed at the reaction her cake was receiving and avoided any eye contact as she proceeded to distribute large slices around the table. Janice and Madison protested that the slices were too large, that they would share one, which prompted David to look up. "Too large?" he asked. "I'll eat the other piece," he volunteered, to which his mother responded, "One piece is enough for you, young man. Remember what I told you about being greedy?"

"This isn't greedy. I'm just helping out," he replied, in full realization that Janice wouldn't see his offer as the generous gesture it was intended to be.

After the children had retreated to their respective rooms, Ruby related their apartment hunting adventures, detailing the plusses and minuses of each place. Hannah reported that the last place was promising and that they were going to follow it up later in the week.

Paul announced that he had some information to report. He turned to Ruby and said, "Ruby, the arrangements have been made at the bank. Harold deposited the full amount of the house sale into your special account and you'll start receiving your monthly payments at the beginning of the month, each month. The man in charge at the bank is Robert Fairfax, and if you have any questions or problems he's the one to go to.

"And my other bit of news is from Pete, our PI. He's found your missing Mrs. Bradshaw! She's presently at *Whispering Pines*, a nursing home over in Clinton Township. He wasn't able to talk to her, but the staff there said she was transferred from *Sunset Manor* a few weeks ago. They have an arrangement with *Sunset,* who sends people over when they run out of space. When he asked about payments, the staff clammed up, claiming they didn't know anything about that. He's going to do some more checking on that, but he thinks there's fraud involved somehow. You know, payments to *Sunset*, who then sends payments to *Whispering Pines*, which are considerably cheaper. So somehow *Sunset* pockets the extra money—which if it's federal Medicare money means big trouble for them. Anyway, he's on it like shit...whoops, sorry. Let's just say he's on it."

Hannah, afraid that Ruby would start crying, turned to her and asked, "Were they short of space when you were there?"

Ruby looked confused, wanting both to cry and answer Hannah's question. Focusing on the question, she replied, "No, they had lots of empty rooms. In fact, I remember some rumors about reduced schedules because there wasn't that much work to do. Some of them were annoyed, but some preferred it because it gave them more time with their families. You know, most of them are young women with young children at home and..."

Hannah cut her off. Ruby could go off on tangents if you let her. "Well, that supports what this Pete was saying. They transfer patients out to make a profit, the lousy bastards!"

"Mom," warned Janice. "Enough with the language."

"Sorry, but it bothers me that those places can get away with treating people as commodities to be used for making money. That's the trouble with this country—it's all geared toward profit-making and nobody cares."

"Well, obviously, some people care and something will be done. Just let Paul handle this. Don't get involved."

"What? You want I should just stick to my knitting and not get involved in things? What? I'm just a meddling old woman who should mind my own business? Well, this is my business..."

Paul, not knowing where this was going, interrupted Hannah. "Hannah, you'll know everything as soon as we do. You won't be kept out of the loop."

Hannah nodded and, sheepishly apologized for losing her temper. "I know you didn't mean anything—I just overreacted."

Looking around the table at the shocked faces of Ruby and Charlie, who obviously weren't used to flashes of temper, Hannah smiled and said, "More coffee, anyone?" Charlie took that as an opportunity to announce that it was time for him to leave—an early morning meeting, you know!

Paul followed him out, after making arrangements to call Janice the next day to make plans for the weekend, and after giving Hannah a big hug.

"What was that all about?" Janice asked Hannah as they were cleaning the kitchen. "When did I ever accuse you of being a meddling old woman? And what's this about knitting? When did you ever knit? Where did all that come from?"

Hannah waved her away. "It's nothing," she said. "I just got carried away.

Don't worry; your old mom isn't getting paranoid. Let's finish this up. I need to check on Ruby. I think I scared her—she's kind of delicate, you know."

"Yeah, I'm sure she appreciated your language!" Janice responded, as Hannah went in search of Ruby.

Chapter 29

Hearing nothing from Paul in the following days, Hannah was unusually irritable. Everything reminded her of how messed up the "system" was, how corrupt all public officials were, and how slow Ruby was in making decisions. She had reached the point where she was wondering if living with Ruby would be too trying for her. If it weren't for the cost, she would have preferred moving into a place of her own. Of course, she hadn't raised the possibility of moving in with Ruby; perhaps Ruby wouldn't want that!

The children had noticed a change in Hannah. "Why is Grandma so grouchy?" asked David, one evening after a particularly disagreeable dinner, where Hannah and Janice had loudly argued about the new city-wide proposal on increasing taxes for an addition to the local library. Janice was surprised at Hannah's opposition to the proposal on the grounds that there was no guarantee the money would be used for its expressed purpose. "You can't trust any of those guys," Hannah had said, "they'll just use the money for their own interests—they probably already have decided to give the construction job to their friends—and the library won't be helped at all. There'll just be some more rich people in town! And there are already enough rich people, people who do nothing for this town."

Janice thought that reaction was unreasonable, claiming that Hannah's cynicism was getting out of hand—which led Hannah to expound even further about the evils of the system and how Janice was too trusting and could use a little cynicism.

Ruby just sat quietly, clearly uncomfortable, and the children just looked back and forth between Janice and Hannah, not sure what was happening. When Hannah abruptly got up to clear the table, the children looked at their mother with questions in their eyes. Janice smiled and said, "It's okay. Grandma's having a bad day. She'll be better tomorrow."

David couldn't resist saying, with a mischievous grin, "Is that like having a bad hair day?"—which elicited a groan from Madison, who replied, "You're such a dork. You don't take anything seriously. Can't you see that Grandma's not herself?"

"Oh! Who is she then?" At that point David quickly got up from the table and ran upstairs, laughing all the way. Janice looked at Madison and shook her head. "He's young, yet, Maddie. He'll grow up—I hope! Why don't you and Ruby go watch some TV while I help Grandma with the dishes?"

Janice sat at the table without moving. What was wrong with Hannah? She was usually the one who was reasonable when Janice misunderstood her intentions. Could there be a physical cause for Hannah's behavior lately? With a sigh, she got up, reluctant to enter the kitchen, not knowing how Hannah would react. She didn't want any more arguing.

But she didn't have to worry about arguing. Hannah was standing at the sink, head down, shoulders shaking. "Mom," Janice cried, as she ran over to her. "What's wrong?"

Hannah wiped her tears, and turned to Janice. "Oh, darling, I'm so sorry. That the children should see me that way—I'm so embarrassed. I don't know what's got into me these last few days. I'm so angry about everything."

"When's the last time you saw a doctor? You know, it could be something physical, hormones or something."

Hannah blew her nose and laughed. "What, you think I'm menopausal at seventy-eight?"

"There are other hormonal changes, you know. It's certainly worth it to find out."

"Darling, we need to talk. I don't want you should say anything, just listen. Okay?"

"Sure."

"Well, I'm thinking of getting a place of my own…no, just listen. The kids are getting older, Maddie will be going off to college in the fall, and David is growing up—yes, he really is! They don't need someone at home for them. And, I don't know what plans you and Paul have, but you don't need an old woman around to get in the way. I haven't mentioned this to Ruby, but I was thinking that maybe she and I could find a place together—that way her money would go further, and my social security would pay for my half."

Hannah stopped there. Janice just looked at her.

"No," Janice responded, "unless you're unhappy here. If you really don't want to live here, then that's a different story. But if you think you're not needed or that you'll be in the way—and I don't even know what that means!—you're just wrong. The kids adore you. They'd be terribly upset if you left. And I want you here. It's not so much a matter of need; we could get along without you, perhaps not as well, though, but this house wouldn't be the same without you. I *want* you to stay!"

Both women had tears in their eyes by this time. Hannah handed the box of tissues to Janice, laughed, and said, "Look at us; soon we'll be crying as easily as Ruby does, God forbid."

Wiping her eyes, Janice asked, "Is that what's been bothering you? That you think you're not wanted here? That's just silly. I think you really ought to see a doctor, maybe there is something wrong—you know, depression, stress, something like that."

"Okay, I'll see the doctor. But we have to talk about this again—when we're not so emotional, okay?"

Janice shook her head and hugged her mother. "No, not okay. But we'll see."

....

The next morning Janice woke the children, cautioning them to be quiet as Hannah was still asleep. Maddie looked concerned but was reassured when Janice told her that Hannah was just tired. David, true to form, nodded and said that he hoped she wouldn't be so grouchy when she woke up.

After a breakfast of Cheerios and juice—and coffee for Janice—they quietly left the house. It was after 9:00 when Hannah finally awoke. Worried that the family had also overslept, she was relieved to find a note from Janice explaining that she would pick up some Chinese food for dinner.

Hannah was at the kitchen table when Ruby walked in. "Good morning, sleepy head," Hannah said. "I hope you had as good a sleep as I did. I didn't even hear the kids this morning."

Ruby shook her head. "I can't believe I slept so late. It's almost 10:00!"

"Well, don't feel so bad. I didn't get up until 9:00. But I do feel better—maybe I needed the sleep. Well, what do you want to do today? Janice is bringing Chinese food home for dinner, so we don't have to worry about that. Do you want to go to the bank and check on that new account they set up for you? We could have lunch at that nice restaurant downtown—you know the one I mean?"

"You mean *Clarissa's*? That would be nice." She blushed before saying, "Do you think we could invite Charlie? I don't think he eats out very much, except for the Center."

Hannah hesitated before answering. She had to admit that Charlie wasn't really the problem. He was pleasant enough, even interesting when you got him talking; it was Ruby who was the problem when Charlie was around. But she said, "Okay, but don't eat too much now. We'll have a nice lunch."

Hannah and Ruby were at the door waiting for Charlie. Ruby was worried that something was wrong: "He's never late. I hope he hasn't been in an accident." Hannah thought that was an extreme reaction for a delay of just ten minutes. He arrived shortly after noon and explained that construction in his neighborhood had delayed him. Driving to the bank, Ruby confessed her fears, which caused Charlie to look uncomfortable. He stared straight ahead, jaw clenched, and said, "That was silly. I was only ten minutes later than I said."

Hannah could see that if Ruby didn't pull back she would scare Charlie off. No man, especially one who had lived alone for most of his life, wanted to know that his every movement was being monitored, that he could so easily cause concern for someone else. Hannah would somehow have to raise the issue with Ruby, but she doubted it would make a difference. Ruby seemed to be the sort of woman who invested all of her energy into living for the man in her life. She had done fine as a widow, when there was no man in her life, but this was different. Hannah wondered if Bernie, Ruby's late husband, had felt the same way—smothered. Perhaps that was why he hadn't shared much with her. Not like Leo, she reflected. There wasn't an evening they didn't spend hours after dinner, sitting in the living room or on the small stoop in front of their house, sharing the events of their day. It didn't matter if it was worrying about a problem at work, or arguing about the latest foolishness in Washington, or just relishing the tales of Janice's latest accomplishments. What was in one's head came out one's mouth, and the other responded. That was what marriage was for Hannah. Sadly, she realized that that was not what marriage had been for Ruby.

After a quick visit with Robert Fairfax at the bank, who explained the procedure for Ruby to access her funds, they strolled down the street to *Clarissa's*, a somewhat overly decorated restaurant, with frilly curtains, doilies on the tables, lots of pastel colors and paintings of women with parasols carrying bouquets of spring flowers. It was usually filled with women eating salads, but there were a few brave men indulging in heartier meals; the food *was* extremely good.

Hannah thought that Charlie might have bolted if he hadn't seen men in the restaurant. But one look at the menu convinced him that he would be able to find something to eat. Ruby ordered the house salad, Hannah a chicken salad, and Charlie a super-sized burger with fries. All were pleased with their lunches, which they extended by ordering dessert.

As they lingered over their desserts, the conversation quickly turned to the investigation of the missing women. Hannah expressed her frustration with how slowly the investigation was going, but Ruby chastised her for her impatience. After all, they had just heard that Mary Bradshaw had been found—wasn't that good news? "In fact," Ruby suggested, "why don't we go to that place—*Whispering* something—and see her? We don't have to worry about dinner tonight, so we'd have plenty of time. Charlie, do you know where that place is?"

"Sure, it's down by the river. It's only about twenty minutes from here."

Ruby looked at Hannah for a response, which she quickly received. "Great idea! Maybe she can tell us about other women who were shipped there by *Sunset*. You know," continued Hannah, "it's strange that it's only women who are missing. They have men at *Sunset*, too, but we haven't heard anything about them missing."

"We don't really know who all is missing, though, do we?" said Charlie. "We just know the women who Ruby knew there. There could be lots of others that we don't know shit about...sorry, Ruby."

"Well, I don't think they're going to let us back in to question the other patients there," Hannah replied. "We'll have to settle with what we have. Perhaps when this Pete guy finds out more, the police will do a more thorough investigation. But, let's go talk to Mary now, before she disappears again!"

The rest of the afternoon was spent tracking down Mary Bradshaw, who seemed to always be somewhere else when they inquired at the various units at *Whispering Pines*. When she wasn't in her room they were told she was at therapy; when she wasn't at therapy, they were told she was having lunch; when she wasn't in the cafeteria, they were told she was in her room; and when she still wasn't in her room, they gave up and positioned themselves there until she returned. It was almost 5:00 when they finally caught up with her. She was delighted to see them and proceeded to relate how she had been taken there.

"I didn't know what was happening. One minute I was in my room having breakfast, if you can call it that. You know, Ruby, what their breakfasts were like: cold oatmeal, a slice of orange, and coffee. And the next minute I was told I was being transferred. I'd never seen so many staff people —usually, you never saw any!—and they got me up and dressed, packed up all my stuff, put me in a van and brought me here."

Mary stopped to catch her breath, tired but eager to tell her story. "But I'm not complaining; this place is actually better than *Sunset*—at least you see some of the staff here—and the food's not much better, but it's not any worse. But I don't think I should have been moved without telling anyone where I would be. It's a good thing I know some of the people here, though; they were at *Sunset* when I first was there, so it wasn't so bad that no one could get in touch with me. Except for you, and Alice, I don't miss anyone from *Sunset*."

Hannah tried to get Mary to talk about the money, but all Mary knew was that everything was paid as before. Since she had long ago used up her regular benefits and savings, she assumed that Social Security and Medicare took care of everything.

They left her, promising to visit and bring her some fruit and cookies.

"Well, that's a happy ending, isn't it?" exclaimed Ruby. "She's actually happier here than at the other place. Maybe we shouldn't make a fuss."

Hannah cast her a piercing glance. "Maybe she's happier there, but what about the others? Don't you think people should have a say where they're shipped off to? They're not UPS packages, you know."

Ruby looked chagrined. Charlie came to her rescue, saying, "She didn't mean we should stop the investigation—did you, Ruby? Just that she's glad Mrs. Bradshaw is okay. Right?"

"Whatever," said Hannah, who seemed to be resorting to that expression more often these days. "Let's just go home. The kids should be there by now."

. . . .

The kids were there. Madison was doing homework while listening to her iPod and David could be heard blasting away at his latest video game. Hannah called up to them, but neither one could hear her over their respective gadgets. Sending Charlie away with a brusque, "Charlie, go home," she went upstairs to check on the kids. When she returned, she proceeded to convince Ruby to put together one of her "no bake" concoctions for dessert. Chinese food was okay, but she believed the old adage that you were hungry again a half hour after eating it.

Dinner was subdued, the children extra careful not to say the wrong thing and get Hannah upset. The conversation focused on Mary Bradshaw, with both Hannah and Ruby sharing their surprise that she was happy at the new place. Hannah made sure to emphasize, in case Ruby needed reminding, that that fact wasn't a reason to rethink the need for the investigation.

Whether Hannah was right about Chinese food or whether it was the lure of Ruby's special no bake cheesecake cookies, she couldn't say, but the cookies were devoured within seconds of appearing on the table.

Chapter 30

THE RESTAURANT WAS ONE of their favorites, a small, out of the way place, where the ambiance enhanced the already splendid food, the aroma of freshly baked bread mixing with the subtle bouquet of herbs infusing the air.

It was a special occasion: the first anniversary of their relationship. Janice and Paul were seated at a corner table by the window overlooking one of the small lakes in the area. The light from the outdoor lamps on the patio spread dancing sparks on the surface of the water. The glow from the candles on the table cast a warm flush on their faces, adding to the effect of the wine.

Paul turned to Janice and said, "It's been a wonderful year. I hope to have many more like it."

Janice smiled. "So do I."

"So, what do we do?"

"What do you mean? Why not just continue as we have been?"

"I want more. I want to know that we're working toward something—that we each want the same thing. It's been great. But seeing you on this somewhat random basis, trying to coordinate your schedule with mine, isn't enough for me. I want more."

"Paul, I want more, too. But you have Sandy to think of, and I have Maddie and David—not to mention my mom. It just makes planning for a future impossible."

"No, not impossible. Difficult, yes, but not impossible. There are things we can do. Sandy's weekends aren't problematic; she could spend them with me wherever I live. And once Ruby and Hannah move out, there'll be plenty of room." Paul stopped, a sheepish grin appearing on his face. "I know I'm assuming a lot. Perhaps you don't want to live together. But I want to know that when I come home at night you'll be there, and when I awake in the morning you'll be there…. I love you, Janice, and I want to make a life with you. That's the 'more' that I want."

"Paul," she said, as she reached for his hand, "I want that, too, but…"

She was interrupted by the waiter, eager to take their order. Using the intrusion to gain time to collect her thoughts, she perused the menu and ordered the salmon; Paul, displaying his annoyance at the interruption, ordered the pork chops, with only a cursory glance at the menu.

"So, you were saying?"

"I just don't know. You know I love you, and I want to spend more time with you. This trying to find time to be together certainly isn't enough. I just don't know if I'm ready for a change right now. And my mom is going through some strange stuff right now. I don't know how she'd handle a change."

"Look, I was making an assumption I shouldn't have made. I'm quite fond of your mother. She's a smart, feisty old gal. I wouldn't mind at all if she lived with us. I just assumed, the way she was talking the other night, that she and Ruby were making plans. You know, we don't have to make any decision tonight. Just think about it. Okay?"

"Okay," she replied.

Reluctantly accepting this as an end to the discussion, Paul concentrated on his food, making small talk. After a few minutes, he looked up and asked, "What's this about your mom, though? Is she all right?"

"I don't know. I want her to go to the doctor—to make sure everything's okay—but she's stubborn. I think she's suffering from depression, but I don't know why. That's why I think it might be physical. Nothing's changed to make her depressed that I know of."

"Hold up there. You don't think that Ruby's moving in is a big change? Sure, she handles it well, but you don't know what she's really feeling, do you?"

Janice thought for a few moments. "Well, we need to check the physical first—then I can focus on what's bothering her." She smiled at Paul and said, "Let's eat. Then we can decide: your place or mine?"

Paul laughed. "My place; yours is too crowded right now!"

. . . .

Janice returned home the next day after a leisurely breakfast with Paul. They had not returned to the conversation of the previous evening, but had spent their time professing their love through actions, not words. They awoke late, showered together, returned to bed, and finally made their way to the kitchen an hour later. After breakfast, Paul drove Janice home, promising to call later to make plans for the week.

It was after 2:00 and the house was quiet. The children were out and there was a note from Hannah: "We went to the Center for Bingo—be home around 4:00—we've got dinner planned so don't worry."

Janice didn't worry; with Hannah around, there would always be something good to eat. She changed into jeans and a sweatshirt, all set to work on the new teaching schedules, but found herself thinking of Paul. Last night's conversation had unsettled her. She didn't realize how much Paul meant to her. Oh, sure, she knew she loved him, that she wanted to be with him. But the thought that they could have more never entered her mind. Did she want more? Was she content to continue as they were? She really didn't know. She thought so, but now....Maybe she was afraid of change; maybe she was afraid of commitment; maybe she was just so overwhelmed by her responsibilities that she couldn't think long enough to know what she wanted!

Well, she would have to think now. One thing she was sure of was that she didn't want to lose Paul, and he didn't seem content to continue as they were. And then there were the children and her mother. How would they react to Paul's moving in? She assumed Paul would be the one moving, not her. His place was quite small and she came with family. Besides she wouldn't consider uprooting the children even for a mansion with a pool—though they might disagree.

Being part of the sandwich generation, caught between being a daughter to an aging parent and a mother to children, with all the responsibilities that involved, was tiring. Add to that having a career and being a single mother, and it all seemed at times unreasonable. How could anyone be expected to do it all? Would Paul understand her frustrations, her need to have time to herself, her need to spend time with the children? And Hannah—would he understand her relationship with her mother? And would that relationship change if Paul moved in? She felt she was just getting to know her mother, that her returns to childish reactions were lessening. She was getting to really like, not just love, Hannah. She didn't want to lose that now.

Well, one bright spot, she thought: she didn't have financial problems, as so many other women had. She was well paid and her job was secure—even the superintendent had written her a glowing annual review!

She was seated at her desk when Madison returned home from her sleep-over at Suzanne's. She plopped in the chair next to the desk, dropped her backpack on the floor, and yawned. "It was awesome, Mom. We went to the party at Terry's and everyone was there, and this guy talked to me—he's into poetry, too—and he kind of liked me and..."

Madison would have continued, but David announced his arrival with banging the door and shouting, "I'm home!" Madison shook her head, clearly disapproving of her brother's behavior, but Janice ignored her. "We're in here, David," she shouted, as she smiled at Madison. "Now, honey, he means well. At least he's talking to us these days."

Madison shrugged and dragged herself out of the chair. "I'm going to change. I'll be down for dinner....Where's Grandma?"

"She's playing Bingo at the Center. She'll be home soon."

David entered the room and, hearing that Hannah wasn't home, he asked, "What'll we do for dinner?"

Madison started to say something, but Janice interrupted with a laugh. "She left a note saying that dinner was under control. So don't worry, you won't starve!"

"I wasn't really worried, but I am hungry—it takes a lot of energy to get to level five, you know."

Janice didn't know, but just smiled at him. He was her little boy. He frustrated her, he worried her, but she didn't want him to grow up too quickly. She wanted something to remain the same.

. . . .

Hannah and Ruby returned to find Janice on the phone with Paul. Hannah's curiosity was at high level: How had their weekend gone? And had he heard anything from the PI? She didn't have long to wait to hear about the PI.

Janice was pleased to report that Pete had found the missing Mrs. Johnson. "They found her at *Whispering Pines*, only under the name of Jackson. Pete said that he never would have found her except that Mary Bradshaw kept referring to another woman from *Sunset*. When he tracked her down he found that her real name was Johnson, but that they had mistakenly listed her as Jackson. Since she was so hard of hearing she never noticed they called her by the wrong name."

"Anyway," she continued, "with these two women, and with the mother of the man who was here for dinner—Greeley?—Paul thinks he has enough to go ahead with the lawsuit. He'll be over later this week and he can give you all the details then."

"Wonderful, darling...And how was your weekend?"

"Fine. Here, let me help you set the table."

Hannah couldn't let it go at that. "That's it—'fine'? So what did you do? Where did you eat? What did you talk about?"

Janice's glare clearly told Hannah to back off, but Hannah wasn't in a backing off mood. "What, I can't ask my own daughter where she ate, what the conversation was about?"

"We talked about you, if you must know! About how moody you've been lately."

"Ah, and you two experts decided what? That I'm depressed, losing it, maybe even senile?"

"Stop it, Mom! I'm worried about you, that's all. You've never been like this before—so touchy, so quick to misunderstand. Usually I'm the one to overreact. It scares me when you start doing that."

Hannah looked down and sighed. "Okay, let's get the food on the table before it should get cold."

"Yeah, I'll call the children. David's probably starving by now."

. . . .

That evening, after the children were in bed and Janice was preparing for the week's activities, Ruby turned the TV off and turned to Hannah. "Something's bothering you, I can tell. Is it me? Is my being here causing problems between you and Janice? You know I wouldn't want that. This has been wonderful for me, being here with you and your family, and I am going to get that apartment…"

Hannah interrupted her. "No, no, it's nothing to do with you. Believe me, this is something that I should have seen before but I just didn't think. I need to move out, get a place of my own. I'm just going to be in the way with the kids growing up, and Janice and Paul getting serious—maybe they should even get married, God willing."

Ruby listened quietly and shyly asked, "Maybe we could move in together—you know, get a two bedroom place at those new apartments?"

Hannah smiled, tears threatening to overflow, "That would be perfect, but what about you and Charlie? I get the impression that the two of you are getting—what should I say—close?"

"Well, he is a lovely man; but I'm not going to live with him!" she replied, shock written all over her face. "I couldn't possibly do something like that."

Hannah sighed. "Maybe I've been listening to the young people too much. They seem to do that all the time. Who knows? Maybe it's better their way, less complications. You move in, you move out. But, you're right, we're too old to change after all these years."

Hannah got out of her recliner and extended a hand to help Ruby off the couch. "Let's sleep on it, okay? We'll talk tomorrow. I'll take another look at that brochure," she said. She gave Ruby a hug as she went into the kitchen to get a glass of water before going to bed.

Chapter 31

R<small>UBY FOUND</small> H<small>ANNAH IN</small> the kitchen, brochure in hand. Hannah rose to get coffee and toast. "You never told me that those apartments are for retired people, for those fifty-five or over," she said, as she poured coffee for Ruby.

"You don't think we're old enough?" asked Ruby.

Hannah laughed. "No; but it also says there's a reduced rate for those with low incomes. Now that we qualify for, too!"

"I didn't notice that. So it might be even less money than they told us?"

"I don't know, but we should check it out. We should drive over there this morning…talk to someone in the office. Okay?"

"Fine. I guess we can go without Charlie, right?"

Hannah held back a groan. "Of course, we can," she sweetly replied. "He's already checked out the place, so it's just a matter of getting more information. I think we can do that without him."

Ruby didn't pick up on the sarcasm, and the two women finished their breakfast and were out the door by 10:00. Hannah drove Ruby's Lincoln, hoping that she wouldn't have to parallel park the big car. Fortunately, the parking lot was quite empty and Hannah was able to glide the car into one of the many spots available. She helped Ruby maneuver the curb—Ruby could now get along with just the cane—and they entered the manager's office, where they were told by the receptionist to please be seated and that Mr. Wisniewski would be with them shortly.

Comfortably seated, they looked about the room, commenting on the unusual assortment of pictures on the walls. Some were photographs of flowers, some were reproductions of famous paintings, and some seemed to be pictures drawn by children.

When the receptionist noticed their interest, she smiled and explained. "The reproductions were donated by some residents and the others are all original works by the residents themselves. We have some quite talented people living here. In fact, some of them teach classes in painting and photography, things like that. Since so many of our residents are retirees, we can offer all sorts of activities free of charge—except for supplies, of course."

Ruby seemed enthralled by the information, perhaps seeing herself as the next Grandma Moses; Hannah, however, was less enthusiastic about taking classes from people who painted like that!

Mr. Wisniewski opened the door to his office and beckoned the women in. He was a large man with the best hair Hannah had ever seen. Oh, what a shame, she thought, all that beautiful hair wasted on a man.

"What can I do for you lovely young ladies," he asked, with a wide grin. Hannah took an immediate dislike to him and, if the apartments hadn't seemed so desirable, would have walked out right then. But she stayed, trying to forestall an unnecessary sales pitch. "We were here the other day and looked at some of the apartments. We know what we're interested in; we just need to get some more information. We're interested in a two-bedroom apartment. What would that cost for the two of us—as you can see we're over fifty-five?"

"You certainly don't like to waste time. I admire that in a woman. Well, as to the price, it'll depend on whether you qualify for federal assistance…"

"No, we're not on any welfare programs, just our social securities," Hannah replied.

The man looked at Hannah before responding. Seeing that a more direct approach was wanted, he got down to business and took a chart from one of the folders on his desk. "Here is the breakdown on costs. For those not on any supplemental federal or state programs, we pro-rate the cost depending on the amount of income of the person. So if you could let me know what your combined social security benefits are—I'm assuming the two of you would be the residents?— I could let you know the cost."

Hannah, without looking at Ruby, replied, "approximately $1,500/month."

Ruby looked puzzled, but let Hannah continue. "Most of it comes from our husbands' benefits."

"Ah, of course. Well, according to our latest figures, a two-bedroom, which is available right now, would come to $950/month. Now that doesn't include utilities, you know. That would be extra, billable to you. But it does include all the other amenities we have to offer—there's a lounge where residents can play cards, take classes, things like that. There's a laundry room—in fact, here's a list of all the amenities we offer," he said, as he handed them a pink sheet of paper. "And, of course, we have our beautiful garden area. Have you seen that? Many of our residents like to sit out there in the warm weather. Some, in fact, help with the gardening themselves."

At this point, Ruby couldn't contain her excitement any longer. "Oh, could I see the garden? I so love to work in the garden. I had a beautiful one at my house, something for every season..."

Hannah stood up. "We have an appointment to keep, but perhaps we could see the garden now before we leave?"

"Why, yes, of course." Mr. Wisniewski rose, opened the door, and called out to the receptionist, "Sally, would you show these lovely ladies the garden area?"

Thanking him for his time, Hannah and Ruby, accompanied by Sally, went out to the garden. If Ruby had needed any further persuasion, this did it. She was sold. Even in late fall the area was alive with color: the rust of sedum, the gold of hardy mums, and the pale pink of autumn crocus, against the bright green of the holly bushes, with its red berries and glossy leaves. Ruby turned to Sally and asked, "Could I work in here? You know, do some planting, weeding, things like that?"

"I'm sure you could. In fact, that would be really appreciated." With a conspiratorial look at Ruby, Sally said, "They might even pay you for it—or give you a discount. I'd check into that once you're here," she whispered.

"Oh, my. To have a garden again. I could add some viburnum and heather for the winter, and there's so much to do for the spring and summer. This could be a magnificent garden." Hannah could see the excitement on Ruby's face, flushed with visions of spending hours creating a profusion of colorful arrays of flowering bushes. Yes, this place would be good for Ruby, she thought. She wasn't sure about herself, though.

The weather had changed, threatening rain or, more likely, snow as the temperature plummeted. But none of this was having an effect on Ruby, whose excitement was still apparent as they walked toward the car. Rattling off the names of plants Hannah had never heard of, Ruby was already envisioning what the garden could look like in the spring. "If we move in before the ground is frozen, I could plant some bulbs so that it would be beautiful in the spring. Oh, I'm so anxious to get my hands in the soil again."

Hannah smiled. Getting her hands dirty was not something that had ever brought her pleasure, but then she had always lived in an urban area where the only things growing were the weeds between the sidewalk cracks. She enjoyed having flowers around, but knew nothing about how to grow them.

Ruby, having exhausted the possibilities for future gardening, finally turned to Hannah. "Why did you tell him our combined income would be $1,500? Mine alone is almost that."

"I know. I don't know why I said that! The number just came to my mind and jumped out of my mouth. But at least we know the prices are reasonable. I'm sure whatever it is we'll be able to afford it."

It was only 11:00, too early for lunch, but not too early to drive to the Senior Center to visit with friends. As they drove into the parking area, Ruby spotted Charlie's Grand Marquis parked close to the entrance to the building. "Oh, look," she said, "Charlie's here. I wonder what he's doing."

"Probably playing cards," answered Hannah. "You know how he likes to play poker. I think he actually comes out ahead in the long run."

"I'm worried that he might have a gambling problem."

"I don't think the nickel and dime games they play here will cause any problems. At worst, what could he lose? $20? Even if he occasionally lost $100—and I don't think it ever gets that steep—it's a cheap form of entertainment. And there's no booze allowed, so at least it's not likely he should become an alcoholic," Hannah explained.

Ruby didn't seem convinced, but just nodded. Hannah was starting to wonder if her attempted matchmaking between Ruby and Charlie was such a good idea, after all. They seemed to have little in common except a liking for each other. Was that enough? Would that lead to serious problems once the thrill of courtship ended? Well, it wasn't up to her; they were adults and could decide for themselves. At least they were enjoying themselves now, and it had taken Ruby's mind off of her son's shameful behavior.

The cafeteria at the Center had been turned over to card players: bridge, poker, euchre, and a few people playing gin rummy. Charlie could be seen, and heard, at the poker table. From the look on his face it appeared he was agonizing on whether to fold or call. Hannah took Ruby aside. "You shouldn't bother him right now. Serious card players don't like to mix business with pleasure," she advised, assuming that being interrupted by Ruby would be pleasurable to Charlie.

They helped themselves to the coffee provided at the counter and sat down at one of the unoccupied tables. Within a few minutes, people started to arrive and Hannah and Ruby were joined by friends.

The weather was the first topic of conversation, as it always was, then followed by reports of each person's health. Comparisons of ailments, doctors, and prescriptions were made, each person claiming that their ailment was the worst and their doctor was the best. Hannah didn't contribute much to this part of the conversation as she had no serious ailments. She did, however, find it interesting that they all were convinced of the superiority of their own doctor, even though the respective treatments differed. She concluded that their beliefs, however unsupported by evidence, gave them comfort.

By the time the staff had put out the food, the card playing had been terminated and the tables were set up for lunch. Charlie, seeing Ruby, came over and sat down on the seat she had reserved for him by placing her cane on the chair. Ruby smiled at him, but said nothing. Hannah, on the other hand, asked, "Well, did you win?"

"Not enough to write home about," he answered. "What's that song?— 'You gotta know when to hold 'em, and know when to fold 'em'—something like that. Well, I should've folded!"

Hannah laughed. He really was a nice man. Too bad he wasn't her type!

After lunch, Hannah rose, waved goodbye to the others at the table, and left for the parking lot. Ruby, anxious to tell Charlie about the garden at the apartment complex, stayed behind, assuring Hannah that Charlie would drive her home later.

. . . .

Hannah had the house to herself. She hadn't realized how much she missed the luxury of being alone when she wanted solitude. Even with a houseful of people, she had always been able to go off by herself, usually in her sitting room, where the children knew not to bother her. Now it seemed there was no place she could be by herself.

Sitting in her recliner, with a book on her lap, she thought back over the day. Nothing had happened to upset her. In fact, it had been a pleasant, productive day. The apartment issue was decided; lunch had been fine, although perhaps too filling; she was looking forward to reading her book. What could be wrong? Why did she have this feeling of...she didn't know what? Having an analytical mind, she sought to find out when this feeling started. She had been fine at the apartments, although a little annoyed at the manager; she had been truly pleased to see Ruby's reaction to the garden; and she had enjoyed seeing friends at the Center....Ah, yes, she thought. That was when it started. The conversation bored her! Was that what her life was going to be? Talking about the weather and comparing ailments! And watching Ruby make goo-goo eyes at Charlie!

All of this analyzing was making her tired. She put down the book, which she had yet to open, and closed her eyes, only to be awakened an hour later by a door slamming and David's voice announcing, "I'm home!" He came into the room and asked, "Do we have any food?—I'm starved."

"Starved, huh? Look in the refrigerator. There should be some cheese. Or make some peanut butter crackers. But don't eat too much—you'll spoil your appetite."

David dropped his backpack on the floor as he bolted for the kitchen, causing Hannah to yell after him, "Pick up your stuff!" Returning to put his backpack away, he saluted her, saying, "Aye, aye, captain!" and scampered off again. Hannah smiled at his retreating back. She would miss him.

Chapter 32

THE REST OF THE week passed uneventfully, Hannah's anxiety about the investigation increasing each day until she finally exploded. "When are we going to hear something?" she asked Janice. "It's almost two weeks since Paul told us about Mrs. Bradshaw—and Mrs. Johnson."

"Mom, I don't know any more than you do. Paul's coming for dinner tomorrow night. I'm sure he'll have an update for us."

"Well, the wheels of justice certainly don't move very fast. That place could be covering up all sorts of things by now," Hannah retorted.

Janice ignored that comment. Hannah had always been impatient, but now the impatience was often accompanied with anger. "Mom, are you all right?" she asked.

"Of course I'm not all right. I'm angry. I want something should be done. Who knows how many other women are being 'transferred'—and what if they're not all transferred, but something worse? People could be killed while we wait."

"Now you're sounding like David and his 'harvesting parts' scenario."

"Well, who knows? Maybe he's on to something."

"Mom…."

"I know, I know. I'm being foolish. I just feel so useless. What if Ruby had 'disappeared?' Who knows what could have happened to her? Her son would have never known and if I hadn't pushed to find out where she was, she, too, could have gone missing."

"Well, we should know more tomorrow. Speaking of Ruby—how is her romance with Charlie going?"

The question brought a frown to Hannah's face. "Funny you should ask!

I think she sees it as a romance, but I'm not sure about him. I get the feeling he's getting cold feet, like maybe he's not ready for anything serious."

"Well, a lot of men shy away from commitments."

"Speaking of commitments—what's with you and Paul, may I ask?"

"Yes, you may ask! But there's nothing to say. Things are as they are, and we're both content with that, at least for now. If things change, you'll be the first to know. Okay?"

Hannah sighed. "I guess it has to be okay—as long as that's what you both want."

Hannah would have pursued the topic, but Madison came in just then. She hung up her coat and backpack, went over to her mother and grandmother, and gave each one a kiss on the cheek. Janice looked up at her. "Okay, what do you want?" she asked.

"Why do you always think I want something just because I give you a kiss?" Madison responded. "Because you always do," Janice answered.

"That's so not true," Madison cried. She turned to her grandmother and said, "Mom is so unfair. I can never be nice to her without her thinking I want something."

Hannah knew not to take sides, but she was waiting to hear what Madison was going to ask for. This was not a demonstrative family; kisses usually came with a price.

After reporting on the day's events at school, Madison came to the point. "You remember I told you about this boy at Terry's party—the one who kind of liked me? Well, he asked me to go to the movies tomorrow. Is that okay?"

"Ah, finally the truth emerges! She wants something!" Janice exclaimed. "Well, of course you can go to the movies with him. A matinee, I assume?"

"No, of course not!" Madison frowned. "He invited me to the 7:00 show, and then maybe we'd go out for pizza afterward."

"And how old is this boy?"

"He's a senior, too—but a year older than me. And he's very nice—you'd approve of him, Mom."

"Well, I assume he'll pick you up here? That way I can see if I approve of him! What's his name? Where does he live? Who else will be going with you?"

"It's just the two of us going. His name is Jamie Ramirez, but he spells it 'Jaime' and he lives in that gray house on Washington…and he's real cute," Madison reported.

"I know him," Janice said, "and that means that he's been in my office, and that means that he's been in trouble."

"That was last year—see, he told me about it. He knows my mother's the principal so he wanted to explain. He told me he got into a fight with this guy and that both of them got sent to your office. He hasn't had any problems since then, though."

"Do you know what the fight was about?"

"No, he didn't tell me, only that something the guy said got him angry and he lost his temper. But that that was the only time. He wasn't bragging or playing the tough guy, Mom. He's really sweet—he wants to be a writer. He actually reads poetry!"

Janice laughed, and looked at Hannah, who was smiling. "Well, that settles it, then. Anyone who reads poetry, and can actually write, has got to be worthy of going out with my daughter!"

Madison looked concerned, not knowing if Janice was being sarcastic.

"Honey, I'm just teasing you. I know Jaime, and he's a good kid. The fight he got into was with a boy who called him a nasty name. They both got detentions—I can't allow fighting on the school grounds—but Jaime was just responding to a racial slur. The other kid got a more serious reprimand. So, yes, I have no problem with movies and pizza with Jaime. Just be home before midnight."

Madison jumped up, hugged Janice, and ran upstairs, most likely to phone Jaime with the good news.

"Well, that went well," said Hannah. "She's growing up fast; she's a special girl, you know."

"I do know," Janice replied. "Both of the kids are growing up—at times, I think, too fast. Before you know it, Maddie will be off to college. And maybe by then David will have matured!"

Hannah laughed. "Don't hold your breath. Boys take longer than girls to mature. Look at Charlie—in a way, he's still a boy. When he has dinner here, who does he talk to? David! They're both on the same level, interested in the same things: cars and those video games David is always playing. Why, I don't know what Charlie would do if he should have to talk to us."

Janice shook her head in amazement. "Yeah, you're right. He's just a really *old* little boy!"

Hannah laughed. "He was really helpful in dealing with Ruby's son, and in checking out apartments for her, things like that—but he is funny!"

· ·

The next evening—Madison off to the movies with Jaime, David spending the night at Billy's—Janice, Hannah, Ruby, and Paul were having a simple dinner of roast chicken and rice. Paul pushed back from the table, patted his stomach, and announced that that was a meal equal to any he had had in the expensive restaurants he'd been taking clients to. "In fact," he said, "it brought back fond memories of meals my mother used to make when I was a boy. And," he added, "she was a terrific cook."

Hannah had curbed her impatience throughout dinner, but as she served coffee and a dessert of angel food cake with raspberries, her curiosity got the best of her. "So," she asked, as she placed the cake in front of Paul, "what's happening with the investigation?"

He grinned. "I was wondering when you would get around to that. Janice told me you were getting worried that we would let the ball drop. Well, things are going quite well. I think you know that Pete found two of the women at that *Whispering Pines* place. Well, when he followed the money trail, he found evidence that social security checks were being cashed by *Sunset Manor*, and that *Sunset* then paid *Whispering Pines* for the care of the women. There are two irregularities here. The first issue is forgery: for one of the women, someone at *Sunset* is obviously forging the signature on her checks—the other woman has the checks signed over to *Sunset,* so there's no forgery there. The second issue is fraud: the government is paying more than is actually being used for the care of these women. So you've got two federal cases involved. He's met with the feds and at least these two cases will be turned over to them. So, thanks to you ladies, *Sunset* will probably be closed down and someone there will serve prison time."

Paul looked at the women seated around the table. Ruby, unexpectedly, appeared concerned, but didn't say anything. Hannah, nodding her head, burst out, "Those bastards! I knew they were up to no good." She turned to Ruby and said, "You were right, kiddo. You knew something was rotten from the beginning." When she didn't get the smile she expected from Ruby, she asked in exasperation, "What's the matter? It's over. We've won!"

Ruby gave her a wan smile, but then, in a soft voice, said, "But what will happen to all the other women at that place? Where will they go? And what about the women in the past? How can we ever find out what happened to them?"

Paul, in a calm, clear voice responded, "As to the other women who are currently at *Sunset*, they'll be transferred to other facilities—like *Whispering Pines*, perhaps. No one will be turned out on the streets, Ruby, so don't worry about them. From what Janice has told me they weren't getting the best care at *Sunset*, so this may be for the best. As to the women in the past, there's probably nothing we can do about them—I assume they've all passed away? It would take a major investigation to dig up all the records for them, and all that would accomplish would be more evidence to support the case against *Sunset*, which we don't need…"

Hannah interrupted Paul and asked if there were at least some way to find out if those other women had been transferred to *Whispering Pines*. "Paul, you'll think we're overreacting, but Ruby and I—and David!—have wondered if perhaps some of the women weren't sent someplace else, but either died, as Mrs. Greeley did, or even something worse."

"Like sold for parts?" Janice suggested sarcastically.

"Well, maybe not that, but…" Hannah shrugged, not knowing what alternative scenarios would sound reasonable enough for Paul to consider plausible.

"Look," he responded, "we can do a search for those women—you'll have to give me their names—to see if they were at *Whispering*; maybe even extend the search to some of the other local nursing homes. We can also check for death certificates for them—I assume that since we're talking about the past, they're probably gone by now. But we can check dates of death, how they died, etc. What we can't do is determine if they died a natural death. Most medical examiners don't do autopsies on elderly people who die from apparent natural causes. For that, we'd have to do a much more intensive, and expensive, investigation—get medical personnel involved, exhume bodies, stuff like that—which we probably wouldn't get permission to do without evidence that there was some foul play. But I can get Pete to dig a little deeper on the other women, see what he can find by simply checking records. Is that okay?"

Ruby and Hannah nodded agreement. Hannah got up to get the coffee pot for refills and on the way over to the counter stopped at Paul's side and hugged him. "Thank you for everything. We couldn't have done this without your help. You're a *mensch*!"

Paul laughed and said, "I hope that's good!"

....

Later that evening, after Paul had left and Ruby had retired, Janice sat down on the sofa next to Hannah. "Mom, can I ask you something?" she said.

"You're asking me if you can ask me something! Of course you can. What's wrong?"

"Nothing's wrong. It's just that you've been so involved in this missing women thing—more so than Ruby, who actually knew some of them. I just wondered *why*. Is it simply concern about Ruby? I hope you don't see yourself ever being in that situation."

Hannah was silent for a minute. When she spoke, her voice was low and her face was sad. "Let me tell you a story—you have time?"

"I have all the time you need," Janice smiled, as she settled back on the sofa.

183

Hannah took a deep breath. "I don't know if you remember Irene Matsoff. She lived next to us in the apartment—an older lady…she used to crochet those doilies that I never used, except if she came for coffee, then I'd pull one out of the drawer so she should see I'm using them—but that's not important. Anyway, she was a widow—no children—and no family that I knew of. She kept to herself, didn't mix with the other women in the building; we all had young children, she didn't have anything in common with us. But I liked her, I felt sorry for her, living all alone with no family or friends. Anyway, she ended up in a nursing home in Brooklyn—I don't remember why: heart, kidney, who knows? Anyway, as I said, she didn't have anyone, so I would visit her every once in a while—it's not so far to Brooklyn, I took the train and a bus—and I would take her a little something—you know, cookies, a cake, something that she wouldn't get there…."

Seeing Janice's look of impatience, Hannah said, "I know, get to the point, right? Well, I would visit her like every other week—on Wednesdays, because that was the day your father worked late—and one day when I went to visit her, she wasn't there. They told me she had died and that was that. Well, she probably did die—she was old, and sick—but all this missing women stuff has got me thinking. How did she die? Was she receiving good care? Without anyone to check on people in these places, how do we know what's happening to them? I feel I should have done more for her, but, in all truth, I don't know what else I could have done.…So, in answer to your question, I guess this is just bringing back painful memories of how vulnerable many old people are—and no, I don't see myself ever being in that situation. I just wish I could do more."

Janice got up and hugged her. "You've done quite a lot already. You can't solve all the world's problems. You're not Wonder Woman, you know."

"No, not Wonder Woman—she's too young. But maybe an older one, less active, with aches and pains—but no fancy outfit: I don't look good in tights," Hannah laughed as she got up from her recliner. "Good night, darling; sleep well."

Chapter 33

MONDAY MORNING. THE SUN was shining, the weather unusually warm. Hannah awoke feeling well rested for the first time in many weeks. The feeling was so unusual for her lately that she had to think why she was so contented. What had happened to relieve the heaviness in her heart?

She got up, took a quick shower, and proceeded to start breakfast. The family would be up soon and she liked to have everything ready. She knew there would be last minute frantic searches for shoes, backpacks, and keys—and, now that winter was approaching, gloves and coats. At least breakfast would not add to the chaos.

When the children and Janice came down, the food was already on the table. David, true to form, was the first to grab a plate and fill it with scrambled eggs, bacon, and muffins. By the time Madison and Janice sat down, he was on his second plate. Janice looked at him. "Are you all right? I've never seen you eat so much in the morning."

"Yeah, I'm just hungry."

"Well, don't wolf it down. You'll make yourself sick."

David looked at his mother as if she had spoken a foreign language and proceeded to devour the food on his plate.

"Don't come to me if you have a stomach ache later. I'll have no sympathy for such a little piggie."

Madison just looked at her brother with disdain, shaking her head while she nibbled on a piece of toast.

Preparing breakfast took thirty minutes; consuming it, five. The next fifteen minutes were spent in a flurry of activity: "Have you seen my keys?" "I know I left my backpack right here." "Mother, I can't go to school without my blue sweater." Hannah just sat at the table, drinking coffee, oblivious to the chaos around her, making plans for the day.

When the house had quieted down, Ruby emerged from her bedroom. "I thought I'd stay out of the way until they left. My, there's a lot of activity in the mornings here."

"It's chaos, but it seems to work. I've learned to stay out of it. Everything usually gets sorted out."

"But it's nice to hear children's voices. That's something I miss. I never really had it, even when Harold was a child. And I always thought I'd have lots of children—and grandchildren. Well, some things aren't meant to be."

Hannah didn't buy the "meant to be" analysis, but agreed that there were some things one had no control over. Changing the subject, she sighed. "It's going to be a beautiful day. We should get some fresh air, go someplace. What do you think?"

"Oh, yes," replied Ruby, clearly delighted to make plans for the day.

"Well, what should we do today? Some shopping, maybe? The paper says that there's a big sale going on at the mall."

"I was wondering. Do you think we could go over to the apartment and look at the rooms more carefully? You know, measure where furniture would go, things like that?"

"Sure. I'll take a tape measure. Have you decided on signing a lease?"

"I think so. What do you think?"

"I think it's a lovely place, and the price is reasonable."

"Hannah, I've been thinking. I'm going to get the two bedroom apartment. If you decide not to move in, I can still easily afford it, and an extra bedroom would be nice anyway. So, you don't have to make a decision right now. Give yourself some time."

Hannah felt herself choking up. Ruby might be timid and she might be overly sentimental, but she was a good woman and a dear friend.

"Thank you." Sniffling back a tear, Hannah suggested they clear the breakfast dishes, get ready and go. Feeling gratitude toward Ruby, she asked if they should include Charlie in the adventure. The smile on Ruby's face was answer enough.

Charlie arrived shortly after receiving Ruby's call, equipped with a large tape measure, a level, and a toolkit filled with a hammer, screw drivers, pliers, wrenches, and who knows what else. Hannah raised her eyebrows, but Charlie warded off any criticisms by saying, "You never know what you're going to need."

Ruby nodded her head in agreement, looking at him as if only he would have thought of such a wise course of action. Charlie blushed under her adoring gaze, but clearly enjoyed it. Hannah shrugged, said, "Whatever," and got her coat.

Once in the car, Ruby brought Charlie up to speed on their plans, leaving it open as to whether Hannah would be moving in with her. He looked surprised, but just nodded, saying, "That'll work."

When they arrived at the apartments, Mr. Wisniewski was in the front office talking to Sally, the receptionist. Seeing Ruby enter first, he smiled and went to greet her, only to be taken aback when Charlie and Hannah entered. He recovered quickly, extending his hand to Charlie and smiling at Hannah. "How nice to see you ladies again. I hope you've decided to join our little family here."

"I don't know about that," snapped Hannah. "We're here to rent an apartment."

Ignoring Hannah's retort, he replied, "Wonderful. Let's go into my office where we can be more comfortable."

Hannah put up her hand, stopping him. "We'd like to look at the apartment first, before signing anything. You know, make sure it's what we remember."

"Of course. I'll get Sally to show you around," he said, turning to Sally. "Would you mind showing them…let me see, I think it's 42K?"

"I'd be delighted," she said, as she got up to get the keys.

The apartment was as they remembered: two average sized bedrooms, one and a half bathrooms, a galley kitchen, and a living area which opened onto a deck overlooking the garden. The walls were painted white with a tint of peach, and there was track lighting in all the rooms. There were windows on only one side of the apartment, but they faced southwest, providing sufficient light for the living area even on sunless days.

Charlie set to measuring the rooms, making sure to note in his pad the dimensions of all the nooks and crannies. He measured closets and cupboards and checked the appliances. Having assured himself that everything was in working order, he closed his pad, put away his tape measure, and nodded approval to Ruby.

They took the elevator to the main floor and sat down at the table in Mr. Wisniewski's office, where he had assembled all the forms that would need to be filled out.

Hannah noticed that Ruby appeared flustered. "You don't have to do that now," she reminded her. Looking at Mr. Wisniewski, she continued, "She can take those forms home to fill out and we can return them tomorrow, right?"

It was clear that Mr. Wisniewski had hoped to settle everything right then, but he made an appointment for them for the next day. Hannah wasn't convinced an appointment was necessary—after all, they had just walked in today without an appointment—but agreed that 10:00 tomorrow would be fine.

Back in the car, Ruby held on to the package of forms as if it were in danger of disappearing. She talked about the garden and the plans she had for it, turning to Charlie for his response. He responded, keeping his eyes on the road and occasionally muttering "Uh huh." "Oh." "Sounds nice." Hannah, on the other hand, was more concerned about Ruby's furniture: What would she use in the apartment, what would she keep in storage, and what should she get rid of? However, getting Ruby to focus on that was proving too difficult for the moment. Perhaps after a nice lunch, they could get down to business.

"Why don't we go back home, have some lunch, and make a list of what you'll need to buy. Then we can go check out that sale at the mall. Okay?"

"That sounds lovely," smiled Ruby.

"But we should look at those papers, too," interrupted Charlie. "You know, make sure you have all the information you'll need." Ruby nodded her agreement.

By the time they arrived home, the list had already been started. Beds, dressers, dining table, sofa and chairs would come from storage, as would dishes and other kitchen equipment. Ruby's house had been large: four bedrooms, three bathrooms, a large kitchen with a separate dining room, and a large living room—not to mention an attic filled with "stuff." Clearly all that furniture would not fit into the new apartment. It was clear to Hannah that it was going to be difficult for Ruby to decide to sell anything. She would just have to try to convince Ruby that it didn't make sense to pay to store stuff she was not going to use. She hoped her friend would see the foolishness of that.

After lunch, Charlie pushed aside his plate, took out his pad, and started drawing. He took a small ruler from his shirt pocket, quickly diagrammed the rooms from the measurements he had taken. Looking at Ruby, he asked where she wanted the various articles of furniture placed. Realizing that he would have to get actual measurements of her furniture, he approximated the sizes to get a general layout.

Ruby wavered back and forth.

"I think I'll need the mahogany bedroom set...no, maybe the maple one. Oh I can't decide—I adore them both. Maybe I should take both?"

"You have two bedrooms," Charlie answered, "but one of them is smaller. I don't know if a big bed would fit in there."

"Oh, that's right. How silly of me to forget. Well, let me think...."

This went on for over thirty minutes until Hannah spoke up. "Why don't we go over to the storage place? Maybe Ruby can decide better when she actually has the furniture before her."

Charlie quickly agreed, nodding his appreciation to Hannah. "Do you have some tags, or something we could put on the stuff we'll be moving out?" he asked.

"There might be some in here," she answered, as she rummaged around in one of the kitchen drawers. "Ah, here they are. We used these for the garage sale last summer. I told Janice we might need them again."

Tape measure, pad, and tags in hand, they were once again on the road. Ruby was as excited as if she were going to visit a long-lost lover! She described the features of her beloved furniture, causing Hannah to wonder about the priorities of her friend. When Hannah had moved to Brewster, she left most of her household furnishings behind. They were just "things"—easily replaced. What she brought with her were photos, letters, and special pieces of jewelry that her husband had given her. Unbeknownst to Janice, though, she had packed away into her suitcase Leo's shaving kit: the aroma from his cologne had gotten her through many lonely nights after he died, and keeping that olfactory memory alive was important to her.

The items in the storage unit were neatly organized, which made it easy for Charlie to take measurements. He took the dimensions of the four bedroom sets, the dining table and chairs, the living room sofas and chairs—he took the dimensions of nearly everything in the place! He was a man on a mission, a mission he did not want to have to repeat.

Taking out the tags, he turned to Ruby. "Okay, now you have to decide: what do you want to take for the apartment? Put a tag on everything you want."

Tears filled Ruby's eyes, threatening to run down her pale cheeks. She looked bewildered, unable to make any decisions. Hannah quickly took her arm and led her around the unit. "How about starting with the living room," she suggested. "You'll want that sofa, right? So let's put a tag on it. And how about those chairs? And the coffee table—I think they'll all fit in the new place."

Once started, Ruby seemed able to focus.

"I know I can't take the dining room set with me—there's no separate dining room. But then I'll need to buy a small table I can use in the living area…and I'll need some small lamps—that track lighting isn't going to be enough."

"We can look for those things later," contributed Hannah. "Remember, there's that sale at the mall going on."

"Okay." Ruby dithered about the bedroom furniture, finally deciding on the queen-sized maple bedroom set for her room. "But what about the other bedroom, the smaller one? Another queen-size or twin? What do you think, Hannah?"

"The twin beds, I think. A single bed would be enough for me and, if I don't move in, twin beds are better for a guest room—you never know who's going to be staying over. It could be a couple or just friends...and besides, a queen-sized bed won't fit!"

The boxes with the dishes and kitchen gadgets were tagged, as were the boxes holding bathroom supplies. Vases and other decorative items were also tagged, as were the linens and towels. All in all, it looked as if many of Ruby's possessions would find a new home in the apartment, although it might be more cluttered than she pictured.

The next chore was to decide what to do with the items left behind.

"Why don't you sell the stuff you're not going to be using?" Charlie asked. "Or you can donate them to Goodwill, or the Salvation Army—you get a tax break that way."

"What does she need with a tax break?" Hannah demanded. "She's going to have such a large income she needs deductions!"

"I was just telling her the options she has. She has to do something with all that stuff!" Charlie replied.

Hannah looked over at Ruby and could see that this discussion wasn't helping. Afraid that Ruby would start crying, she suggested that they leave that decision for another day. At least they knew what she wanted moved into the apartment. Now Charlie could see if it would all fit.

All that decision-making had taken more than two hours, at the end of which it was clear that Ruby was exhausted. The decision to go to the mall was abandoned and the three of them headed home. Charlie's impatience was apparent to Hannah, but Ruby seemed oblivious to it, continuing to agonize over the decisions she had had to make. When she started to rethink which bedroom set she wanted to use, he showed signs of a temper Hannah had not seen before. Usually that would have disturbed her—Leo never lost his temper!—but, in this case, she sympathized with Charlie. It was difficult dealing with Ruby's indecision. But what made it worse was that one felt so guilty about feeling that way. Ruby was completely unaware of the effect she had on them, and would have been devastated if she realized she was annoying her friends.

After settling Ruby on the recliner, with a cup of herbal tea and some cookies, Hannah and Charlie set to working out the placement of the furniture on his floor plan. After assuring themselves that everything would fit, they took the plans to Ruby who, whether out of conviction or exhaustion, smiled her acceptance and suggested only a small change in the placement of the coffee table.

Charlie picked up the package with the forms for the apartment that had been thrown on the hall table. He looked at Hannah for advice, received a shake of her head, and put them back. This obviously was not the time to fill them out.

Hannah smiled at him and said, "You must be exhausted, too, Charlie. Why don't you take off. I'll work with Ruby on those forms after dinner, when she's rested a bit."

Charlie responded as if he were a student being let out of school early. He could hardly contain his delight as he bent over Ruby to give her a kiss on the cheek. To Hannah, he mouthed, "Thank you!" and dashed out the door.

. . . .

The forms were put aside. No mention was made of them until after dinner when Janice and the children had retreated to their respective rooms: Janice to deal with budget issues; Madison to work on her French verbs; and David to fight the latest challenge to attaining level six.

Ruby was seated on the sofa when Hannah joined her, carrying a pot of herbal tea and some biscuits. She poured the tea into the two flowered tea cups she had set down on the coffee table, sat down in the recliner, picked up her cup, bit into a biscuit, and sighed.

"Well, this has been quite a day. I know you're overwhelmed, but we really did accomplish a lot today. The next thing we should do is fill out those forms—but it doesn't have to be tonight. We can wait until the morning; you'll feel stronger then."

"No, we can do it now—at least start it. I'm okay. It was just hard realizing that I'm going to have to get rid of so much—things I've had for over fifty years. Some of it from my mother, some even from my grandmother!"

"But we didn't go through the little things, today. I bet you'll be able to keep a lot of them. It was just the big items that you wouldn't have room for. Think of it this way: you're doing a big house cleaning! When I moved here, I went through all my things and do you know what? Most of what I left behind—selling or giving away—I haven't missed. And I actually threw out a lot of stuff that I wondered why I had kept all those years. They didn't have any sentimental value; they were just things I accumulated and forgot about—*tchotchkes* I didn't need."

Ruby nodded, as she nibbled on a biscuit. "You're probably right. But first I need to get the apartment. Let's get at those forms."

The two women poured over the forms, Hannah making notes on what they would need to pull out from the various papers Ruby had stashed in her room. In less than an hour, they had filled out most of the information required, the rest to be finished in the morning. Ruby shook her head. "That wasn't so bad," she declared. "Maybe tomorrow we can look for a dining table?"

"Sure. The sale is still on at the mall—and we have the measurements Charlie took. I don't think we need to involve him in the shopping, though. I don't think he's the shopping type," she said, pleased when Ruby nodded her agreement.

Chapter 34

DAVID CAME HOME TO find two old women asleep in front of the TV. It was his day to walk Max. Trying not to wake the women, he made more noise than if he had entered in his usual bombastic manner. In the process of putting the leash on Max, he'd knocked over the umbrella stand, uttered a few profanities, and startled Hannah and Ruby awake.

"I'm sorry," he said. "I was trying to be quiet."

"That's okay. We weren't sleeping," said Hannah.

"Yeah, I know," he grinned.

Ignoring his comment, Hannah asked, "Why are you home so early?"

"Soccer practice was cancelled—something about the coach's wife—I don't know."

"Maybe she's sick; he should be with her if she's sick."

"Nah. I think she's having a baby."

"Well, that's certainly a good reason for him to be with her!" Hannah replied, hoping to impart a little sensitivity to her grandson.

"Grandma," he said, "can I talk to you after I take Max out?"

"Of course, darling. You don't need to ask. I'm always here you should need to talk."

David nodded and, with an excited Max on the other end of the leash, went out the front door, banging it as he left.

Ruby smiled. "At least he picked up the mess he made in the hallway," she said.

When David returned with a panting Max, who ran immediately to his water dish, slopping water all over the kitchen floor, Hannah suggested they talk in the kitchen, leaving Ruby to watch another *Walker* rerun. Retrieving juice from the refrigerator and cookies from the cupboard, David sat down across the table from his grandmother.

"Grandma, what's happening with that guy we were checking up on?" he asked.

"Oh, that turned out just fine. The information you got helped Charlie to figure out what was what. And now Ruby has enough money to live on. Her son—he was the guy we were checking up on—was trying to gyp her out of her money. But we stopped that and she's okay now."

"You shouldn't say 'gyp,' Grandma."

"'Gyp?' What's wrong with that?"

"We learned in class that it's short for 'gypsy' and it says all gypsies are thieves."

"Oy, the things I'm learning! I don't know any gypsies, but I certainly wouldn't want I should hurt their feelings. Thank you for telling me. I'm glad you're learning these things.…So, is that what you wanted to talk about—the guy we were checking up on?"

David hesitated, breaking the cookie into smaller and smaller pieces.

"If you keep doing that, you'll end up with crumbs. Out with it; what's the problem, darling?"

"The other night I heard Mom talking to Paul on the phone. She said something about your moving in with Ruby when she moves out. Are you going to leave us?"

The expression on his face brought tears to Hannah's eyes. How could anyone doubt that he would grow up to be a caring, kind man—he was halfway there already!

"No decision has been made, David, but I'm thinking through my options. After all, you don't want an old lady around forever, do you? Sometimes things change and that can be good."

"You wouldn't be here forever; you're going to die someday," David replied, oblivious to tact. "It's just that, well, I kind of like it the way it is now. I like you living with us—it's more fun than before you came. Then Mom wasn't home very much and Maddie bossed me all the time. You're bossy, but not like her."

Hannah smiled, and took the hand that had crumbled the cookies in her own and kissed it. "Darling, even if I should move in with Ruby, that doesn't mean that we wouldn't see each other. I wouldn't be sleeping here, but I would certainly be here for when you get home from school and I'd probably still be making dinner—your mother's too busy for that. So you see it needn't be any different than it is now."

"So why move out, then?" David asked, showing the analytical mind that Hannah so enjoyed seeing in him. He looked so serious, so confused, Hannah was tempted to unburden herself and tell him all her fears. But he was only a child. He didn't need to be burdened by her worries. And if she brought up the possibility of Janice marrying Paul, who knew how that would be received by him, especially since there had been no talk of marriage yet. No, she had to simply put him at ease by reiterating that no decision was made, that she was just considering her options.

Just then, Maddie came into the kitchen, eyes shooting daggers at her brother. She was still wearing her coat and backpack, which convinced Hannah that something important had happened in order for Maddie to forget the house rules.

"What have you been telling Jaime, you little twit?"

"Huh?"

"You heard me. He says that you told him I had a thing for Kenny. That's so not true!"

"I didn't say anything. He asked me if you were dating anyone and I told him you used to date Kenny—you did, you know! What's so wrong about saying that? I'm not going to lie for you!"

"Why are you talking to him, anyway?" Janice continued. "Where did you meet him?"

"He's the new assistant coach for my soccer team. He's a real neat guy. You should date him, he's even cooler than Kenny—and he's a real good soccer player. You should see him…"

"Oh, it's useless talking to you. You just don't understand. Stay out of my personal life, please," she shouted as she stormed out of the room.

"Gees, I didn't know I was *in* her personal life," he muttered.

Hannah took this as an opportunity to avoid a continuation of their earlier discussion and got up to start preparations for dinner. "Darling, maybe you should do some homework before dinner? Then you can play with your games, no?"

"Okay," he replied, as he grabbed another cookie, obviously having forgotten, at least for the moment, about the unfinished discussion.

. . . .

By the time Janice came home, the aroma from the meatloaf that Hannah had thrown together after her talk with David wafted through the house, leading Janice to comment, "Smells good, Mom. What is it?" as she hung up her coat and came into the kitchen. Nodding her approval, she launched into helping Hannah mash the potatoes and set the table.

The conversation at the table focused on Ruby's detailed recounting of the day's activities: finalizing the leasing of the apartment, with an in-depth description of the apartment and her plans for the garden; shopping for a new dining room table, with again an in-depth description of what it looked like and how it would fit into the living area space; and, finally, explaining the decisions she had made regarding what to do with the furniture she wouldn't be using, again describing each article in loving detail, almost coming to tears at the idea of parting with them.

Hannah didn't know how much more of these details she could handle. In an attempt to change the topic and, at the same time, fend off the tears, she interrupted Ruby, praising her for having successfully made the appropriate decisions, and then turned the conversation to other matters. Following up on Madison's earlier mention of Jaime, she inquired about his coaching David's soccer team. "He must be pretty good if he's coaching, no?"

David corrected her. "He's an assistant coach, not the real coach."

"Well, he must be good enough then to be an assistant coach. That's pretty important for someone still in school, no?"

Madison chimed in. "He is good. He's the best one on the high school team. That's why he was asked to help with the kids." She glanced at David to see if he would react to being called a kid, but he was oblivious, no longer interested in the conversation, just anxious to return to his video game and the challenge of level six.

Chapter 35

Tʜᴇ ꜰɪʀsᴛ sɴᴏᴡꜰᴀʟʟ ᴏꜰ the season and it was not yet Thanksgiving. Charlie was due any minute to drive them to the new apartment, where the moving van was delivering Ruby's furniture from storage. Ruby, ever protective of her possessions, wanted to be there when they were delivered to make sure they were handled properly.

"Do you think they'll deliver in this weather?" Ruby asked.

"Why shouldn't they? It's just snow," answered Hannah.

"Yes, but I don't want my furniture to get wet."

"I'm sure they know how to cover them so they shouldn't get wet. Stop worrying; it'll be fine. And see, it's stopping already. By the time Charlie gets here, it'll be over."

Hannah was anxious to get the move over. Ruby wouldn't be moving into the new apartment yet, but at least she would be able to settle things into their proper places, something she was constantly talking about. Hannah knew she was being unreasonable, but she just couldn't understand why Ruby was so concerned about her possessions. They were just things! But when she had made this comment to Janice the other night, Janice had looked at her strangely and shook her head, as if it were Hannah who was the odd duck. Well, maybe she was, but at least she had the satisfaction of not having to waste time on what seemed to her unimportant details. More time for important things—like fighting injustice and cooking!

The snow had not stopped falling when Charlie arrived, but he echoed Hannah's assurance that the movers knew what they were doing and that the furniture would be protected. Even Charlie seemed anxious to get going, refusing Hannah's offer of coffee and something to eat. He helped Ruby into the car, as she continued to comment on what appeared to her to be an increasing snowfall, Charlie looked at Hannah and shook his head, leaving Hannah to wonder again if her plans for them were at all realistic. Maybe Janice was right: she should leave matchmaking to others.

They arrived at the apartment just as the moving van drove up. If Ruby had been able, she would have jumped out of the car and run up to the van to give instructions on how to handle her furniture. Since that was not possible, she shouted "Wait!" as she struggled to get out of the car before Charlie could get to her door. Once out, she braved the snow, not bothering to use the umbrella to protect her hair, and strode as rapidly as she could to the van, where she proceeded to deliver her instructions to the two men who were already unloading the furniture.

"No, no, no," she shouted. "That cover isn't tied properly. That's going to get wet."

"Lady," one of the men replied, "we know what we're doing. Get out of the way—you'll get hurt."

"Charlie, do something!" she cried, looking around to see where he was.

He was standing by the car, with Hannah, both of them amazed at the sight of Ruby, gesturing wildly, hair dripping wet. He looked at Hannah, shrugged, and walked over to Ruby. "Ruby, let them do their work. They know what they're doing. Come on, let's go inside and wait."

"They're going to ruin everything," she cried. "It's all going to be ruined."

Charlie, clearly uncomfortable with the scene she was creating, looked at the men with a sheepish grin, and shrugged helplessly. Hannah's tolerance for Ruby's behavior had slowly ebbed until it was non-existent. She marched over to the van, took Ruby by the arm and said, "Kiddo, let's go. You're in the way." To Charlie's amazement, Ruby allowed Hannah to lead her into the building, all the while continuing to complain. By the time Hannah succeeded in getting Ruby to calm down, the furniture had all been carried into the apartment and placed where Charlie's diagrams indicated. All that remained to do was remove the contents of the boxes that had been delivered.

Hannah looked at Ruby's flushed face. "How about we leave the boxes for now—maybe have a little lunch? Charlie? What do you think?"

Charlie quickly agreed, anxious to remove himself from any more potential scenes. "Yeah, sounds like a plan. But I just remembered I have an appointment this afternoon. I won't be able to help with the boxes."

Ruby looked worried, but Hannah quickly replied, "That's okay. I think Ruby and I are up to handling the boxes." Turning to Ruby, she said, "It's just a matter of opening the boxes and deciding where things go. There's no problem. We'll go the house, have a little lunch, then Charlie can go to his appointment and we can come back and unload the boxes."

At first Ruby argued that they needed Charlie to help unload the boxes, but she was overruled by Hannah who convinced her that Charlie's help wasn't needed, that they could easily—and more efficiently—deal with the boxes themselves. Charlie sent her a look of gratitude.

Lunch was quickly put together from leftovers in the refrigerator and then they left—Charlie to his probably fictional appointment and the women to the boxes in the new apartment.

By the time they arrived home, having sorted through ten boxes of dishes, pots and pans, linens, and assorted gadgets, they were exhausted. With tea and cookies, they settled into their respective chairs in front of the TV and fell asleep before the first commercial aired, tea and cookies barely touched. And that was how the children found them when they arrived home from school.

"See, I told you," David said. "You owe me a dollar. I knew they'd be sleeping."

"I never made the bet," Madison claimed. "I just didn't agree with you—that's not the same as taking your bet."

"Cheater!"

"Oh, go soak your head, you twit."

"What's going on?" yelled Hannah. "What are you two fighting about now?"

"We're not fighting, Grandma," said David. "We're having a business disagreement."

"Oh, a business disagreement. Sounds serious. So, come tell me about it."

Madison preceded David into the living room, wanting to get her side of the story in, but David's voice was heard first. "She's a cheater. She made a bet with me and lost and now she won't pay up."

"I didn't make a bet—he's lying."

"Oh, my—a liar and a cheat! Well, I don't know who's right, but I suggest you both cool off before your mother gets home. And, David, a bit of advice: next time you bet someone something, make sure they accept it. And, Maddie, maybe you should make it clear that you're not accepting the bet. Sometimes a handshake, or something like that, makes it clear that you both agreed on the bet. That way there's no misunderstanding."

David looked at his sister and then back at Hannah. "Okay," he mumbled, and ambled into the kitchen for a snack. Madison shook her head and sighed. "He's such a nuisance, Grandma."

"I know, darling, but he's your brother. And he is young. Give him a little time—he'll grow up. In the meantime, try to see the humor. He can be quite funny!"

"Yeah, funny like a fungus!" With that, Madison turned and, with what she hoped was a dignified exit, went up to her room.

....

Ruby had sat silently, apparently fascinated at the cooking show on the screen, but, in truth, all her attention had been on the conversation between Hannah and the children. When Madison left the room, she turned to Hannah and said, "I envy you. The children come to you with their problems as if it were the most natural thing in the world. What I wouldn't give for that."

Hannah looked uncomfortable, not wanting to tell Ruby that it was her son-of-a- bitch son, and not her grandsons, who was the problem. After all, if Harold had maintained a decent relationship with her, the boys would have gotten to know her. She was confident that had they known her, they would have loved her. After all, even in the short time she had been living with them, Madison and David had taken to her. Hannah felt sorry for Ruby, but what could she do? Well, she could be a friend, and friends had to be honest with each other, so she turned to Ruby and asked, "What's with you and Charlie? Anything there?"

Ruby blushed, initially denying any interest in Charlie but, under Hannah's persistence, finally admitted that, yes, she had come to like him.

"Like? Toots, it seems more than 'like' to me. And if I'm right, we have to talk. You're going to scare him away if you're not careful."

Now she had Ruby's attention! "What do you mean?"

"Well, it's clear he has a thing for you. And, I think, you have a thing for him…No, let me finish. I need to say this and you need to hear it. Charlie's been a bachelor for all of his life, as far as I know. I don't think he was ever married, although I'm sure that he's had his lady friends—such a good looking man. But I get the feeling that he's not in the market for marriage, and your depending on him so much I think is scaring him."

"But I'm not even thinking of marriage!" Ruby blurted out, looking embarrassed and confused at the same time. "Why would he think I wanted to get married?"

"Because he's a man—they always think that's what women want. Even when they want it, they always act like they were trapped, you know, pushed into it. And I don't see Charlie as the marrying kind."

"Well, I can't simply tell him I don't want to get married—he hasn't even asked. In fact, he hasn't really said anything about us; he's just there when we need him. Oh, Hannah, I feel so foolish. Things were fine before all this happened. I was happy in my house, with my garden and friends like you.

Now, I don't know who I am anymore! I've become so—I don't know—weak, I guess. I don't feel in control of anything, certainly not my own life."

Hannah got up, went over to her friend, and put an arm around her shoulders. "But you're not weak, and you are in control—you just had a little setback. Once you're in your new place and able to get around on your own, you'll see—you'll feel different, strong again. And Charlie will see that you're okay on your own, that you don't *need* him, but maybe *want* him around. Remember, that's what got him interested in you in the first place: you were interesting, attractive—and independent. You still are, or can be, all of those things again. And you will be, once you're in your own place with a beautiful garden to take care of."

"So what do I do?" wondered Ruby, as she wiped her eyes with a tissue. "I don't know how to say any of this to Charlie. I'd be so embarrassed."

"Well, I don't think you say anything—leave that to me...No, don't worry, I won't say anything about marriage! I'll simply call attention to the way you've become stronger, more independent, things like that. Which means that you have to stop being so wimpy: no more tears, no more depending on him for everything. We'll still have him over to dinner—I think he looks forward to home-cooked meals. In fact, once you're in the apartment you could invite him over for an occasional dinner. And we can all go to the Center together. But you play it cool, as the kids say—or I think they say. I can never keep up with their language....Do you think you can do this?"

Ruby wiped her eyes and smiled. "I haven't had a talk like this since I was in high school and my friends would get together and talk about how to get boys to notice us."

"Well, I'm sure it didn't take much to get them to notice you—that's not changed much," she smiled. "But, as Sherlock Holmes says, 'The game's afoot, Watson,' so let's go."

Ruby laughed. "What does that mean?"

"I don't know but I think he says it when he has a plan—and we have a plan now."

Just then Janice entered the room. "You two were so engrossed you didn't even hear me come in, did you? What are you up to, Mom?"

Hannah looked at her, feigning indignation. "Why, what a thing to say! We're just having a little 'girl-talk.' Just because we're mature women doesn't mean we're not interested in things."

"Things, huh? You're either plotting something or you're talking about Charlie." Janice's eyes opened wide. "Or both!" she said, smiling.

"Oh, she's good," chuckled Hannah. "Come, let's get started on dinner. We'll fill you in on our plans later."

Chapter 36

Ruby's new apartment looked as if she had lived there for years. Most of the furnishings had come from her former house, only a few things were new, and within a week she had created a comfortable home for herself. She had taken Hannah's advice and hadn't asked Charlie to help her settle in. After a day apart, he had invited her to lunch at the Center. She accepted, of course, and they spent the time in conversation with friends, Ruby never mentioning that she could use his help in repositioning some of the larger pieces of furniture in the living room. It was only on the way back to her apartment that he had asked if she needed help with anything. She thought Hannah would agree that it was okay to accept his help!

Hannah still hadn't made a decision about moving in with Ruby, but she could see that Ruby was finding living alone quite pleasant. She had been reassured by Ruby that if she decided to move in, that would be wonderful; but, if not, Ruby would be fine. After all, Ruby had said, she still had Hannah and her friends. And then there was Charlie, who seemed to be more interested in being with her these days. She still had difficulty controlling her tears, but at least she could laugh when they started to flow, claiming "I must have something in my eye," which allowed Charlie to nod and ignore the tears.

She and Hannah had established a routine: they would lunch at the Center a few times a week, and once a week Ruby came to dinner at Janice's. Charlie was usually invited along for these events, as was Paul—who was becoming a more visible part of the family.

At one of these weekly dinners, Paul announced that the case of the missing women was solved. *Sunset Manor* was closed, pending a federal investigation of fraud, and the residents had been transferred to other nursing homes in the area.

"Pete, the PI, was able to trace some of the missing women to other nursing homes. But, what's even more important is that he found that there was fraud involved in issuing death certificates for some patients. In at least two cases, there was evidence the person had died—natural deaths, it was assumed—but that a death certificate hadn't been filed until two years later. All the time *Sunset* was accepting insurance payments. So not only was the place in trouble with the feds; it was in trouble with various insurance companies."

"So what happens now?" asked Hannah.

"Well, the place is closed and the higher ups in management are being charged with felonies. And with the evidence against them, they're going to be doing time...and," Paul went on to say, "it was all due to two persistent women, who wouldn't let up the pressure."

Hannah and Ruby blushed; Janice brought out a bottle of champagne and, glasses raised, proposed a toast to "two stubborn old gals." David, realizing that she had mistakenly poured a glass for him, chugged it down before his mother realized her mistake. Madison, ever alert to what David was doing, called this to Janice's attention, but by then the glass was empty. He gave her a look of triumph and responded to Janice's questioning gaze by saying, "I don't see what's so special about champagne, anyway. I think beer tastes better."

"We'll talk about that later, young man," his mother replied, casting a look at Hannah to see her reaction, surprised to see a smile on her face. Her mother never ceased to amaze her: the smallest transgression could lead to a lecture and yet a twelve-year old drinking beer raised nothing but a smile.

Dinner was eaten with gusto, conversation was lively, and spirits were high. Even David enjoyed himself, as was evidenced by the fact that he stayed at the table, neglecting the call of his video games. When Charlie asked him what level he was now at, David proudly announced that he was now at level seven—the only one in his group to get that far. He proceeded to describe the difficulties in getting to that level, only to be interrupted by Madison, who showed her lack of interest by turning the conversation to Ruby's new apartment.

"How do you find your new place, Ruby?" she asked.

Ruby beamed. "Oh, it's lovely. It overlooks a beautiful garden, and I've got all my own things in there so it's just like living in my house again—except it's so easy to keep up. You know, I never realized how much time I spent cleaning the house; here it just takes a few minutes each morning and it's done! Gives me more time to do other things."

"More time to spend with me, that's for sure," chimed in Charlie, looking pleased.

Hannah and Janice exchanged conspiratorial smiles. Maybe her mother's matchmaking was working, thought Janice.

Eventually David's interest in adult conversation waned. No more mystery about missing women, no gory details about human chop shops—therefore no need to remain at the table. He asked and received permission to leave, rounded up Max and coaxed him up the stairs. He slammed the door as he entered his bedroom, but opened it immediately and shouted down, "Sorry!"

Janice sighed, Madison grimaced, Hannah smiled, and the men laughed.

. . . .

Monday morning it snowed, and snowed, and snowed. Hannah hadn't seen so much snow since she was a little girl visiting an aunt in Minnesota for Christmas. Of course, in her case it was Hanukkah, but she always called the holiday Christmas as the decorated trees and Santas all over town clearly said "Christmas." It didn't matter to her. In fact, she rather preferred Christmas over Hanukkah: prettier, more exciting, and better presents—even though not as many. Fortunately, her Christian friends didn't mind her rather irreligious version of their holiday—probably because they agreed with it!

School had been canceled and the children were sleeping in. Janice, braving the elements to get to work, had ignored Hannah's warnings of the dire consequences of driving in this weather, but promised to call home once she arrived at school.

The phone call received, Hannah relaxed and was preparing a special breakfast of French toast—testing out a recipe she had seen on the Food Channel—when Madison came down.

"Wow, look at that snow. You can't even see the trees across the street."

David announced his arrival with a loud "Hurray! No school today!"

Hannah placed the French toast on the table and sat down to join them. "Well, what are you two going to do today? Catch up on homework? Clean your rooms?"

Madison gave her grandmother a "you've got to be kidding" look, while David stared at her as if she were an extra-terrestrial in human form. Hannah shook her head, admitting defeat. It was clearly going to be a free-for-all day. At least, she thought, she would use the day productively—although she didn't know what that would involve. She had no homework, her room was clean—in fact, the house was clean—and she had no projects to work on. For the first time in many months, there was nothing that she had to do. But the problem was that there was nothing that she wanted to do. That was unsettling. She would have to find something to keep her active. She had heard what happened to people when they got old and settled down: they became senile or died!

Her thoughts were interrupted by the phone ringing. It was Ruby, reporting that Harold had called and was planning to visit her once the weather improved. "Isn't that lovely?" she had asked. "Yes, lovely," Hannah had replied, but thought: What does he want now? She had a sinking feeling that Ruby was going to be convinced to "share" some of her money, but she said nothing, resolving to treat Ruby as a competent adult who could look after herself. Of course, that needn't prevent her from casually mentioning it to Charlie the next time she saw him. Perhaps he could be more influential in protecting Ruby from herself.

The French toast proclaimed a success, David ran upstairs to call Billy and discuss plans for later in the day. Madison offered to help with the dishes, which alerted Hannah to the discussion that she knew would follow. Madison at the age of seventeen was making a graceful transition from childhood to adulthood, with occasional lapses manifesting themselves in increased insecurity. She needed encouragement but was reluctant to ask for it, thinking that it somehow diminished her independence. Hannah, having experienced this with Janice at Madison's age, knew not to push the issue, but to let Madison reach out for advice when she felt comfortable doing so. This morning seemed to be one of those times, and Hannah patiently waited for the opening.

Dishes done, Madison lingered in the kitchen as Hannah poured herself another cup of coffee. "Sit, darling, sit. Keep me company. I'm all *fartummelt* today. It must be the weather."

Madison laughed at the Yiddish word, not knowing what it meant, but getting the gist from Hannah's hand gestures. "Yeah, me, too," she responded.

"Why? What's bothering you?" Hannah asked, using the opportunity to allow Madison to determine the direction of the conversation.

"Grandma, how do you know if someone likes you? You know, *really* likes you?"

"Oy, that's a hard question. There's 'liking' and 'really liking,' as you say, and sometimes it's hard to know what's what. Does this have anything to do with that boy—Jaime, is it?"

"Yeah. He says he really likes me and we have a really good time. He's fun and we're interested in the same things, and he really listens when I talk. But, I just don't know...."

"How do you feel about him? Like or *really* like?"

Madison hesitated before replying, "I think I *really* like him."

"So, the problem is...what? He wants more than friendship? He wants sex? You know you shouldn't have sex just because the boy wants it. Any boy who drops a girl because she won't have sex with him isn't worth it."

"No, it's not that. He jokes about it—about our not having sex—but he doesn't push me or anything. It's just that I'm going off to State next year and he's probably going to the community college here at first—his family can't afford State and he'll have to try to get a scholarship to go to State the next year. His grades aren't good enough for a scholarship now. He's going to try to get a good GPA his first year and then transfer. But we won't be able to see each other the way we do now. I'm thinking of going to the community college, too, and then transferring to State when he does. But I think Mom will go ballistic if I mention that."

"Yes, she will! And so would I," replied Hannah. "You can't put your life on hold for someone else—especially at this age. If not seeing each other as frequently as you do now is going to cause problems, then it's not a good situation. If you two really like each other—if you love each other—you'll find a way to make it work. The university is only two hours from here, right? So, what's the problem? He's got a car; there's a bus, no? Besides, both of you will be busy with your studies, so even if you were at the same school you'd have to spend time apart."

"But we could see each other, catch up with what's going on."

"And with all the fancy, schmancy technology you two have, you couldn't spend some time each night calling or writing each other—you know, the way you do on that gadget you have? You know, darling, sometimes time spent apart makes the time together more special. And if you're worried that he'll find someone else, well that could happen even if you're at the same school. That could happen even if you were living together! And the same possibility exists for you, too. So, don't go off like a chicken without its head. If he's as serious as you think he is, you two can make it work. If not, there's nothing you can do about it."

Madison sighed. "I know you're right, but…"

"Darling, life is full of 'buts'—you just have to work with what you have. And you have a lot to work with. I don't believe in 'meant-to-be', so I can't say that whatever happens was meant to be. But—there's another 'but'—there's a lot you can do to help things along. You know, I think most marriages fail because people don't put enough energy into making them work. The same is true of relationships. If you and Jaime are serious about wanting to make this relationship work, you'll both need to devote time and energy to it. That means, keep up your schoolwork and don't spend time partying. Instead spend the time doing that 'texting' thing you do. Then you should have some free weekends when you can visit each other. Believe me, darling, those times will seem more special."

Madison rose and went over to hug her grandmother. "Thanks, Grandma."

"You're very welcome, darling," Hannah replied.

Chapter 37

THE WEEKS PASSED, EVERYONE caught up in the daily routines, the preparations for the holidays in full swing. Paul was spending more time with the family, and Janice was spending more evenings at Paul's. The house was filled with the aroma of freshly baked cookies—half eaten before they could be put in the freezer—and freshly made strudel. Boxes of decorations were brought down from the attic, opened with oohs and aahs as long-forgotten ornaments were removed, producing remembrances of past holidays.

"Remember this one, David? You made it in kindergarten," smiled Janice, as she held up a strangely shaped lump of clay, painted dark brown.

David examined it and frowned. "It's stupid," he groaned. "Look, it's all uneven. What's it supposed to be, anyway?"

"It's a horse, silly," answered Madison. "And look at this one! I remember when Grandpa made this one for us." She held a wooden sled painted bright red in her hands. "See, he put our initials on the side."

"Where?" asked David. "Oh, yeah, I see it. Cool!"

Hannah and Janice watched as the children pulled out the rest of the ornaments, occasionally commenting on the history of the various pieces. Some were from Janice's childhood, which allowed her to share her stories once again with her children. After so many years of relating the same stories, she had perfected them—enhancing them by leaving out the boring details and exaggerating the rest—so that the children didn't mind hearing them again. Hannah knew not to correct her daughter's increasingly unrecognizable accounts, enjoying the children's increasingly exuberant reactions to the stories.

Ornaments sorted, garlands spread out, lights untangled, what was now needed was a tree! They were waiting for Paul, who was on his way over to help them cut down their "special" tree, when Ruby and Charlie arrived.

"I hope you don't mind our barging in like this, but we thought we'd go along with you. Charlie thinks I need a tree in my apartment—a small one, though." Ruby, who had never had a Christmas tree in her life, was like a little girl eagerly anticipating opening a birthday present. Her cheeks were rosy, whether from the cold or the excitement wasn't clear, and she looked happy and healthy. She walked without a cane, but kept it handy. "Just in case," she said—but Hannah knew she kept it with her because it was a gift from Charlie.

"Nonsense," said Hannah. "The more the merrier. Come, have some strudel—fresh from the oven—before Paul gets here. Of course he can have some, too," she added, looking at Janice.

"Strudel? Did I hear strudel?" shouted David, as he ran down the stairs.

"There's clearly nothing wrong with his hearing!" Janice laughed.

By the time Paul arrived, all that was left of the strudel were crumbs—thanks mostly to David's and Charlie's appetites. With a short delay after David searched for his hat and gloves—they were found at the bottom of his closet—the group, each one dressed in coat, hat, scarf, gloves, and boots, trudged off to the cars. After convincing Charlie that, even though seven people would fit into his car, two trees would not, two cars took off, leaving Paul's Mustang behind.

When they reached the tree farm, David leapt out of the car and ran to the tallest tree in the field. "This one, this one," he cried, jumping up and down in the snow.

Janice looked up at the tree—at least ten feet tall—and laughed. "And where do you suggest we put it? Or should we cut a hole in the ceiling? How about something a little smaller?"

The disappointment on David's face was quickly replaced by excitement as he found another tree to his satisfaction. This one was only seven feet tall.

Madison, however, less impressed by size than by quality, pointed out that it was crooked and had bare spots on one side, to which David replied, "So, we'll put that side against a wall—no one will notice."

Madison shot him a look, clearly implying that he knew nothing about Christmas trees. Hannah came to the rescue before the disagreement escalated into an argument, and suggested that they break up into groups to find a tree. She and David would go to the left and call out if they came upon the perfect tree—tall, but less than ten feet, and perfectly symmetrical. Everyone seemed satisfied with this suggestion and they paired off—Ruby and Charlie to the right; Janice, Paul, and Madison straight ahead.

It didn't take long for David's shout to be heard by all: "We found it! It's the best one here!"

The others quickly joined Hannah and David, who were standing in front of a beautiful, seven foot, perfectly symmetrical blue spruce, big grins on their faces.

Paul was the first to speak. "You did it, David. You found the special tree. Good work!"

The others all agreed that it was, indeed, the perfect tree. Paul and Charlie then set to cutting it down with the chain saw provided by the tree farmer, while the others went in search of a small—but perfect—tree for Ruby.

Both trees finally securely tied onto the cars, the group headed home, each car to its own destination. Hannah's insistence that the decorating of the tree be delayed until after lunch was received by David as a violation of his basic rights, only to be told by his mother to wash his hands and sit down at the table. Hannah had prepared a large pot of beef stew, which had been set on a low simmer before they left the house that morning. By now it was thick, the beef tender, the vegetables perhaps a little too soft, but the spices beautifully blended. With some baguettes, the meal was a welcome treat to melt the remaining chills from their morning adventure.

. . . .

The tree placed near the window, secured by rope so that ever exuberant Max wouldn't topple it, lights and ornaments carefully placed in their agreed-upon positions, Hannah and Janice were seated in the living room, TV turned on but ignored as they chatted about the events of the day.

"Ruby and Charlie seem to be getting along better, don't you think?" asked Janice.

"Yes. It's nice to see. She's her old self—a little too ladylike at times, but she's got her independence back…and Charlie's not so afraid! He has his own place—so does she—but they can see each other as often as they want, without tying each other down. An ideal situation, if you ask me."

"And what about you, Mom?" asked Janice, looking straight at Hannah. "Still feeling useless?"

"Well, not useless. But I'm still keeping my options open. We'll see how things go."

"What does that mean?"

"It means we'll see how things go! That's what it means. Madison goes off to college in the fall. Who knows what's going to happen with you and Paul. We'll see….By the way, what is happening with you and Paul? You know it's no secret that you two are, what they call, an 'item.' Are you making plans?"

Janice sighed. "I don't know. It's all so complicated—he has his family, I have mine; he's busy, I'm busy. Things are fine the way they are. I don't see the need for any changes."

"And what does Paul think?" Hannah asked, turning to face Janice.

"You'll have to ask him," she replied, getting up to turn off the TV. "I'm exhausted. Tomorrow is a big day at school—I'm going to bed. Don't forget to turn off the tree lights before you leave."

Hannah sat in the room a while longer, marveling at how a simple thing like a lighted tree could make a room cozier. Her Jewish friends could never understand why she and Leo had a Christmas tree every year. How could she make them understand that it wasn't a religious thing for her; it was just pretty!

She turned off the lights, went into the kitchen for a cup of herbal tea, and retired to her suite. With Ruby's belongings removed, she had restored the room to its former function as a sitting area separate from the bedroom. She looked around the room, at all the familiar objects which made it her place. Fighting off a feeling of nostalgia, she undressed, sipped her tea, and went to bed.

Chapter 38

CHRISTMAS DAY HAD GONE without the usual chaos of holidays. David had waited to a respectable hour before waking the household; presents were opened with the appropriate comments: "Oh, it's beautiful!" "Wow, this is great!", "Darling, you shouldn't have;" a late breakfast of waffles, with plenty of syrup and fruit, was enjoyed. All in all it was one of the better Christmases for the family.

Ruby and Charlie came over in the afternoon to exchange gifts and share some eggnog, and Paul arrived later, to join them for dinner, which turned out to be a feast.

Hannah had outdone herself: an assortment of pre-dinner bruschettas and drinks; a rib roast instead of the traditional turkey; potatoes au gratin; two green vegetables; a salad; and the cookies and pies she had been baking for days—along with a Death by Chocolate tart she had made for David, but large enough to be shared.

As everyone sat down to the table, Paul stood up and tapped his wine glass. All eyes turned to him as he turned to Janice.

"Janice and I have an announcement to make. I've asked her to marry me and, to my delight, she has accepted."

He leaned over and, taking her face between his hands, kissed her to a chorus of *mazel tovs* and congratulations, and one lone "gross" from David. Janice then took from her pocket the pearl ring that Paul had given her earlier in the day, which he proceeded to finally put on her finger.

Hannah joined Ruby in tearing up. Sniffling and reaching for a tissue, she got up and hugged Janice and Paul. "I knew it!" she exclaimed. "You kids couldn't hide your feelings from me. I'm so happy."

Charlie then stood up and raised his glass. "A toast to the couple. I've only known you folks a short time, but you've made me feel like family. I wish you all the happiness you deserve and hope that you'll continue to include Ruby and me in your lives."

Ruby proclaimed that her allergies were acting up, as she quickly wiped away her tears. Charlie laughed. "She has a lot of allergy problems at times like this."

Madison was ecstatic, already making plans for a big wedding—in which she would obviously play a major role. Janice had to rein her in, reminding her that this was an engagement—they had not yet set a wedding date—which prompted Hannah to ask, "When are you thinking for the wedding? Soon? Or you want I should be a really old lady at your wedding?"

Paul laughed. "Hannah, you'll never be a really old lady, even when you are a really old lady!"

"Paul and I haven't decided that yet, Mom, but believe me, you'll be the first to know. Now, let's eat this magnificent feast you've prepared."

David had been quiet since his comment on the kiss. Now he looked at his mother, puzzlement in his eyes. "What does this mean, Mom? Is Paul going to be my father, now?"

Paul quickly responded. "David, I can never take the place of your father. That's a special relationship between you and him. But I would be honored to be your stepfather and friend, if that's okay with you."

David frowned, considered this for a moment, and then looked up and replied, "Yeah, I guess that's okay."

. . . .

That evening when everyone had left and the children were upstairs—Madison on her new Blackberry with friends, comparing gifts, and David playing his latest video game—Hannah and Janice were once again settled in the living room.

"So, darling, what are your plans?"

Janice smiled. She knew her mother so well she had been expecting the question. "Nothing definite, but we're thinking of the summer. Once school is out, I'll have more time to organize something. It's going to be a small affair, you know; nothing elaborate. Probably just have some friends come here after the ceremony for some snacks, things like that. It's the second time for both of us, so I don't want a shower, and I certainly don't need any gifts. It'll just be a party with friends and family—and the family is already here!"

"Yes, we don't have a big family, and what we had is gone—except for you and the children. Well, whatever you and Paul decide is fine with me. Just let me know so I can get a new outfit," Hannah joked.

"You'll have plenty of notice....Mom, do you think David's okay with this?"

"David's going to be fine. Paul handled him just right—David will have a father and a stepfather, each with their own relationship with him. Of course, your no-good-nik ex-husband doesn't really have a relationship with him, but that's another story. I wouldn't be surprised if, after a little time, David starts to look at Paul as his *real* father."

Janice rose, kissed her mother goodnight, and turned in. Hannah sat for a while and, with a sigh, rose and turned off the lights on the tree. She already knew that sleep would not come easily tonight.

. . . .

"Ruby? I need to see you today. How about lunch?...No, nothing's wrong; I just need to talk with you...yes, yesterday was lovely...yes, I'm delighted about Janice and Paul....Look, we can talk about all of this later. What time do you want I should pick you up?...Okay, 11:30—I'll be there."

It was just 8:30 and the children were still sleeping. Janice had risen early to help Paul prepare for his daughter's visit. Sandy had celebrated Christmas with her mother and was going to do the same with her father today, so last-minute details needed to be attended to—like food and finalizing plans on how to spend the day. It was also an opportunity for Janice to get to know Sandy, and vice versa. They had agreed not to mention their engagement: Janice wanted time for Sandy to get to know her a bit before announcing she was going to be her stepmother!

Hannah hadn't slept well. And she knew she was drinking too much coffee—she was already on cup three. But she couldn't settle down. She had made a decision and was anxious to get on with it. But first she had to talk to Ruby—and that wasn't for three hours! What could she do to fill up the time? She knew she wouldn't be able to concentrate on her novel. She had already finished the crossword puzzle. The recent sudoku puzzles in the local newspaper were too hard to finish. Ah, she knew: she'd sort the clothes in her closet. If she was going to move, it would be good to have sorted through what to take and what to give away.

And that was how Madison found her when she came down at 10:00—amidst a pile of clothes on the floor and another one on the bed. "What are you doing, Grandma?" she asked.

"Oh, good morning, darling. It's an early spring cleaning. I just realized that there's a rummage sale at the Center next month, and I thought I'd get a head start on it. Can you believe that I ever wore this?" she laughed, as she held up a lavender polyester pantsuit. "What was I thinking?"

Madison smiled, remembering when Hannah wore that pantsuit. She was pleased that her grandmother seemed to have developed better taste since coming to live with them.

"Are you hungry? Is David up?"

"Yeah, he's in the kitchen getting something to eat."

"Well, let's join him before he eats all the food."

Madison laughed and followed her grandmother out of the room.

"Good morning, darling. Are you hungry?" Hannah asked, as she eyed the crumbs on David's plate.

"No, I just wanted some cereal."

"Then what are you doing with that chocolate cake, my little dumpling?"

"There was just a little left. I didn't think anyone else would want it," he sheepishly replied.

"Well, I might have wanted it," said Madison, with a look of exasperation.

"You? No way! Too many calories!" he teased. "You don't want to get fat," he continued in a mocking tone.

"Enough," interrupted Hannah. "If you're done eating, clear your place and let your sister sit down. You've got your stuff all over the table."

David got up, put his dishes in the sink, and started to leave the room when Madison asked, "Where's Mom?"

"She's over at Paul's. She's going to spend the day with him and his daughter," Hannah replied.

David stopped in his tracks. "Whose daughter?" he asked.

"Paul has a daughter—I think her name is Suzie, Sandy—something like that. She lives mostly with her mother, I think, but spends some weekends with Paul."

"Is she part of the package?"

"Package?"

"Yeah, you know—part of the marriage thing."

"God, you make it sound like she's a piece of furniture Paul's going to bring with him. You're so immature," scolded Madison.

"Well, if Paul's going to live here, and she's going to live here—this place is going to get pretty crowded," said David, with his brow furrowed.

"You're just being selfish and..."

"Now, both of you stop it. We don't know what your mother's plans are yet. I'm sure she'll work out things to everyone's satisfaction. So don't go jumping the horse."

David looked at his grandmother with amusement. "Jumping the horse?"

Hannah gave him a look and responded, "Whatever!"

David hooted, "Jumping the horse! That's a good one," he laughed as he left the room.

Madison gave her brother a withering look and sat down to a breakfast of cereal and juice. Hannah joined her with a fourth cup of coffee and listened to Madison outline her plans for the week. Most of it seemed to involve Jaime.

Kitchen cleaned, Madison off to her room, Hannah got ready to meet Ruby. Yelling goodbye, she gathered her purse and went out to the car—to find it missing! She had completely forgotten that they had only one car now that Ruby had moved out and that Janice had taken it that morning. Embarrassed, she walked back into the house, phoned Ruby and, without any explanation, asked her to do the driving.

. . . .

"So, what's bothering you, dear?" Ruby was clearly worried about Hannah, who seemed more flustered than she had seen before. They were driving to *Clarissa's* and Ruby kept looking over at Hannah until Hannah finally blurted out, "Keep your eyes on the road. I'll tell you when we get there—if we don't get killed first.…Watch out for that car!"

Ruby meekly complied, driving even more slowly, eyes straight ahead. After many attempts at parallel parking in front of the restaurant, she managed to maneuver the big car into the space only twenty four inches from the curb. Hannah got out, looked down and shook her head, but said nothing.

By the time their lunches arrived, Hannah was well into the questioning of Ruby's relationship with Charlie.

"So, tell me. How often do you see each other? Does he stay over? Is he planning on moving in?"

All of this bewildered Ruby. Too polite to tell Hannah that it was none of her business, she struggled to figure out *why* Hannah was asking these questions. The answer came shortly. Halfway through her chicken salad, Hannah put down her fork, took a deep breath, and came straight out and asked if Charlie was using the extra bedroom in Ruby's apartment. It finally dawned on Ruby that Hannah was asking if she could move in with her.

"No, we're fine with the arrangement as it is. He has his place; I have mine. And, you know, dear, that I would love to have you move in. But, are you sure that's what you really want to do? Have you talked to Janice about this?"

"No; I wanted to know what my options were before I talked to her. It's just clear to me that they're going to be married this summer, that Paul will be moving in, and that his daughter—he has a little girl, you know—will be spending time there. There's just not enough room for everyone if I stay. Even if they wouldn't mind having me around—which was my first concern—there's just not enough room."

"Well, if you're sure that's what you want to do, you know you have a place with me. But I still think you should talk to Janice before doing anything definite. Okay?"

Hannah smiled and reached out to squeeze Ruby's hand. "Okay—let's have dessert."

. . . .

That evening, after the children were in bed, Hannah sat down next to Janice on the sofa in the living room, and said, "We have to talk."

Janice quickly turned off the TV program she had been watching, and turned to her mother. "What is it, Mom?"

"I've been doing some thinking and I've made a decision. I'm going to move in with Ruby. She has that extra bedroom, I can afford the rent, and that'll give you the room you're going to need when Paul moves in."

"Whoa! Wait a minute! Where is this coming from? Who says Paul is going to be moving in? And even if he does, I think we'll be sharing the same bedroom! So what's with the room problem?"

"Of course he's going to be moving in. A husband doesn't live with his wife—in the same town? And what about his daughter? You have to have a room for her—she should feel like she belongs, no?"

"Why don't you let me worry about the details. I think you're going off half-cocked and making an important decision without thinking. Look, it's late. Sleep on it. We'll discuss it again tomorrow. Okay?"

Hannah sighed. "Okay. I am tired; I'm going to bed."

Chapter 39

Four days into the holiday break and the children were still wired. David was up bright and early, anxious to show Billy how far he had gotten on his new game. Madison was getting ready for her first skiing lesson from Jaime. Even Janice seemed jittery this morning, as if she had so much to do but didn't know where to begin. Hannah realized that this was not the time to return to their last night's conversation.

"Well, darlings, what's it to be? Cereal, eggs, pancakes, chocolate cake?" This last suggestion was made with a wink at David, who grinned back at her. "Is there chocolate cake?" he asked.

Hannah laughed. "No, my little dumpling. You ate it all! How about some scrambled eggs and toast—give you energy for the next level? In fact, how about I make up a batch of scrambled eggs for everyone? Maddie, you'll need something substantial if you're going to be out in the cold all day. Okay?"

Nods all around, Hannah started on the eggs, while Janice tended to the toast. Breakfast done, the children off to their respective activities, Janice surprised Hannah by declaring that she had some errands to run and wouldn't be home until dinnertime.

Hannah had the house to herself. She tidied the kitchen, showered and dressed, and sat down to think. Last night's conversation had left her with a bad feeling, but she didn't know why. There had been no argument, no hurt feelings, no resolution. Maybe that was it—nothing was settled. For the first time since those months after Leo had died, she felt adrift—no goals, no purpose, no desires, nothing . Would she feel any better living with Ruby? Probably not! But at least she wouldn't be a burden to Janice.

But that was the problem! Wherever she lived, she had to do something—she couldn't just sit and watch the world go by: she was a doer! But what to do? She spent the next few hours sitting at the kitchen table with a pad and pencil jotting down ideas, crossing out some, adding others, until she had a fairly short list of things she wanted to accomplish before she died—or at least in the next few months. Some of the items were clearly long-term (preparing for her death), others were quite short-term (get rid of some of her old clothes), and others were in-between, assuming she wasn't going to die tomorrow. It was this last category she knew she had to work on. Well, there was no sense in procrastinating; she would start today.

She spent the rest of the morning going through every item in her suite, ending up with a large pile of donations for Goodwill and an organized clothes closet. Feeling virtuous and somewhat more upbeat, she called Charlie and invited him over for lunch. As usual, he accepted without any questions.

When the family returned home that evening, they found her fast asleep in front of the TV, with cookie crumbs and cold tea beside her.

"Watch," giggled David. "She's going to say, 'I was just resting my eyes'"

"I'm not asleep—I'm just resting my eyes," said Hannah, getting up from the recliner and looking straight at David, who responded by saying, "Grandma, you're a corker!"

"Oy, another word I don't know. Okay, now that you're all here, what do you want I should make for dinner? I was so busy, I forgot all about that."

"Tonight's going to be pizza—Paul's treat," chimed in Janice.

"What kind is he getting?" asked David. 'I don't want anchovies touching my piece. You know I don't like…"

"Oh, for heaven's sake," interrupted Madison, "it's not always about you."

"Look, Paul knows what to get—he's seen you eat pizza before, you know. He should be here soon, so wash up. And Maddie, put all those wet clothes in the laundry room before they mess up the floor." Janice turned to Hannah and said, "Come on, Mom. Let's put together a salad and maybe some of those pepper bruschettas you made for Christmas dinner."

"Yeah, they were decent," yelled David, as he started up the stairs to wash up. Hannah and Janice exchanged smiles. "He sure likes his food," said Hannah, laughing, as they entered the kitchen.

Paul arrived with three large pizzas, each one earmarked for particular persons: pepperoni for David, vegetarian for Madison, and a third with everything, except anchovies, for the rest of them. With all the likely leftovers, there would be no problem about what to serve for lunch the next day.

The conversation at dinner was lively. David had reached a new level on his game—to hear him talk, it was a level never reached by a mortal before. Madison had managed to get down the bunny hill without falling, and had decided that she was really a natural athlete who had not had the opportunity to develop her talent. She credited Jaime with pointing this out to her, relating that he thought she did brilliantly for the first time on the slopes.

When Madison had finished describing her skiing adventures and David had tired of interrupting with reports of how extraordinary his accomplishments were, Hannah announced that she had something to say. They all turned to her.

"What is it, Mom?" asked Janice, concern on her face. "Are you all right?"

"Yes, darling; I'm fine. I didn't mean to worry you. It's just that I've been working on something and I wanted to share it with you." She looked at Janice. "You remember I told you about Irene Matsoff—our next door neighbor? Well, that—and the missing women here—got me to thinking. So today I had Charlie drive me to the Senior Center and told them about my concerns. Well, to make a long story short, they were interested in what I had to say. I got them to agree to set up a program—a pilot, they called it—where someone would go into the various nursing homes and visit with the people there—really check up on them, especially those that don't have regular visitors. It would probably be mostly volunteers in the beginning, but they said they would ask the county for some money—a grant, they called it—if this idea worked. They thought they would be able to get volunteers from those who use the Center. And I am going to be the coordinator. So next week I'm getting a lesson on how to set up a 'database,' I think it's called."

This announcement brought expressions of surprise and congratulations—and a guffaw from David, who expressed his doubt that Hannah's computer skills would not be up to the challenge of dealing with a database. She assured him, however, that she was not too old to learn new skills, especially something that didn't appear to be very high-tech.

Paul looked at Janice, awaiting some reaction, but she just said, "Mom has always been a political activist. When I was growing up, she was always out protesting some injustice that was going on. It's nice to see you getting involved again, Mom."

. . . .

It was 8:00, the children upstairs, the grown-ups relaxing over another glass of Chianti. Janice looked at Paul, who nodded. "Kids, come on down. We're having a family conference," she shouted up at them.

David was first to arrive, slightly out of breath in anticipation. Madison was right behind him. "What's up?" he asked.

"We have a serious issue to discuss and I want you two to just listen and not interrupt until I'm finished. Then you can have your say. Okay?"

"Okay," they said in unison.

"You know Paul and I are getting married—probably this summer. Grandma has been worried that she'll be in the way once we get married and has decided to move in with Ruby…"

"No, Grandma," blurted out the children. "We don't…"

"Hush, let me finish. If Grandma wants to move in with Ruby, that's her decision and we'll have to accept it. But I thought she ought to hear our views before she makes her decision. Is that okay with you, Mom?"

Before Hannah could answer, Madison sniffled back a tear and asked, "Why would you want to leave us? It's been perfect with you living here."

"I could keep my room neater, and I promise I won't slam doors anymore," contributed David.

Hannah reached for the tissues nearby. "Oh, darlings, that's not it at all. I love being here with you, but things are going to have to change. Your mother and Paul are going to need time for themselves. And you're both growing up—Maddie's going off to college next year, and David, you, too, are growing up. You all need more space; you don't need another person here."

She turned to face Janice and Paul. "Marriage, as you both know, is difficult enough without extra baggage," she said. "You need your privacy; you need to run the household the way you want to. You don't need an extra person around. I'm fine now, but I don't kid myself. I'm going to need more care as I get older and you shouldn't have that extra burden."

"Mom, that doesn't even make sense!" cried Janice. "That's like saying you're going to die someday so we should bury you now!"

Paul put his arm around Janice, who was also reaching for the tissues. "Hannah," he said, "I appreciate your concerns. I do know what marriage, a good marriage, requires. I made one mistake and I don't want to make another. But I know that my marriage didn't fail because of a lack of space. It failed because of a lack of love. And what I see in this family, in you, is certainly not a lack of love. In fact, I have never felt as 'belonged' as I do with this family, and that has a lot to do with you. I know Janice feels the same way: you are what makes this house a home. Without you it wouldn't be the same."

Janice blew her nose and started to speak. "Paul and I have talked it over and we're thinking of selling both our houses and buying a bigger one so that we'll all have our spaces, including a space for Sandy when she comes to visit. There's a house we've been looking at on Crawford Road. It's got four bedrooms—so everyone would have their own—but it also has what they call a 'mother-in-law' addition, which, in our case, could be a 'granny' addition. We'd like you to stay with us, but in your own place—to come and go as you please, but to be with us. You'd have a little apartment, it's attached to the house so you just open the door and you're in the house. You'll have the run of the house—nothing changes there—but when you want to get away from it all, you'll have your own place. And we think you'll need your own car, especially now that you'll be working with the people at the Center. And when you get 'old', we'll worry about that then! But if you *really* want to move in with Ruby, that's okay, too. It's your decision."

Tears were running down Hannah's cheeks, as she reached for another tissue. "I don't know what to say. I love you all so much, and I'd miss you if I didn't see you every day. And, I know this isn't nice to say—she's been so kind to me—but I don't think I could take Ruby's 'sensitive nature' for very long."

"Does that mean you're staying?" asked David.

"Yes, my little dumpling, it does. But," she asked, turning to Paul and Janice, "can you two afford that new house?"

Paul laughed. "You obviously don't know how much a successful lawyer makes. And we can afford a car for you, too, so don't worry about that."

"But I still contribute my social security checks—I insist on that."

"You're a tough cookie, Hannah, but, okay—it's a deal."

Madison ran to Hannah and hugged her. "I'm so happy, Grandma."

David, in what was a serious tone for him, declared, "So that's why you've been so crabby lately. I'm glad that's over."

Hannah laughed as she rose from the recliner. "Well, that's settled then. Anyone for a snack? By the way, the people at the Senior Center want I should run for the City commission next year. Can you imagine that? They must be desperate for candidates! Of course, I said no—but I maybe wouldn't mind the School Board. There's a lot to be done there."

Janice shook her head, hugged her mother, and walked into the kitchen with her to get the snacks.

THE END